SHADY GROVE

Other books by Janice Holt Giles
published by The University Press of Kentucky

Act of Contrition

The Believers

The Enduring Hills

40 Acres and No Mule

Hannah Fowler

Hill Man

The Kentuckians

The Land Beyond the Mountains

A Little Better than Plumb

Miss Willie

The Plum Thicket

Tara's Healing

Wellspring

SHADY GROVE

JANICE HOLT GILES

With a Foreword
by Wade Hall

THE UNIVERSITY PRESS OF KENTUCKY

Publication of this volume was made possible in part by a grant
from the National Endowment for the Humanities.

Scholarly publisher for the Commonwealth,
serving Bellarmine University, Berea College, Centre
College of Kentucky, Eastern Kentucky University,
The Filson Historical Society, Georgetown College,
Kentucky Historical Society, Kentucky State University,
Morehead State University, Murray State University,
Northern Kentucky University, Transylvania University,
University of Kentucky, University of Louisville,
and Western Kentucky University.
All rights reserved

Editorial and Sales Offices: The University Press of Kentucky
663 South Limestone Street, Lexington, Kentucky 40508-4008

02 03 04 05 06   5 4 3 2 1

Cataloging-in-Publication data available
from the Library of Congress

ISBN 0-8131-2238-4 (cloth: alk. paper)
ISBN 0-8131-9023-1 (pbk.: alk. paper)

This book is printed on acid-free recycled paper meeting
the requirements of the American National Standard
for Permanence of Paper for Printed Library Materials.

Manufactured in the United States of America

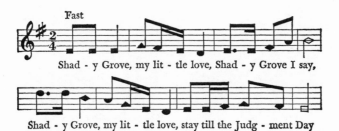

Fast

Shad - y Grove, my lit - tle love, Shad - y Grove I say,

Shad - y Grove, my lit - tle love, stay till the Judg - ment Day

Arranged by Henry Giles

Cheeks as red as the reddest rose,
  Eyes of deepest brown,
You're the darlin' of my heart,
  Stay till the sun goes down.

Shady Grove, my little love,
  Shady Grove, my darlin',
Shady Grove, my little love,
  Stay till the sun goes down.

Wisht I had me a big fine hog,
  Corn to feed him on,
And a pretty little wife to stay at home,
  And feed him when I'm gone.

Shady Grove, my little love,
  Shady Grove, I say,
Shady Grove, my little love,
  Stay till the Judgment Day.

FOREWORD

Wade Hall

Shady Grove, published in 1967, is Janice Holt Giles's last book of fiction about her adopted Kentucky homeland. In this book she again claims the ridge country of Adair County—here called Broke Neck, Kentucky—as her literary property, and, writing as a native narrator, Frony Fowler, she also becomes a forceful and eloquent spokeswoman for the region's people and way of life.

The feisty and articulate widow Frony tells the story of "what happened during the time of our trouble," and she also participates in its action. She is a masterful storyteller, reminiscent of nineteenth-century southern frontier yarnspinners, real and fictional, whose heroes survive through strength and strategy. *Shady Grove* celebrates such characters in tales of raucous practical jokes and capers that litter the landscape with laughter, embarrassment, and sometimes pain.

Frony creates a lively, vibrant world teeming with her people and their feuds, fusses, fights, politics, and religion. She invites us to their dinner tables, their elections, their churches, and their moonshine stills. We meet people with roots in the ridge soil that are generations deep. We go to their impromptu parties of fiddling, singing, and dancing and hear such folk favorites as "Shady Grove":

> Shady Grove, my little love,
>> Shady Grove, I say,
> Shady Grove, my little love,
>> Stay till the judgment Day.

Frony paints a full canvas, detailing the food they eat, the clothes they wear, the houses they live in, and the language they speak. Above all, she introduces us to people who, despite poverty, ignorance, and unwelcome interruptions from the outside world, remain unbroken in spirit and dignity.

Set in the 1960s with the Vietnam War in the distant background, the novel chronicles the adventures and misadventures of Frony's kinsman, the thrice-married farmer Sudley Fowler, and his extended family. He is well respected for his honesty and know-how by relatives, neighbors, and politicians, for whom he can deliver the votes of his large family—in return for a piece of political pork. Likely modeled on the author's husband, Henry, he is a ridge man to the core, muleheaded and "long on hunting and fishing and short on hoeing and plowing." Nonetheless, Frony testifies that Sudley is a good man and, moreover, "a good Christian" in his own way. But he sometimes gets "tangled up with the wrong people," such as the preacher who has come into the community to improve their morals and elevate their religion.

Admittedly, Broke Neck is not a utopia; but the residents like it the way it is. As Sudley says, "God made Broke Neck first and then used the leftovers to make the rest of the world." Into this old-fashioned, self-satisfied society steps the new preacher from a fancy, city-based denomination. The mission he heads is several classes above the holy-roller, nondenominational church to which most of the native "Bible Christians" belong. Although everyone is polite and indulgent of his fumbling overtures, it soon becomes apparent to the natives that the new minister is "all brain and no heart." The frequent butt of local jokesters, the preacher is once injured when a pack of dogs chases a polecat into a home he is visiting and trees him. He is not used to such lawless behavior and asserts that such goings-on don't happen "in a civilized world." Sudley replies proudly, "This ain't the civilized world, Preacher, this is Broke Neck, Kentucky. If it *can* happen, around here it does."

Imported religion doesn't fit the natives of Broke Neck, nor do imported government laws and make-work antipoverty projects. While most of Kentucky might be Democrat, this ridge country is rock-ribbed Republican and suspicious of government handouts, though willing to accept "pensions" and "benefits" if offered. Frony's own son, Barney Sadler, is certified mentally challenged and is "on the draw." It's the people who come in from "off," however, who confuse and complicate life for the ridge people, whether it's a salesman with an unneeded product or a road-grader who gets a woman pregnant and then skedaddles.

But the outsiders wreaking the most havoc in Broke Neck are the federal revenue men who break up Sudley's son Tate's whisky still and a group of four lonely men hell-bent on marrying a presumed Kentucky heiress, Sudley's daughter Darkus. Past thirty and desperate to get married, she solicits a husband from the ads in a lonely hearts magazine, exaggerating her assets. When Darkus's four suitors, who call themselves Lonesome, Anxious, Texas Ranger, and Brokenhearted, converge on Broke Neck—along with the federal men—all bedlam breaks loose. It is a comic fiasco that ends with poetic justice for all, including the preacher, who leaves the county to have a nervous breakdown.

The federal raid on Tate's still, a comedy of near-fatal errors and mishaps, is distorted into a media event. A Louisville newspaper plays the final interloper by twisting the facts of the raid and painting the people of Broke Neck as ignorant, foolish, backward, lawless, and lazy. Newspapers in Lexington and Nashville carry the stereotypes even further.

In *Shady Grove,* Janice Holt Giles attempts to smash media caricatures while portraying the ridge people honestly and realistically, dirt and warts included. It is her final tribute to her husband's people and culture, which she had learned to respect and love. She took his "old-timey" people and their colorful metaphors, folkspeech, and wild humor, combined them with generous pieces of folk wisdom, and threaded them into a story as warm and comfortable as a homemade quilt. People behave like people everywhere. As Sudley says, "From the Rockefellers to you and me, every-body pulls the quilt over on his side." Only a person who has slept in a crowded bed under a single quilt could give such good advice.

Indeed, Arkansas native Janice Holt looked closely at the backwoods world into which Henry Giles had brought her shortly after World War II, and she listened intently to the people. The author distilled all she had learned about her ridge country neighbors into words that will outlast the real people. Frony ends her storytelling with a plea to the writing woman, Janice Holt Giles, to "get it down straight." Well, Frony, you'd be proud to read how she wrote the story you told her.

SHADY GROVE

I

THE FIRST time that preacher came he got tangled up with Nebuchadnezzar and old Belshazzar and they had to take twelve stitches in his head. Last time he came he got tangled up with the Texas Ranger and a guitar and they had to take twelve stitches in his head. Six years between. Now, anyway you look at it, that is standing still. In six years, that man just strictly never did take a step forward.

Ask anybody. Ask just anybody at all. Go on out the ridge. Go up the holler. Go down the creek. Go to the crossroads and the post office. Go anywhere in the Broke Neck settlement. Go further than that. Go plumb to Pigeon Roost. Go to Sawbuck Ridge and Little Lost Creek. Go over to the river to Cartwright's Mill. Go wherever you want and ask them all. Take that tape recorder machine along with you and get it all down in black and white so the whole world can hear what they say.

They will tell you the same. Sudley Fowler is a good man. He is a good neighbor and a good family man. They will tell you that according to his lights, he is a good Christian. Since he was saved the time of the raining tree he has backslid but very little. But few know the Bible better than him. You won't hear evil of Sudley Fowler. He has done a lot of favors for a lot of people and I have confidence that if the time has come to collect them up, he hasn't cast his pearls before the swine.

Oh, they may tell you, and I'll agree, that he is on the mule-headed side. Gets his head set, gets his mind made up, you can gee in one ear and haw in the other and he won't even hear you. But if a man doesn't have a mind of his own to *make* up, he's in a poor way. Give me a good, strong-minded man any day of the week. At least he don't stand still in the middle of the road pulling and hauling both ways. He *goes,* one way or the other.

About things that don't matter much, Sudley is notional a little. Easy distracted. Sets out to hoe the corn and ends up on the river fishing. Begins to gather corn and winds up with a sloped gun hunting squirrels. He's dawdly, no use not admitting it, and he likes to traipse. But there never was a Fowler man yet that didn't. Their feet were made to walk and a fishing pole or a gun fits their hands a sight better than a hoe or a plow. Since Fowlers first came to these parts the men have been long on hunting and fishing and short on hoeing and plowing. That is in Sudley Fowler's bones, born there and bred there and nothing he can do about it.

I ought to know. I've lived a neighbor to Sud Fowler all my life and most of his. Truth is, we both live on places heired from the old Fowler land. I'm part Fowler myself. My grandmother was a Fowler. Sister to Sudley's grandfather. Sud and me are a little kin, though I wouldn't undertake to try to unravel it for it isn't only on the Fowler side. My mother married a Cartwright from over at the Mill, and Sudley's father married a Cartwright and they were cousins of some kind. We make the generations seven, of Cartwrights, Coopers, Fowlers, Pierces, Harbins, McKittredges, Camerons, Powells in this settlement, and one way or another, a little or a lot, we are all connected.

But we are Muley Fowlers, Sudley and me. Folks from off couldn't be expected to know the difference between Muley Fowlers and the rest of the Fowlers, but around here we do. You don't get to be a Muley Fowler but one way. If you're not born one, you never get to be one. And it's no good anybody trying to lie about it. We know who's who here.

If I have got the straight of it, back in the olden times there come two Fowler brothers into the country and settled. As far as I've ever heard they were both good men, but it was Muley turned out to be the pick of the two. He was the one took up the land and stuck with it and was able to hand it down to the generations. If you come down on the Muley Fowler side, then you're a Muley Fowler and so will your children be.

I wouldn't want to appear mouth-proud, but if you're a Muley Fowler you have at least got a good name to begin with. A Muley Fowler is generally held in good regard. All that feuding that went on between the Fowlers thirty, forty years ago — it was always between plain Fowlers and Muley Fowlers. Used to, there was bad blood between them.

The worst thing about Sudley is that he can agitate up a storm quicker than you can walk from here to there. Just standing, doing nothing but breathing, he is agitating more than most men pitching hay. He is the all-*outest* man, whatever he does, the Lord ever made. That had a lot to do with all the ruckus and the trial and tribulation. Give a man time to think and he can usually think of something to do. Make him mule-headed and he won't turn loose of what he's thought up. Give him the nature to agitate up a whirlwind and something is going to blow. But it's no sin.

A bad man, a mean man, a hateful, spiteful, harmful man, Sudley Fowler is not. Never, on purpose and of his own intention, did he do anybody any harm. To lay it all to Sudley is not true, no matter what the preacher told, and what the newspapers and television did was a pure shame and the truth was so buried nobody could have dug it out. You couldn't put a bit of dependence in what they said. I don't know what was so all-fired *funny* about it all, anyway.

There *was* an indictment and a trial. But it wasn't Sudley being tried. We were mixed in with it, I'll admit, but mostly by accident. And there was some shooting up here on the ridge one night, but that was all a mistake. We got it straightened out. And nobody was bad hurt, much less killed. Not even one of those Lonely Hearts men, to say nothing of the preacher. He got bunged up, but he did it himself. Nobody touched a hair of his head.

As for Sudley being the cause of that preacher having a nervous prostration and having to quit his job at the mission and go back up north where he came from, I never heard such foolishness in my life. It just flatly is not so. For a while there was considerable commotion going on around here and I'd be telling less than the truth if I didn't admit it. But if the law hadn't put their noses in, and if the newspapers and the TV hadn't got into it, and if that preacher hadn't been mixed up in it, we would have straightened it all out amongst ourselves, the way we're used to doing. It was family business and nobody else's.

But any time you get outsiders mixed into your business, it spells trouble. No good ever comes of them coming into the country. They are either looking for ways to cheat you out of something or they aim to have the law on you. I have seen but few outsiders that weren't ignorant, foolish, pushy, braggy, nosy, and bad-mannered. We don't like them. We just plain mistrust them and we have had good reason to.

As for the preacher, to begin with he wasn't worth the trouble it would have taken for Sudley or anybody else to send him into a nervous prostration. None of those preachers the denominations send in here are. They don't even make a riffle on the pond. We don't hold with the denominations here. We are Bible Christians. There is nothing in the Bible that says anything about denominations. They are man's vanity, is all. The Bible doesn't say there shall be denominations and church organizations and church boards and printed literature and headquarters and preachers taking pay for preaching when it's a grace from the Lord and they ought to make their living in a common ordinary way, like the Apostle Paul. I don't suppose they could get very far making tents nowadays, but there is always houses to be painted and handy work to be done, or they can teach school or even raise a crop now and then. It wouldn't hurt them.

Truth is, the denominations go strictly against the Bible, for in the Book of Revelations it says nothing shall be added *to* the Bible. The denominations add on all the extras the load will hold and then some. They run it over. We hold it is a sin to belong to the denominations — whatever name they go by, Methodists, Baptists, Presbyterians, Catholics, and all six different kinds of Brethrens and Churches of God and Christ. If they are a denomination they are adding *to* the Bible and it is wrong to belong to them. They think they know better than God's Book, but they are an abomination to the Lord. All it takes to be saved is to see the light, confess your sins and be baptized. The Bible don't say one word about joining a denomination.

We are good Bible Christians here and always have been as far back as the generations go. The oldest of us had the right ways from his father, and from his, and from his. It goes un-telling how far back. It takes a mighty proud-walking man, or a foolish one, to come into this country and let on his reli-gion is better than ours and he has come to save us. We are not benighted heathens and we don't appreciate being treated as such. We know we have laid hold of the truth and they are false prophets.

That denomination that built the mission up Broke Neck Creek has, to my certain knowledge, never had more than a hundred members, in the forty years they have been here. A hundred that stayed with them, that is. Some foolish people thought maybe they had brought a new gift of prophecy and they'd better listen, but most of them saw the light and came back to the true faith in time. They have got a lot of build-ings up there and they have spent enough money to have saved half the heathen in darkest Africa, but if they picked up and left tomorrow they wouldn't be missed.

They have had several preachers, one time or another, sa-shaying up and down the roads. Their preachers don't work to save souls. They put in their time flying up and down the roads. Going to town to the *Ministerial* Association. Speaking on the radio. Chaplaining out at the town hospital. Conferencing here and conferencing there. Trying to organize this and organize that. They don't have time to save souls. They are too busy organizing and conferencing. In a month of Sundays you can't tell them we don't like being organized, we don't want any community center, and we won't send our boys and girls away to any Youth Camp. We have our own ways and they have suited us for a long time and likely will go on suiting us long after the denominations have given up and closed their missions and gone back where they needn't have left from as far as makes any difference to us.

That last preacher of theirs — the one they are saying we drove out of his mind — we couldn't have. That man was just one jump ahead of a fit when he came here. He had the nervous fidgets the worst of anybody I ever saw. Never was still a minute. On the go all day every day. He didn't know *how* to just set and ponder and enjoy being a child of God. There wasn't any enjoyment in him. There was just a mess of wires strung up too tight. If the whole settlement hadn't coddled him along and pulled him out of the trouble he got into faster than they could haul him out, he wouldn't have lasted as long as he did. But whatever we think about a man, we know our manners here. We don't shame him before the people. The men were hard put to it, many a time, to keep him from looking foolish, and sometimes they couldn't because he was a natural born fool.

Like the time the mission was going to build the new parsonage. He drew up the plans big as you please. Said he was going to have a big basement under the whole house. For a recreation room, he said, for the young folks. Well, anybody with the sense God gave a goose would have known, just by looking, that the water level was the Broke Neck Creek running right by. You think he did? No. He brought in a bulldozer and they commenced gouging out a big hole in the ground. They hit water two foot down. Regular gusher. He went running for an irrigation pump. He ended up with six irrigation pumps that got behind more every day. He tried for two days, then he gave up and had them to shovel the dirt back in and did without his basement.

He said *why* didn't the men tell him the water was just two foot down? Saved him all his trouble. Now, how would that have looked? To be telling him he was ignorant. To be going against him and letting on they had more sense than he did. Which they did, but we don't like to walk proud here. We don't let on to be better than others. The men never did open their mouths one way or another. He ought to've known by their silence it wouldn't work. Fools, though, will rush in where angels wouldn't ruffle a feather. The worst of it was, he not only made a fool of himself before the whole settlement, he made fools of his congregation. It was a year before they could hold their heads up, it was such a shame to them. That their preacher should be such an ignorant and foolish fellow. Some of them even left the congregation on account of it.

Another thing he was so foolish about was what he called folk music. He had a tape recorder and he ran about the country with it trying to get the people to sing the old songs in it. Said they were priceless. Said they were dying out. Said

somebody had to record them for posterity. As if he had dis-
covered them. People have been traipsing these mountains
for over thirty years recording our old songs. They had been
well saved for posterity long before that preacher ever came
into the country. What they do with them when they get
them on the TV, you wouldn't recognize, though. They
don't sound the way we sing them, I can tell you that for sure.

The Fowlers have always been master hands at making
music. Picking and singing runs in the family. We all sing
and some of the men have been good song leaders. Sudley is
mighty good with a guitar. But the best hand of all of them,
this generation, is Sudley's boy, Tate. Anything with strings,
Tate can pick — banjo, mandolin, guitar — and he can make
a fiddle walk to town. But the preacher pestered Sudley a lot
to pick and sing for him. Sometimes he would — sometimes
he wouldn't. It's a notional thing with him. And there's
nothing would dry him up quicker than somebody pestering.

He was an ordinary looking fellow, that preacher. No different from any other man. Plain and common. I wouldn't
know his age but he wasn't an old man. He was able. He
had a house full of young ones and when they left, his
woman was due again. Which don't signify. Sudley is sev-
enty-five and he has children that go from a boy nearly fifty by
his first wife to one that's only four by his third. But the
preacher and his woman both looked to be around forty, give
or take a year or two. She looked older than him. But women
generally do, given eight children *and* a man to see to. Besides having to missionary on the side. Missionarying is awfully hard on the women, they say.

It was in October. Late October, I remember, for Sudley

and Lissie had just been married a few days. People were commencing to gather the corn, and apples were ripe and the frost had come and the leaves were falling. Sudley and the boys had begun running the hounds of a night.

I was over at Sudley's helping Lissie and Darkus make apple butter. Lissie is my stepdaughter that I raised from a babe in arms and Darkus is Sudley's girl that was still at home. Well, making apple butter is a tedious job. You have to stick right with it and if you leave off stirring it for one minute it will scorch. Both Lissie and Darkus were as flitter-headed as girls ever get to be, though in raising Lissie I did my best to teach her to do up her work right. Her mother was a McKittredge, though, and they were all flighty people. Darkus wasn't much better. On the wrong side of thirty, she had her mind on just one thing. Catching a man. There wasn't room for anything else in it.

I knew in reason those girls would ruin a whole kettle of apple butter if I didn't take a hand. My place joins Sudley's on the back side and it came handy for me to run over and help out. The footpath cuts across the neck of the holler by the spring, goes through the pasture and orchard and into the back lot. Five minutes and I'm here.

We had got an early start and had as nice a batch of apple butter cooked off by dinner time as you ever saw. And not late with dinner, either. Straight up eleven o'clock and the soup beans were done, the meat was fried, the bread baked and the coffee made. I had even beat up a stack cake which Sudley dearly loves. Put it together with hot apple butter. I was just getting ready to dish up when we heard a car drive up out front.

Lissie and Darkus nearly fell over each other getting in the front room to see out the window. I followed on. "Who is it?" I said.

The girls were creening their necks to see. Lissie said, "I never seen him before. He's strange."

"Is he getting out?" I said.

Darkus said, "Yes, he's getting out. He's getting some papers and things from the back seat."

"Well," I said, "quit twitching that curtain and mind your manners. He'll see you peering out. Who do you reckon it could be?"

"Somebody taking orders, maybe," Darkus said. "He's gathering up a whole bunch of papers."

"Selling something, more than likely," Lissie said. "Linoleums or house paint or washing machines."

I was misput, thinking of the menfolks needing their dinner soon. People from off don't ever seem to know when dinner time is. They come just when it's ready and if they won't eat, it's got to set and get cold. I was downright outdone. Sudley and Witchie — that's his boy that was still at home — and my boy, Barney, had been shocking corn since good daylight. They would be as hungry as lean pigs. To have to wait on their dinner till this fellow took a notion to leave would give them the weak trembles. "I'm just going to step out and tell him we don't need nothing," I said. "I'm not going to have dinner getting cold while he sets around on the porch and jaws." I took off my apron.

Darkus said, "Frony, he could be a new Watkins man. If he is, I need another jar of cold cream. Maybe we ought to all go out and talk to him."

"That last jar didn't do you no good," I said. "It's a pure waste of good money. Buttermilk will do as much for you and lot cheaper."

"It don't smell as good," she said.

"You paying to smell good?" I said.

"It don't hurt none," she snapped at me.

"No," I said, "you girls stay inside." I stepped out on the porch and pulled the door to behind me. "If you're selling linoleums," I said to him, "we got all we need already. Four of 'em. One in every room."

"No, ma'am," the man said, "I'm not . . ."

"We don't need no house paint, either," I said. "Sudley painted last year. And he's got a good roof on, so we don't need no roofing. We got two washing machines — one that works and one that don't . . ."

"Ma'am," he said, "I am . . ."

"We don't need any more Bibles," I said. "There is four on the place already. And we take the *Progressive Farmer* and the *Grit* and they are the only magazines we ever read."

He had stopped at the gate to figure out that piece of baling wire Sudley fixed for a latch. He shook his head, "No . . ."

"Well, if you're a new Watkins man," I said, "we don't need no products, either. Between us, we have got enough vanilla and liniment and salve to last us the rest of our lives."

He laughed, a little embarrassed. "I'm not selling anything . . ."

Then it came to me he might be another of those survey men from that college. There has been some kind of committee or council had their headquarters at that college and for several years they have been going through the country asking some of the foolishest questions and having people to fill out questionnaires and such. Said the Ford Foundation was putting up the money. I would think they had it to spare, seeing the Ford Motor Company took several billion dollars out of the country. On account of the coal. At one time the Ford Motor Company owned a whole country nigh us. It went right quare that that committee was using Ford money to find out some of the things Ford Motor Company had helped do to the country.

It's not hard to tell the way people like that *want* you to answer their questions. All you have to do is listen close to the way *they* talk. Generally you know what the right answer is — according to them. According to us, it none of it made much sense.

"Oh," I said, "are you taking another survey? Well, we have done been interviewed six times. I don't know as we have got ary other opinion to give you."

He had got the gate open and was coming on toward the porch. He took off his hat and held out his hand for me to shake. I shook it, for all I'll never get used to that way of doing. A man and a woman don't touch flesh here, unless they have got a right to. My man like to run a preacher off one time for patting me on the shoulder. He had thought the most of that preacher, too. Wouldn't miss a time he held a meeting. Then one time the preacher took dinner at our house and I could have gone through the floor when he put his hand on my shoulder and said what a good dinner it was. William went plumb white around the mouth. Told the man to begin picking up his feet and putting them down and not to come back again. The fellow acted real strange, as if he didn't know he had insulted William. But if he hadn't gone, and quick, William would have got his gun. It may be proper *off* for a man to be free of his hands with another man's wife, but it's not here. It is a mortal insult.

"Ma'am," the fellow said, and he told me his name. "I am the new pastor at the Broke Neck Mission. I am trying to meet all my good neighbors. I just stopped by to see you and get acquainted. I want to meet all the good people of the Broke Neck community." He was smiling all over his face by now.

Well, my soul and body! I never felt so mortified in my life. I could have gone right through the floor if it had opened up for me. I just wanted to sink down out of sight. To think I had been so unmannerly to a preacher. Denomination or not, I wouldn't have served him so had I but known. I was so flustered I couldn't say a word. Couldn't make a squawk. Just stood there and gawked and fidgeted my feet and tried not to look him in the eye. I don't know as I ever in my life was more ashamed.

"Are you Miz Fowler?" he said, finally, "Mrs. Sudley Fowler?"

"My name's Sadler," I said, "Frony Sadler."

"Oh," he said, "you live next door. I was planning to stop at your home next. I'll just kill two birds with one stone, won't I?" He laughed and cleared his throat. "Is Mr. Fowler at home?"

"He's in the field," I said.

"Miz Fowler here?" he asked.

"She's inside," I said.

"May I come in, then? I would like to meet her." I wished he had brought his woman. It don't look right, a man going inside alone where there's only women. But there wasn't a thing to do about it, since he'd asked. I said, "Come on in." And when he had got in, I said, "Git you a cheer."

He didn't, though. He went towards Darkus with his hand held out. "Miz Fowler, I'm very glad to meet you."

Darkus looked scared enough to run. "That ain't her," I said, "this'n is Lissie. Lissie Fowler."

He looked astonished, on account of Lissie being so young, but he walked over and shook hands with her. Then he turned towards Darkus again and said, "You must be Miss Dorcas then." He said her name proper, the way her school-teacher used to. We don't talk proper here. Even the ones that know how, don't. It goes like they were trying to copy folks from off. Trying to put themselves up above all the rest. We all talk just alike, the way we're used to.

"Darkus," I said, "just step outside and tap the bell for your father. He'll come right to the house," I said to the preacher, "when he hears the bell."

"Oh, don't bother him," the man said. "I don't want to interrupt his work."

"He would be misput," I said, "if we didn't bring him to the house with you here."

He was talky and mouthy, like they all are. Never stopped for a good breath hardly. Smily and knowing, like he owned the earth. Me and Lissie just set. That was all we needed to do, for even if we had been of a mind to talk, he didn't give us a chance. With one ear I was listening for the bell and finally it rang. Darkus must have given the rope an extra hard tug,

for it bonged so loud it made us all jump. And it excited the
hounds and they started barking and we could hear Darkus
trying to make them quieten down.

Sudley keeps a big pack of hounds. Too many, I say. But
he's a fool for a good dog and can't pass up the chance to get
another one. At that time he had eight in the pack, if you
included Bathsheba and since she run as good as any dog he
ever had, you couldn't count her out.

The preacher had to quit talking for a minute, but Darkus
got them stilled and came on back in. She set over by Lissie
on the sofa. The preacher sorted out the papers he had
carried in with him and they turned out to be tracts and
leaflets and such. He passed them out to us. Gave some to
Darkus and some to Lissie and some to me. He said he would
like to share them with us and hoped we would read them. I
felt exactly like I was handling the devil's own work, but it
wouldn't have been polite not to take them.

The preacher said he wanted us to know how much they
wanted us to come and worship at the mission. "You'll find a
warm welcome there," he said, smiling big at us. "We are
planning a big program of work for this next year. Many new
things." He took off his glasses and got out his white handkerchief and cleaned them. "What church do you belong to,
Miz Sadler?" he said.

"We don't belong to *no* church," I said.

He put his glasses back on and smiled all around the room
at us. "Well, then, perhaps you will visit the mission and perhaps you will join with us in the Lord's work. The Lord," he
went on, "has need of us all, Miz Sadler, to do His work.
None of us should hold back."

As if we didn't *do* the Lord's work, the way we see it and the way we are called to! Somebody in the denominations ought to teach those preachers manners before they turn them loose on people. But I kept a decent tongue in my head. I just said, "You think you'll like?"

"Like?" he said.

"Like pastoring at Broke Neck," I said.

"Oh," he said, "oh, I'm sure we will. The country is beautiful. The hills are so pretty. The valleys . . . the streams. And the people are so good. When we get to know them better, I'm sure we will find our work with them challenging. Those pamphlets I gave you tell about the work of our denomination and what we want to do here in Kentucky. We go where we are called, Miz Sadler. We go where we are called."

I wondered who had called him. Broke Neck hadn't, that was certain.

He was standing in front of the mantelpiece, just on the edge of the hearth, teetering backwards and forwards on his heels. He'd go up on his toes and then back on his heels — up on his toes and back on his heels. Made a body dizzy just to watch him. Well, he hadn't much more than finished his last words, all smily and teetering, when I heard Sudley yelling at the dogs and all at once there was the biggest ruckus you ever heard out back, every hound in the pack giving tongue. I knew Sudley had run up on something in the back yard and had cast the hounds. They were baying and howling and running, and Sudley and Witchie and Barney were yelling them on.

Lissie and Darkus ran out the door to see what it was all

about, and to tell the truth I would have loved to gone, too, to see what varmint they had got up. But *somebody* had to stay with that preacher, though much good it did for there was so much noise, what with the dogs baying and Sudley and the boys yelling and then Lissie and Darkus screeching, you couldn't have heard a clap of thunder in the house, much less somebody talking. The preacher just stood there looking at me, sort of astonished like. He did leave off his smiling and teetering.

Then something hit the back porch with a thud and next thing I knew the dogs had pelted around the porch and through the dogtrot and then they poured into the kitchen and circled around and you could hear things being knocked over. I had the biggest notion to go and stop it all, but there was that preacher. I did step over to the door and look down the dogtrot. But by that time I didn't need to see what is was the dogs had got up. You could smell it a mile. The whole house was drenched with it. Polecat.

They came out the kitchen door, made another round of the dogtrot and went into the back room. Sudley and Witchie and Barney hit the back porch about then and they were howling as loud as the dogs. They all come out of the back room and circled the dogtrot again, then headed into the front bedroom. Anything got in their way was knocked over.

I yelled at Sudley to quit that foolishness, but a tornado blowing through the house wouldn't have caused more noise and confusion. He couldn't have heard a cannon. I looked around at the preacher and he was standing there with his jaw dropped down and his nose squinched up, and little wonder for the smell was sickening by now.

Something crashed to the floor in the front bedroom and I said to myself, "There goes the Victrola." Then the skunk came tearing out the door, the dogs right behind him, old Belshazzar leading, his deep old drum voice shaking the walls, Nebuchadnezzar on his heels. Solomon and old King David were coming along fast and Bathsheba wasn't far behind. The pups were doing real well, too. You could tell they had good stock in them. They were nosing right on the floor. Sudley and Witchie and Barney were on their tails, all of them stomping and whooping and shouting. Lissie and Darkus weren't lagging much, screeching for the pups to lay with it.

The polecat went tearing down the dogtrot and back up again, then down and I thought maybe he would scamper off through the back yard. But, no, he come back up again and next thing I knew he come flying through the door in amongst us. He ran across the room and right between that preacher's legs and he went to ground up the chimney. The soot flew and nearly blinded us. Then the dogs hit the preacher while he was trying to get the soot out of his eyes, all eight of them at once, and he went down like a pole-axed steer, in a bunch of tails and legs and flopping ears, to say nothing of all of them dogs barking treed right on top of him. It was something to witness, now, I'm telling you.

Sudley and Witchie and Barney come flying in. Sudley yelled, "Where'd it go? Where'd it go? Where's that polecat at?"

"Up the chimney," I screeched back at him, "but that polecat'll keep. Handle your dogs, Sud. They got more'n a polecat treed."

"Where?" he yelled. "Where at? Is they another varmint loose in the house?"

"There's a preacher under that mess of hounds, Sudley," I said, "and you better handle 'em before they tromp him to death."

Sudley stopped dead still and just stared at me. He swallowed a time or two. "A preacher?" he said. "Did you say there was a preacher here? A real, live preacher?"

"He *was* alive," I said, "but he likely ain't now. Call them dogs off so we can see."

"O-o-h, God's little britches," Sudley said, weak-voiced. Then he groaned real loud. "Frony, I think I'm going to faint."

I yelled for Lissie to lead him to the sofa, and me and Witchie and Barney and Darkus got the dogs pulled off. "Now, take 'em out and tie 'em up," I told the boys, "and make sure they can't git loose again."

I had already seen the blood on the preacher's head and I was scared Barney would begin giving me trouble. Barney is my boy. Barney is a natural and I've not ever denied it. But he's not crazy. Not real crazy like the ones in the asylum. He's just not real bright. But his wits aren't addled. What sense Barney has got is good sense. That boy knows enough to come in out of the rain. Times, I think he knows enough to be right aggravating mean. But any time he saw blood he started howling and running around in circles. I told Witchie, "Stay outside and keep Barney with you."

Witchie said he would and he scooped up the pups with one hand and with the girls helping they got all the dogs out. The preacher was laying there looking like death warmed over. The stillest and palest I ever saw, but with the blood spilled from his head running on the hearth. I was so scared he was dead I was almost afraid to look, but somebody had to see what made all that blood so I lifted his head. There was a big gash in it and I figured he must have hit the corner of the mantelpiece when the dogs knocked him over.

About that time he gave a big groan and it was the welcomest sound I ever heard. He wasn't killed, anyway. I got a pan of cold water and bathed his face and head and when the girls came back inside we got Sudley off the sofa and the preacher on. Sudley was taking on like he was mortally wounded, too. Lissie took him off into their room.

Well, the preacher finally come to himself and he wanted to go right home, which was natural. But Sudley's car had a flat tire. It usually did for neither Witchie or Darkus would ever bother to change a tire. And the preacher's car was one of those little cars — a compact, Witchie called it. Didn't look to be room to load him into the back and he sure as sin couldn't drive himself, the state he was in. He was sort of wringing his hands together and moaning, "Let me out of here. Let me out of here. I want to get out of this place." And the polecat smell was awfully strong on him and making him sick and he was commencing to heave.

We wanted to get him out as bad as he wanted to go, but we had to do some figuring. I called Witchie and told him to go look at that little compact and see if he thought we could lay the preacher out on the back seat. He come back and said likely we could but it would be a tight fit. It was lucky the preacher was a short man, he said, a tall one wouldn't have went in. I had bandaged his head with some clean rags but the blood was seeping through, so I took some towels to lay on the seat to keep from ruining it.

Then the four of us, Witchie and Lissie and Darkus and me, carried him out. We got him in, him groaning and moaning and taking on something terrible. I felt the sorriest for him. "Witchie will drive you home," I told him, "but you'd best have the doctor right straight with that head. You got a bad lick on it."

I don't know if he heard me or not. He didn't let on. I told Witchie to take care driving and not jostle him up no more than he had to. He said he would. But not one of us had thought that the little compact would have a gearshift. It had been a time and a time since Witchie had driven a car with a gearshift. He stalled the engine three times and when he finally got it going he bucked along a piece and stalled it again. He got the hang of it then and went sailing on down the road.

"I could of drove him better than that," Darkus said. "Witchie'll have him so shook up his insides won't settle down for a week."

"I a little doubt that," I said. "I've not forgot, nor won't to my dying day, the time you drove that old Cadillac. It had a gearshift, too, in case *you* have forgot."

She just sniffed at me.

Upon my word and honor, that girl nearly killed us all the first time she drove. It was Sudley's first automobile. A Cadillac. He got it from the funeral home. It was the car they drove families in. They bought a new one. Sudley was the proudest of that car, but Darkus kept deviling him to let her learn to drive. He finally give in and taught her. Or thought he did.

Then come a day when me, and Barney and Lissie, who were just little things, were over there and Darkus wanted to take us driving. I didn't know but what she was good at it by then, so me and the young ones got in the back and Sudley got in the front beside Darkus. She drove us around all the roads up here on the ridge, then she wanted to go to the cross-roads. Sudley said, well, he guessed so.

Everything was fine till we come to the hill that winds off down from the ridge onto the pike. Sudley said, "Now, Dar-kus, you'll get to going too fast down this hill you don't watch out. You'll have to use your brake, or put it in low gear one."

"I will," she said.

We started down the hill, which has got three horseshoe bends. Pretty soon we got to going faster and faster. The windows were rolled down and we got to going so fast I had to hang onto my bonnet. It excited Barney and he started crawl-ing over towards the window and I had to hang onto him for fear he'd try to crawl right on out.

"Use the brakes, Darkus," Sudley yelled at her, "use the brakes. You're going too fast and that first curve is right ahead."

Darkus nodded her head, but it didn't seem to me she slowed up at all.

"The brakes, Darkus, the brakes!" Sudley yelled again.

We took the first curve with the tires screeching. Darkus looked down then, for a second, and when she looked up again we purely took wings and commenced to fly. Sudley covered his face with his hands and groaned. "Frony," he said, "git down. She's done froze her foot to the accelerator."

She had froze to something, that was certain, so I gathered Barney and Lissie together and shoved them down on the floor, but I wanted to see, myself, so I just braced for the worst and hung on. Sudley kept yelling at Darkus and wrestling the wheel with her and it may be he got a good enough grip to keep the car in the road. Something did, though we went backwards and forwards across it considerably. There was a deep holler on one side and the big high cliffs on the other. When we weren't brushing the edge of the holler, we were scraping the cliffs on the other side. I told the Lord that He was a witness to the fact that I had brought two little innocent young ones into danger and He ought to spare them anyway, seeing they had nothing to do with getting themselves into such a place to begin with.

There is a creek at the foot of the hill that you got to ford. Broke Neck Creek and that day I thought it was right well named. I thought it likely there would be another broke neck in the middle of it. Well, we come swooping around the last bend and went zooming down the bank like the Wabash Cannonball. And gentlemen, I'm here to tell you, we parted the waves. Moses rolling back the Red Sea couldn't have made a cleaner sweep of it. When we hit that creek a wall of water like a spring tide rose up and drowned us. We was blind as bats till it poured off.

When we could see again Darkus had plowed across Ethan Green's front yard and had sheared off half his front porch. The rest of it was hanging by one post and the rainspout. Sallie Green was standing in the front door, turned to stone.

When the car come to a stop we all just set there, like we was paralyzed. All but my insides. They were quivering like jelly. I reckon I was the first one to come to my senses. I crawled out and pulled Barney and Lissie out and set my bonnet straight. Then I looked at the car. The whole front end was stove in. You could tell that car wouldn't ever be anything to be proud of again. It might still run, but it was pleated like an accordion.

Sudley was sitting bolt upright and his eyes, when I noticed, had a kind of glassy look in them. Without turning his head he said, "Frony, I think my neck is broke."

"Fiddlesticks," I said, "if your neck was broke you'd be dead. Here, let me feel."

I retched in through the window and felt up and down and twisted it one way and the other. "It's just creened, Sudley," I said. "What'd you hit with it?"

"The top," he said, "when we jumped the creek."

"That's what I allowed."

For once Darkus didn't have a word to say. She couldn't. She had had the breath knocked out of her by the steering wheel. Sudley got out and walked around the car, holding his neck stiff, looking at the damage. "Well," he said, "I'll have to get somebody with a tractor to come haul her to the garage. I don't believe she's hurt inside."

"If I was you," I said, "I'd have it hauled back to that funeral home and try to get my money back. That car ain't to be trusted."

"It wasn't the car, Frony," he said, "it was Darkus. She got the pedals mixed up."

"That hill ain't the place to get mixed up," I said.

"I wouldn't pick it myself," he said.

Sallie must have called Ethan, for he come around the corner of the house to look at what was left of the front porch. He said, "Reckon I'll have to build a new one."

"It looks like it," Sudley said.

"Better get it done before tobacco-cutting time," Ethan said.

"It would be a good idea," Sudley said.

"Cost a couple of hundred dollars, wouldn't you say?" Ethan said.

"Every penny of it," Sudley said. "Might cost a little more than that, Ethan."

"Well," Ethan said, "soon as you pay me I'll get right to work on it."

"Me pay you!" Sudley said. "It's your front porch, ain't it?"

"It was," Ethan said, "till you mowed it down."

"I never mowed it down," Sudley said. "I wasn't driving that car. Darkus was driving."

"It's your car, ain't it?"

"Sure, it's my car," Sudley said, "but what's that got to do with it? I wasn't driving. Frony can tell you."

"No matter who was driving," Ethan said, "it's your car and you're responsible."

"You mean I got to pay for having that front porch of yours fixed?" Sudley said.

"Well, you don't have to, Sudley," Ethan said, "but if you don't I'll have to take you to court."

"Great blazes, Ethan," Sudley said, "I ain't got that much money."

"You can sell some timber," Ethan said.

"But I ain't wanting to sell no timber," Sudley said.

"Suit yourself," Ethan said. "Sallie, get ready. We'll go see Job Rigdon."

Sudley groaned. "All right, Ethan, all right."

Ethan and Sallie went on in the house.

I said, "Well, come on, you all. Let's go home. The night work is to do up yet and it's a long walk." It took us till full dark to make it.

Sudley never would let Darkus drive that car again. And I never did like it, myself. It was the one Sudley took me in to get some shoats I saw in the paper for sale and we put them in the back end. We had such a time that Sudley wouldn't help me unload them. He said, "Just raise 'em in the back, Frony, then you won't have to load 'em to take to sell." And walked off and I had to get the wheelbarrow and unload them by myself.

But that was why I didn't much believe Darkus could have driven the preacher home. She didn't have too much luck with gearshift cars. Truth is, it's chancy to ride with Darkus to this day — in an automatic transmission.

2

SUDLEY was so mortified over his dogs treeing the preacher that he wouldn't even go see the man. He said, "A man don't handle his dogs no better than that has come to a sorry pass."

I said, "They was cast, wasn't they? They was doing what they have been trained to do . . . foller a trail. How was you to know that preacher was standing on the hearth?"

"Yes," Sudley said, "how was I?"

Truth is, Sudley was so mortified that when the man got better and could stir about he went out of his way to keep from meeting him face to face. Wouldn't even go to the crossroads by the main road — which goes down the hill and by the mission. Sudley went the long way round by the old Coon Den Holler path. Where Tate lives. Tate is Sudley's boy that lived at home till Sudley and Lissie got married.

But I went to ask after the preacher several times. Me and Darkus. We took them milk and butter and eggs, and once a cake I stirred up. Witchie went one time, too. He took them a bushel of new-dug sweet potatoes. You think they knew enough to let those sweet potatoes season out before they cooked them? Not a bit of it. Baked a big mess of them and ate a big bait of them and they all had the trots for three days. We *heard* so, anyway. And it went reasonable. Green sweet potatoes are as good a physic as castor oil.

When he heard about the sweet potatoes, Sudley held his head and groaned. He said, "Them missionaries is going to believe we are trying to kill 'em. They'll have the law on us yet."

I said, "Fiddlesticks. It ain't our fault if they're ignorant. You'd think anybody would have the sense to season out sweet potatoes. Besides, they wouldn't have any case. Not if Job Rigdon has anything to do with it."

Sudley brightened up. "They wouldn't, would they? I have voted the Fowlers for Job every time he's run for a county office. He wouldn't do me a disfavor. He knows he'd lose the Fowler vote if he did."

Sudley has had a big family. Bigger than most and we commonly run to big families here. But he's had three go-rounds at it. His first woman was from off. He married her when he was in the army during the First World War. In Tennessee. Her name was Ordrey. A fancy town name if I ever heard one.

Sudley wasn't really in the war — in the fighting, I mean. He wasn't in the army but three months. They drafted him along towards the last but he didn't ever go across the waters where the fighting was at. Most of the time he was down in Tennessee at a camp — shooting squirrels. But there was some veins knotted up in his legs and they said he had flea-bitis or something like that, and they said he wouldn't be able to march, so they gave him a medical discharge. A while back when he commenced to find out about all the giveaways and pensions and things he put in for a pension on account of his veins and they gave it to him. He draws sixty dollars a month. Says that's the best-paying squirrel hunting he ever did. His veins have not kept him from marching all over these hills, either. He can outwalk any man in the Broke Neck settlement, day *or* night, when those coon hounds of his get to running.

I was as good a neighbor as I knew how to be to Ordrey, but when a man marries from off and brings a woman back here she don't ever amount to much. He would do a lot better to marry amongst his own. Generally, if a man marries more than a hill and a holler away he is in trouble.

Ordrey was a good woman and she tried hard but her ways were quare and she didn't ever really get used to ours. She was a denominationer, too. Presbyterian. The nearest Presbyterian church is in town and in those days, before they built the pike and before we had automobiles, it was a day's journey to go to town. With a good wagon and team. With a sorry oufit, it was two days. Ordrey made out by going to the Primitive Baptist till the mission come in. Then she went to it.

She and Sudley had four young ones — all girls. They're all married now and live close by and got young ones of their own. Ordrey died having the fifth little girl. It and her both died. I was the one that laid them out for burying and I set up in the death watch with her. We put them away in the same coffin. They're in the churchyard right down the road. Mine and Sudley's great-grandpa gave the land for that cemetery. Anybody is welcome to use it, but mostly Fowlers are buried there. There are so many of us.

Sudley took it hard, but he married again straight off, of course. He about had to, with four little girls to raise. His second woman was from up-the-holler, up the Broke Neck Creek. She was a Cooper. Zilpah Cooper, and as good a woman as there ever was. Coopers have been here as long as Fowlers and we're connected. Zilpah was a good Christian woman and you can believe that *she* never had anything to do with those mission folks.

She and Sudley were married thirty-five years. They had eight young ones of their own and Zilpah raised Ordrey's four. Only one they lost was Big Tice, who was killed in the Second World War. On one of those islands in the Pacific. Tate was in the war, too, and so was Witchie. Tate came back without a scratch, but Witchie got shot in the hand and it was left a little crooked and lame. He draws forty dollars a month for it.

All the others lived and except for one have turned out to be a comfort to Sudley. In all that bunch he only raised one to be a rogue. A father don't quit loving his boy because he's a rogue and he don't ever give up on him, but it's hard on him — a grief to his heart. And that is what Tate Fowler has been to Sudley most of his life. Wild and scampy when he was a boy — hateful with his tongue and hardheaded now that he's fifty.

Mostly Sudley's boys and girls are married now and live nigh him, except the three grandboys that are in Vietnam. They are Andrew, James and John. Andrew is in the Infantry and James and John are in the Marines. Whenever this country starts a war there's always Fowlers of an age to go and for us to miss and pray over.

But all our big family is what gives Sudley such a power at election time. Sudley has got a big batch of votes he can deliver any time he pleases, and grandchildren coming on make it several more every year. When they lowered the voting age to eighteen in Kentucky, Sudley added five votes to his batch in one year. He can just about swing Broke Neck precinct any election, and he can go a long way in two other precincts close by. He has to use his influence now that they have put in the voting machines, but when we used to vote by ballot he used to send the boys around and vote the dead Fowlers, too. I have seen Sudley vote seven times, himself. Sudley's a good man to have on your side at election time.

Zilpah died of the T.B. I was the one that laid her out, too, and kept the death watch over her. We put her away alongside Ordrey. Sudley wanted them right together. He said he had married two good Christian women and if the Lord was willing and he didn't backslide too much he expected to spend eternity with them. He wanted them handy for the Judgment Day. I don't know if a Presbyterian could be counted a Christian or not, but Sudley said it didn't hurt to hope.

Sudley's kids were all grown and married when Zilpah died, except Tate and Darkus and Witchie. And Witchie should have been. He had three young ones by Tish McKittredge then. They have got six now. But Tish can draw for them on the Aid to Dependent Children long as she and Witchie aren't married, so they allowed they just couldn't afford to get married. Tish lives on with her folks and the kids stay with her, except when Witchie brings one or two of the boys home with him for a week or two. And Witchie comes and goes, but he counts Sudley's place home.

They get along about like any married couple. Far as I know don't either one of them ever look at anybody else. Of course, not either one of them is any great shakes to look at now. Tish has lost most of her teeth and Witchie has lost all of his and won't wear his false teeth. Tish won't have hers fixed. She don't believe in doctoring, except with herbs. She used to have great faith in a medicine man that used to come through the country. He carried a wild Indian along with him. Tish put the greatest dependence in that man's liniment and tonic. She used it for everything — to rub on or to take. But he's not been through the country in a time and a time. Not since old Sylvester Cahoon drank a whole bottle of that liniment at one time and went stark raving crazy for one whole day and night. Some said Sylvester was just drunk but it was the wildest drunk anybody ever saw. He tried to bury himself — alive. The men ran the medicine man off then. Dusted his heels with birdshot a mile down the road. Told him if he ever come back they would bury *him* alive. Since then Tish has made out with herb doctoring. She strictly don't have the least bit of faith in doctors. I don't see how she can expect herbs to grow her a new set of teeth, but she won't go to the dentist.

Her and Witchie get into it once in a while. Mostly about money. Witchie thinks Tish ought to give him some of the draw money and Tish don't think so. Says it's hard enough for her and the kids to get along on it. She's always after Sudley to see if he can't get it raised. Her and Witchie go at it sometimes, hammer and tongs, and then Witchie will stay away for a week or two until they get over being mad at each other. They always make up. Witchie is as pleasant a boy as ever was. His only fault is he likes to drink. When he gets his pension check the first of every month he always goes on a big toot. If Tish or Sudley don't get their hands on the rest of it and hide it from him, he'd drink up every penny of it. Usually one of them manages to save about half of it for him.

We all knew in reason Sudley would marry again when Zilpah died. He was too used to having a woman do for him to do without. But I must say I got the surprise of my life when he and Lissie come walking in my place one day, Sudley all prancy and roostery and Lissie with her head hanging, and Sudley said, "Frony, I have done and married Lissie."

I could have fainted I was that astonished. I just sunk down in a chair and looked at them. Then I said, "Lissie, is he telling the truth?"

She said, "Yessum, he is."

I said, "Lissie, how come you to do such a thing? I never even knew you was talking to Sudley."

"I wasn't," she said.

"Then how come you to do it?" I said. "Sudley Fowler has married and buried two women and he is old enough to be your grandpa. What favor has he found in your eyes?"

"He wanted me to," she said.

That was all the reason she ever gave. He wanted her to, so she married him. And her but seventeen years old. Lissie was as pretty as an angel, if I do say so myself. Looked like frosting on a cake and good enough to eat with those big blue eyes and her curly yellow hair and deep dimples in her cheeks. I would have thought she could have her pick of any boy in the settlement. But even at his age, Sudley had a way with women. He had kept his looks better than most . . . hadn't run to fat any. But I think what they mostly liked about him was his good nature. He laughed easy and didn't rile up quick. Easygoing and pleasant, for the most part. And he *was* good to his women. Living a door neighbor, I could swear to that. He never in his life mistreated a wife or a young one. Open-handed with them and loving and kind. Some of our men get sour and dark after they're married, but Sudley never did. He *made* over his women, and he loved his kids almost too much. When they were little, you never saw Sudley without his young ones. He took them everywhere with him and was the proudest thing of them. It like to killed him when his boy, Big Tice, was killed in the war. Everybody called him Big Tice to tell him from the others named Tice. It's a name that runs in the Fowler families. Nobody knows who the first one was, but it goes a long way back.

So, it didn't worry me that Sudley wouldn't be good to Lissie. I just thought she was too young to be marrying such an old fellow. I said, "Well, there's no use crying over spilt milk. Be good to her, Sudley."

"I will, Frony," he said, "you know I will."

But a woman's lot is a hard one, even with a good man. I allowed Lissie would commence filling the house up with young ones straight off. She started off like she aimed to, but after Nathaniel and Whitley there hasn't been any more.

Little Tice is not her boy. Little Tice . . . well, there's no use lying about it. He is Darkus's. About the same time Sudley and Lissie got married, Darkus got mixed up with a road-grader. The state was building the gravel road down the ridge. Oh, that road-grader fellow really did set up to her. Darkus made sure she finally had got her a man. He took her around everywhere in his car. Darkus would tell how they went to the movies or to the roller skating rink, or to that tavern out on the pike. How they would eat hot dogs and drink hot pop. I don't even care for the stuff cold and how anybody could drink it hot was more than I could tell, till Witchie told me hot pop was soda pop with whiskey in it. When I found *that* out I knew no good was going to come of it and said so. And I was right. What come of it was Little Tice, about six months after that road-grader left out.

He was born in the preacher's car. I have midwifed considerable in my time, but I must say that the back seat of a compact is about the tightest fit I ever had to work in. Way that happened was that when Darkus's time come, Sudley's car wouldn't start.

Sudley had a Lincoln by then. He has always liked a big car. Says he wants to get his money's worth. I was staying at Sudley's at the time, for Lissie had just had Nathaniel and I was nursing her. Well, Darkus's time come in the middle of the night, the way they usually do. We got ready to go to the hospital and then the car wouldn't start. Sudley ground away at it till he run the battery down. It was weak anyway and didn't take much. Finally Sudley thought to look at the gas gauge. It said "E." Darkus was taking on something dreadful in the back seat. Sud said, "Darkus, have you been driving this car today?"

She moaned that she had. "Just down to the crossroads and back," she said.

"Well, why didn't you put some gasoline in? Darkus, you must think that E stands for Enough. I have told you and told you it means Empty."

Darkus commenced crying. "I never think to look at that there needle, Pap. I just get in and go."

"Well, tonight you won't," Sudley said. "There ain't no gasoline to take you to the hospital. You got in and went just once too often."

"Oh, what'll we do, what'll we do?" Darkus said.

It looked to me like the sensible thing to do was go in the house and let Darkus have that young one the way we have had our young ones since time out of mind. But these modern girls think they have to go to the hospital and Darkus had her heart set on it. Witchie was down at Tish's with his old rattletrap and it was three miles to walk to Coon Den to get Tate and his old truck. "I reckon," Sudley said finally, "that preacher would take us. The mission is the closest place where there's a car and it's on the way to town, too."

"How'll we get to the mission?" Darkus said. "I can't walk that far."

"Well," I said, "if she's got to go to the hospital, Sudley, there's not but one thing to do. Hitch up old Dander to the cart and hope it suits him to pull." Sudley has had that mule so long they have both forgot how long it's been and the mule is notional.

So that's how we got to the mission. The preacher was right startled to be roused up at two o'clock in the morning but he said he'd be glad to help out. When he had got dressed and backed the car out, I said, "Preacher, you drive like one of them boys drag racing down at the bridge all the time, but you'd better floorboard this little compact every inch of the way tonight or the stork is going to win."

He did his best, but we didn't make it. That boy was born and bawling good and loud and I had him wrapped in my petticoat before we got halfway. It shook the preacher up considerably. You wouldn't think it would, him having such

a bunch of young ones himself. But I don't suppose he had
ever been that close to one being born before. Mostly a man's
part of having a young one is a good safe distance away from
the birthing part. I noticed when we hauled up at the hospital he was all broke out in sweat. Sudley said, "Preacher, I
sure am obliged to you. Now, how much do I owe you?" We
always like to pay our way here. You don't ask people to go to
trouble for you and not offer to pay them for it.

The preacher shook his head. "Sudley," he said, "I don't
think you have enough money to pay me for this night's experience. Besides, I wouldn't think of charging for it."

"I like to do what's right, Preacher," Sudley said. "I appreciate your kindness and I want to make it up to you."

But the preacher wouldn't take anything. We sent him
half a pig when we killed hogs later on. We heard they give it
away for fear it would serve them the way the sweet potatoes
did. It wouldn't have, but if folks are ignorant, they're ignorant, and there's nothing to be done about it.

It was several days after the boy was born that the preacher
came in to visit. Me and Sudley were there. The preacher
said it was his turn to chaplain at the hospital and he thought
he'd just see how Miss Dorcas was getting along. We said,
fine. He talked on a while and then, making ready to leave,
he said, "Shall we have a word of prayer?"

We all looked at each other and then Sudley said, "I don't
reckon it would hurt any. Go right ahead, Preacher."

He prayed and it was a right good prayer till on the last.
When he asked the Lord to guide this erring young girl's
footsteps in the paths of righteousness I thought he over-
stepped his place a little. It went mouth-proud for *him* to be

stepping in, seemed to me. Like he had a special line to the Lord.

He had just said the Amen when the doctor came in. He said, "Darkus, what are you going to name that boy of yours? I have to fill out his birth certificate."

Darkus said, "I always wanted to name a boy Junior."

"Junior?" the doctor said. "Junior what?"

"What do you mean, Junior what?" Darkus said. "Just Junior."

The preacher laughed a little. He said, "Miss Dorcas, Junior is not a name itself. It means the second, or the next in line. My name is Junior," he said, "but it's Thomas, Junior, because my father was named Thomas and I was named for him. Junior must be junior to *somebody*."

"You mean," Darkus said, "if I name him Junior I have got to call him after that road-grader? Well, I won't. I wouldn't name a dog after that skunk. Married all the time and letting on he wasn't." She busted out crying. "Pore little feller," she said, "he's not really got a name, has he?"

Sudley leaned over and patted her hand and said, as gentle as could be, "Yes, he has, Darkus. He has got a name, and as good a name as anybody. His name is Fowler. And he's a Muley Fowler, too. I'd better not ever hear anybody slur off on him, either."

"That's right," I put in, "we'll see to this boy and we'll raise him right. He don't need that road-grader's name. You put your mind to thinking of a good name to go with Fowler, now, and hush your crying."

She pondered for a time and she said, then, "I know. I'll name him for Tice. Big Tice didn't have any younguns of his own — not that we *know* of — and won't ever, so I'll just name him after him."

The doctor wrote it down and left. Sudley explained to the preacher how it was a family name and went away back. The preacher listened and then he cleared his throat and said, "I must be going. Shall we have a word of prayer?"

Sudley just stared at him. Then he said, "Are you losing your mind, Preacher, or have you done and lost it? You have prayed over Darkus once and I a little doubt she has had time to err any since." That did me the *most* good. I didn't think Sudley had missed that slur on Darkus.

The preacher looked the foolishest. He turned turkey red and commenced to stutter. Then he said goodbye and sort of scuttled out the door.

So that is how we got Darkus's boy and he has been a pleasure to us all. As good and sweet a young one as we ever had on the place. We don't commonly speak of him as Little Tice, though. We mostly call him Junior. I thought it was a shame Darkus couldn't name him what she wanted to, and I said if he had to be junior to somebody he could be junior to Big Tice. It pleased Darkus, so we just commenced calling him Junior.

Tate was the only one that was ever hateful about the boy. He laughed his scorn at Darkus and said she had commenced the best paying work she could have got into. Said she oughtn't ever to want, with the Aid to Dependent Children paying the way it does. Said when times got scarce all she had to do was have another young one. But Little Tice was strictly a misstep. Darkus wasn't about to make a habit of such. She draws on the ADC, which she's entitled to, but that's all. Darkus wanted to get married and have her young ones legal. She purely didn't want them without.

Tate was still living at home when Sudley and Lissie got married, but he got so mad at Sudley marrying again, especially to somebody as young as Lissie, that he just up and moved out. He said, "I'm not going to stay here and work and sweat for another batch of younguns. I was the oldest of eight and I helped raise them. I ain't doing it for no more."

Sudley said, "Who's got a batch of younguns? Me and Lissie has just got married."

Tate said, "It won't take you long. In nine months she'll drop her first one and in five years there'll be a house full of 'em. And I'll have to do most of the work. I'm not going to. I'm moving out right now."

Tate is the only one of Sudley's boys that would talk to him so. He has jawed back at Sudley all his life. Tetchy and ill, is what he was. Never did have a civil tongue in his head. And he got more mean-tempered after Sudley got Big Tice's war insurance. He wanted half of it and when Sudley wouldn't give it to him but bought more land with part of it and put the rest in the building and loan, Tate swelled up like an old toadfrog. He was just jealous because he came out of the war without anything to draw on.

Oh, he drew that fifty-two twenty for a year after he got home, and he went to that farm school over in the next county on the G.I. bill until his time ran out — but he didn't have something coming in regular for the rest of his life and it itched him considerably. He said he figured he was smart not to get hurt during the war, but now he misdoubted it. Said he ought to have got a little wound that would pay off for him. He was aiming that at Witchie.

Well, Witchie didn't get his hand shot on purpose. He got it shot during the Battle of the Bulge staying with his machine gun till the rest of his squad got away safe. He got the Bronze Star for it. Which is more than Tate ever did. Best I could tell, Tate spent the biggest part of the war in the guardhouse. He was always pulling some kind of foolish stunt. Witchie made sergeant and stayed sergeant all through the war, but the way Tate run up and down from private to sergeant and back again was one more sight. Sudley would get a letter and he'd be a sergeant. Next letter he'd be a private. Next one he'd be a corporal, maybe. Backwards and forwards until it got Sudley so bewildered he threatened to write the President and see if he couldn't get things settled down a little.

The boys didn't really mean to get mixed up in a war, but they had joined up with the National Guards. It hadn't been very long since the depression. Truth is, the depression wasn't over around here. Everybody was still scratching for anything he could get.

Now, *that* was a time around these parts. Tobacco down to seven cents a pound. Corn worth strictly nothing. Hogs sold so cheap they wouldn't pay for their feed and you couldn't *give* chickens away. The boys tried the CCC but they hauled them off to Wisconsin and they had to dig ditches and build roads and it was so cold up there they nearly froze to death. They didn't like at all, so they came on back home. Sudley got them on the WPA then. They got three days work apiece every week. They had to build roads again, but at least they were living at home.

Sudley got the commodities for all of us, and he got me and Zilpah and the oldest girls on the sewing project over at the county seat. We managed to make it, one way or another, but it was a time when if you got hold of a nickel it doubled what was in your pocket. I saw Sudley burn a whole tobacco crop one year — just haul it out of the barn and burn it. It was selling so cheap that when he figured the cost of having it hauled to the warehouse and the warehouse charges for handling it, he not only wouldn't have made anything, he would have lost money. Oh, it was poor-do amongst us in those days, all right.

The only time in our lives we ever voted Democrat was in 1936. Sudley rounded us all up and said we had to. Not that he liked Franklin D. Roosevelt, for he didn't. But he said if it got out we hadn't voted Democrat we'd all likely be taken off the WPA and the projects and maybe even the commodities. So we all voted for him, but that one time was all.

That was the beginning of all these government giveaways, but it was just a drop in the bucket compared to what they've got now. It sometimes goes right foolish to me. Especially paying us for *not* growing stuff. I have got forty acres of corn in the cut-out and Sudley has got nearly a hundred. Thirty dollars an acre for *not* growing corn. It does beat all. Sudley says he could *not* grow a lot of things if he knew just what the government would pay.

Anyway, the boys heard the National Guard was paying for marching and drilling so they all joined up. It went along fine for a year or two, then the war come along and first thing they knew they had to go. Big Tice and Tate got sent to the Pacific and Witchie ended up in Europe. He made the whole rounds — North Africa, Sicily, Italy and France and Ger-

many. I reckon he would have gone to the Pacific with Tice
and Tate and the other Kentucky National Guards, but he
was home AWOL when they left out. He got homesick at
that camp and put in for a furlough. They wouldn't give him
but a three-day pass. My goodness, that didn't do any good.
He couldn't hardly make the rounds of the kinfolks in three
days. So he just stayed on two weeks. While he was here his
outfit left and sailed from California. When he got back to
the camp they put him in the guardhouse for a time, but then
they let him out and put him in an infantry outfit and next
thing we knew he was going across the waters in the other
direction. It was an anxious time, I can tell you, with Fowler boys scattered all over the world. Even as many of them
as there were in the army, so many of them got killed or
wounded I commenced to wonder if there would be any left
to carry on the name. Tate was one of the few that didn't get
hurt in any way.

The day he decided to leave Sudley's roof he backed that
old Chevrolet truck up to the door and started loading into it
everything he had bought and some he hadn't. He took the
TV set. That started Darkus to yelling. "Pap, are you going
to let him take the TV? What'll we do without the TV to
watch? How'll I know what happens in my stories in the daytime?"

Sudley scratched his head. "I dunno, Darkus. I dunno who
bought the TV."

Tate said, "I did. So I could watch the wrestling."

"I reckon he's right, Darkus," Sudley said.

"I know I'm right," Tate said, "for I paid for it with money
I won in a crap game. You like to not let me bring it in the

house. You was uncertain if it was a sin to watch the TV."

"I recollect, now," Sudley said. He nodded his head up and down. "And then we read the Scriptures again and couldn't find where Paul forbid the TV. So I let you bring it in."

Darkus was going in circles, taking on, so Sudley said, "We'll get another one, Darkus. Don't take on so. Soon as I can get to town I'll get us another one."

Darkus dried her eyes and commenced begging for a bigger one and for a color set. "I seen a color set in town one day," she said, "and you wouldn't believe how pretty the pictures are. All that scenery is just grand."

Sudley said, "We'll have the best, Darkus, I promise you."

Tate took the vacuum cleaner and the linoleum off the back room floor. He took the bedstead from there, which wasn't his but one that Zilpah had heired. Cherry. From her ma. All her young ones had been born in that bed. Sudley hated to see it go. "Tate," he said, "that was your ma's bedstead."

"I know it," Tate said, "but I'm the oldest and I reckon I'd heir it in time. I'm just taking it now without waiting."

"Well . . ." Sudley didn't stand in his way.

He took a stack of bed quilts, too, some of which I had made for Zilpah myself. "I need covers, don't I?" he said. "You want me to freeze to death?"

"If you'd stay home where you belong," I said, "that wouldn't be no problem." It did gravel me to see him carrying off those good quilts I'd made.

"No," he said, "I have made up my mind. I'm going."

He took some dishes and kettles and pans and he would have taken the kitchen stove, and it hot where Lissie and

Darkus and me were cooking dinner. But there was trouble over that. Sudley said, "Now, hold on there a minute, boy. You ain't taking that cookstove. You didn't buy that."

Tate went on working on the stovepipe. "Who did?" he said.

"I did," Sudley said. "I plainly recollect the day the old stove fell apart. Darkus got her arm burned. I went straight to town and paid down on this one. Why, it's not been more'n two years."

"Yes, you paid down on it," Tate said, "but I paid most of them installments."

"No, you didn't," Sudley said. "Only a time or two when I wasn't here when the man come to collect. I paid the biggest part of them installments. I ort to know, Tate, for I just finished paying it off a month or two back."

Tate was still trying to get the stovepipe down, but it was fitted too tight. He commenced kicking at the stove. "Tate," I said, "you'll knock over them kettles you don't watch out. If you'll wait a minute till I set 'em off . . ."

I retched over to set the kettles off, and I never have believed Tate did it on purpose, but he did whirl around and fetch me such a lick in the side with his elbow that it knocked me over backwards in the wood box. There I set, my heels higher than my head, the breath clean knocked out of me. If the roll had been called that very minute, I couldn't have answered to save my life. All I could do was heave in and out.

It made Sudley madder than a hornet all at once. "Now, see what you've done," he yelled, "you've overset Frony in the wood box. You have went too far this time, Tate, I'm telling you."

He tried to fistfight Tate away from the stove. They jostled around and pushed and shoved and then with my own eyes I saw what Tate did and no mistakes about it. He just doubled up his fist and tapped Sudley in the belly. Sudley folded up like a piece of paper. He went staggering off, out of the kitchen and across the dogtrot to his bedroom. Darkus and Lissie had got out of the way, but they were taking on enough to wake the dead, crying and yelling, and my Barney was sitting down at the end of the table his eyes bugged out and his mouth wide open. I knew he was beginning to get scared, too. By that time I had my breath back and I yelled to Darkus to come help me haul out of that wood box. She didn't hear me for all the noise, so I had to haul myself out the best way I could. Tate just about had the stovepipe loose by then.

But Sudley come back in the kitchen about that time, and you could have knocked me over with a feather. He was carrying his gun. He was really stirred up. Red in the face and his mouth working and his hands shaking so hard he couldn't hardly point the gun. He said, and his poor old voice was quavery, "Now, Tate, I've done told you. You have went too far. I never have drawed a gun on one of my own boys before and I don't like to now, but don't lay a hand on that stove again."

Tate stood there like he was frozen in his tracks. I was the worst scared. I thought, they're going to kill each other right here in front of our eyes. I knew Tate carried a knife. He'd been cut up more than once in knife fights. I allowed he would go for it and just whittle poor old Sud to pieces before he could get off a shot, *if* he got up the nerve to fire at his own boy. But he never. He stood there a minute, then he started laughing and he walked out onto the back porch. He said, "I'll leave it, then, since you feel so strong about it, Pap. But don't think I'm scared of that old muzzle-loader of yours. I'm not. You couldn't hit the side of the barn with it, anyway."

He had no call to say that, knowing the store Sudley set by that old shotgun, which is not a muzzle-loader, just an over-and-under, and the sun never rose on the day Sudley Fowler couldn't outshoot any boy he ever raised. Tate couldn't have said anything that would have outdone Sudley more. He walked over to the door and without even opening the screen just shot through it and made the dust dance around Tate's feet. "I'll show you what this gun'll do and what I can hit," he said. "You commence dancing, boy, if you don't want to lose both feet."

Now, of course, Sudley wasn't trying to hit Tate. If he had been, Tate would have dropped in his tracks. He was just trying to learn him to have a little respect for his father. He grabbed up a handful of cartridges and walked out onto the porch. "Keep on dancing, Tate. Keep picking them feet up."

He blazed away and Tate picked them up, I mean to tell you. First one side the path, then the other. Finally he broke for the corner of the house and ducked around it and made for the truck, Sudley raising the dust right behind. I stuck my head out the window and yelled at Sudley to stop now. "Leave him be, now, Sudley," I yelled, "you've done taught him a lesson."

I barely did get my head pulled back when Sudley blasted the side of the house. Broke out one of the windowlights and shot a hole in the coffeepot. Nearly scared the daylights out of Barney. When he gets real scared he commences yelling at the top of his lungs and if you can't quieten him down he'll run off into the woods and have to be hunted out. I got him hushed and then I grabbed up a piece of stovewood and marched myself out on the back porch. "Sudley," I said, "if you don't quit that foolishness I am going to quile you down myself with this piece of cookwood. You have done and addled pore Barney's wits and first thing we know we'll be having to hunt the woods for him. Besides," I said, "dinner is ready except you've done shot a hole in the coffeepot and like to scalded Lissie's arm. Let Tate go, now."

Sudley cradled his gun and just stood there. Then we heard the truck start and directly it roared on off. When Sudley come in he had tears in his eyes. He stood his gun in the corner and sat down to the table. "I never thought to see the day," he said, "when one of my boys would be so disrespectful to me. I don't know what has got into Tate."

Darkus was binding up Lissie's arm where the hot coffee had splashed. It wasn't but a little place but Lissie was always one to take on. She always wanted salve and bandage on the least little place. Darkus said, "He has always been mean, Pap. Just plain ornery mean, all his life."

Sudley was still mourning. "A body hates to see his boy leave his roof, though, Darkus. It won't seem the same without Tate. I don't know where I could of went wrong raising that boy. He has had the same raising as all the others, but he has always been a sore trial."

I set the dinner on. "Eat, now," I said, "it'll make you feel better. You've got no call to fault youself for the way Tate has turned out. There never was a barrel of apples didn't have one bad one in it. Tate is just your bad apple, Sudley."

Witchie came in then and went to wash his hands before eating. "What was all the shooting about?" he said. "Dogs get up some varmint?"

Darkus said, "It was Pap. Shooting at Tate."

Witchie raised his eyebrows, then he laughed. "You get him, Pap?"

"I never tried to," Sudley said, "you know that, Witchie."

"It wouldn't of been more'n he deserved," Witchie said, and he straddled the bench and squared around to his plate.

Between Darkus and Sudley they told him what had happened. "I keep a-wondering," Sudley said, "where he aimed to go. He drove off up the ridge, Witchie. Ain't nothing up that way but Coon Den Holler. Road ends there."

"That's where he's going," Witchie said. "He's aiming to buy the old Cameron place down in the holler."

Sudley was so astonished he stopped his fork halfway to his mouth. "He is?" he said. "How do you know?"

"He told me. This morning," Witchie said. "Said he was going to buy the place and live in that old cabin."

"Well, my goodness," Sudley said, "that ain't no place for him to go. That ain't no place for anybody to buy. There ain't no tobacco base on it. And no place to raise much of anything. Just steep old hillsides and that old cabin down on the ledge. Why in the world would he want to buy *that* place?"

"He didn't say," Witchie said.

"It would go cheap, Sudley," I said. "I don't reckon he'd have to pay more'n a couple of hundred dollars for it."

"And that would be too much," Sudley said. "Why, that old cabin has done fell in . . . in places. How long has it been since anybody lived down there, Frony?"

"Oh, it's untelling," I said. "Ed Cameron built it for his least boy when he got married, but they didn't like and didn't stay more'n a year. It's been anyway twenty years, I'd think."

"Anyway," Sudley said. "There ain't no timber on that place, either, is there?"

"Just what's on them steep slopes," I said. "About enough to cut cooking wood off."

"He don't want it for the timber, then," Sudley said. "Tate has always wanted to foller sawmilling and I allowed maybe he aimed to set up a mill. But it ain't that. It's a puzzle, ain't it? What he'd want with that old place. You sure he didn't give you no idea, Witchie?"

"I'm sure," Witchie said. "All he said was he was getting out. And he aimed to buy the Coon Den Holler place. That was ever word he said. I never asked no questions because it don't do no good to ask Tate anything. He'd of just tole me to mind my own business."

Sudley nodded. "That's what he'd of done, all right. Well, he'll strictly starve to death on that place. I'll have to figure out some way to help him."

Witchie laid his knife and fork down. "Pap, now that Tate's gone you ain't going to give him part of the tobacco, are you? That wouldn't be right. We been splitting it three ways, between you and me and Tate, but if Tate has left out and I got to tend it myself, it ain't nothing but right for me to get half." He started laughing. "Besides," he said, "you can't ever tell. Tish and me have got five younguns now. That's all the state pays on. Tish says if we have e'er other one, I got to help out. We can't draw for no more. I might need that tobacco money real bad one of these days."

"Knowing you," Sudley said, "I'd agree. If you stop with

five it will surprise me. No," he said, "I'm not aiming to give
Tate no part of the tobacco. He has left. It's only right you
should have half now. What I meant was, I'd have to see if I
could get him some money coming in. Trouble is . . ."

"Trouble is," Witchie said, "you can't get Tate no job. For
he ain't going to work on public work. You know that."

"And I wouldn't want him to," Sudley said. "No, sir, I
wouldn't want no boy of mine working in a factory or going
over to the mines or doing any kind of hand-to-mouth public
work like that. It would be a humiliation to him and to me.
It's just plain begging and asking for a favor. But if there
was an election coming up I could get him a political job.
There is no call for anybody to feel shame for a patronage
job. You trade out. You do a favor and they do you a favor
and you elect your man and you get your patronage out of it
and you don't owe nobody nothing and you can hold your
head up. Trouble is, there just is not no election right now.
I wish I could get him on some kind of draw. But he ain't
old enough for the Old Age and I don't reckon he's ever paid
into the Social Security."

"If he had, he ain't old enough for that either," I said.

"No," Sudley said, "he's not. And he's not worked out no
place to draw the unemployment."

"And he's too old for the school aid," Witchie said, laughing, "and he ain't hardly a idiot, like Barney there."

This raised my hackles, which they mostly do when anybody flouts off on Barney. Sudley and me had it out about
signing Barney a pauper idiot several years before, when he
wanted to because the county paid ten dollars a month for
them.

Sudley has taken good care of all his folks on the draws and giveaways. Mostly all he has to do is name it to Job Rigdon and he can get them on *something*. But when he came over to my place one day and said if I would sign a paper saying Barney was an idiot *and* a pauper, I could get ten dollars a month, I rose right up on my hind legs. I said, "In the first place Barney is not no pauper, Sudley. He has got a half-right in this place the same as me. It's mine till I die then Barney heirs it. That makes him a property holder."

"He's a pauper till you die, Frony," Sudley said.

"No, he's not," I said. "He has got other property. Didn't I sit by his father's deathbed and hear what he willed for him to have? And didn't I promise to see Barney would get it? William said, with his dying breath, 'I want Barney to have my ma's old feather tick, Frony. And her fruit jars and the old pie safe. I give him the cow and chickens, too.' Now, them was his father's dying words and I promised him to see to it. I am not aiming to break a death promise, Sudley."

I have kept that promise, too. I allowed William didn't mean for me not to have the use of the cow and chickens, seeing Barney had to eat, too. That cow died long ago and I could have got out of my promise by saying the cow his pa give him was dead, but I never. Right down the years I have set aside a calf for Barney, and I have always held that anyway a dozen of the hens belonged to him. I have always given him the egg money from that many of them.

Sudley said, "Ain't nobody asking you to break your promise, Frony. It wouldn't be breaking it to sign Barney a pauper idiot."

"It would be lying," I said, "and I ain't doing it, Sudley."

"You're missing out on ten dollars a month, regular," he said.

"I'll just have to miss it," I said. "I'm not swearing no lie."

There hadn't been any more said of signing Barney a pauper idiot. Now, when Witchie said Tate couldn't be named a pauper idiot, it bridled me. "Barney," I said, "is not no idiot, I'll thank you to remember."

Barney was sitting down at the end of the table catching flies. He loves to catch flies. He'll just flick out his hand, snatch, and there'll be a fly. He don't hardly ever miss. But when he catches them he don't know what to do with them. He just turns them loose. Sudley and Witchie looked at him, sitting there flicking out his hand and catching flies and turning them loose. Witchie said, "He don't miss it far. Look at him. He ain't got no more sense than to turn them flies loose when he catches 'em. Why don't he kill 'em?"

"Barney is softhearted," I said. "He don't like to kill things."

"Softheaded is more like it," Witchie said.

"Witchie," Sudley said, "don't be unkind."

"All right, Pap," Witchie said. "But I sure don't see no way you can get Tate on a draw."

"It's got me stumped right now," Sudley said. "Maybe Job can come up with something. But I can anyway get him on the welfare commodities. He'll have enough to eat, then."

"Whyn't you let Tate worry about himself?" Witchie said. "Maybe he knows what he's doing, Pap."

Sudley looked grieved at Witchie. "A man don't let his boy go without help, Witchie. I got to help Tate if I can. Darkus, put me on a kettle of water."

"What for?" she said.

"So's I can shave," he said.

"It ain't Sunday," she said.

"No, it ain't," he said. "I can read the calendar good as you. But if I'm going to town this afternoon I got to shave, don't I?"

She got up and filled the kettle. "Will you buy the TV this afternoon, Pap?"

"If there's time when I get through, I will," he said. "I got to see Job Rigdon first."

"Get the TV first," she begged, "and then go see Job."

"No," he said, "I got to see to my boy first."

3

MY, BUT THAT COLOR TV was the most pleasure to us. We had
some green-faced people and some red-colored grass until we
learned to set it right, but after that it showed the prettiest
pictures. We knew already the programs that had the undressed girls and the dancing and drinking and carrying on.
We never turned them on. But there was plenty to see without watching them. The ocean and the Rocky Mountains
and California and Florida and Niagara Falls. A body don't
really know how big and pretty the United States is till
they've got color TV.

Me and Darkus tried some of the cooking recipes and they
turned out pretty good. For fancy foods, that is. And we got
us some curtains like they showed one time. They did all
right until they had to be washed and then little sharp pieces
that looked like glass come all in the water and got into the
other clothes. Made us all scratch like we had the itch. We
took the curtains back and the man said they were fiber glass
and had to be hand-washed. "We bought a washing machine
to keep from hand-washing," I told him. "Just take these
back and give us some plain cotton."

The people talked a little about us having color TV. Said we were trying to get above everybody else. Acting proud. But then they all commenced getting color TV as fast as they could, so the talk didn't go on very long.

But I do believe it was that color TV that caused Darkus to be more unsatisfied and begin to want to traipse. "I want to see some of them places," she said.

"Well, look," Sudley said, "there they are."

"I mean go and see for myself," she said.

"That goes the foolishest," Sudley said. "What business have you got traipsing so far? Them places ain't just in the next county, Darkus."

"I know it. That's why I'd love to go," she said.

"Which you ain't likely to do," Sudley said. "Now, hush, and watch the show."

There wasn't a thing Sudley could do for Tate about a draw, though. He was in between every kind of draw and giveaway the government had. Either too old or not old enough, and he wasn't blind, lame or halt, and he had all his faculties as far as we knew. Sudley was right outdone. He said there ought to be *some* kind of giveaway that fitted a boy in Tate's fix.

After the state came out with the Aid for the Totally and Permanently Disabled, he was hopeful he could get him on that. He got Tate to go to the doctor to see if there wasn't something a little wrong with him. But the doctor said Tate was the soundest man in body he had ever seen and he would have to swear a lie, and a whopping big one, to sign that Tate was disabled in so much as a big toe. They tried three or four doctors and they all said the same thing. Witchie said they were wasting their time. He said, "If Pap had a couple of hundred dollars to spare, he could get that paper signed by that old feller down near the Tennessee line. He ain't much better than a horse doctor and he's a dope fiend, but there's some have got their papers signed by him."

"Four doctors," I said, "have sworn that Tate is sound in mind and body. I don't see how that doctor could say any different."

"Oh, he'll sign anything . . . for money. He's got to have money to buy his dope with, Frony."

"Then I'm just as glad Sudley's not got the money," I said. "It don't go right."

All Sudley was able to do for Tate was get his name on the jury list and sign him up for the welfare commodities. I don't know how they work that jury list. Sudley said they drew the names from some kind of wheel. But the same names are always in the wheel . . . the ones that need help. In a year's time most of them get several days' work . . . different times court is in session.

And the commodities gave Sudley a little peace of mind that there would be something to eat in Tate's house. Those commodity things are all right. We all got the commodities and they were good food. You could set a right good table with them. It was handy, too, to get your flour and lard and sugar and meal and such on a giveaway. It was saving for you. Nowadays we get the Food Stamps and just trade with them like money at the store. I reckon the government run out of commodities. Sudley says they are going to run out of money one of these days. He says we'd all best get all we can before they do, the way the Democrats are spending it.

Tate didn't stay at outs with Sudley long. It wasn't but a week or two till he was eating a good hot dinner at home with us three or four times a week, which mostly I had cooked seeing Darkus and Lissie were so flitterheaded. I didn't mind, it was such a comfort to Sudley. And one more don't make any difference when there's already a houseful.

Witchie said to me one day, "Don't Pap know how Tate aims to make his money?"

I said, "No, he don't. Nor do I. I didn't know he aimed to make any, outside of hand-to-mouth work now and then. How does he?"

Witchie laughed. "Well, if you've not guessed, it's not for me to tell you. But I can tell you one thing, Frony, Pap don't need to worry none about helping Tate out. Tate will do all right."

"You ought to tell Sudley," I said. "It would be a comfort to him."

"I a little doubt it," Witchie said, and laughed.

My goodness, little did we know how *little* comfort Tate was going to be to us all in time. Maybe a good thing we didn't, for I don't know as there was one thing we could have done anyway.

It was several months after Tate left that Sudley got my Barney on the Aid for the Totally and Permanently Disabled. "Now, Frony," he said, when he had been over to see Job Rigdon, "if ever anybody had a right to a draw, Barney has got a right to this one. He is about the worst totally and permanently disabled person I ever saw. You can't say, Frony, that Barney is able to work. Oh, he is strong enough and if you set him a task and stay right with him he can turn off the work good enough. But he's not able in his mind, Frony, and no use you saying he is. There wouldn't nobody hire him to work."

Well, that was the beautiful truth if it was ever told. Barney could work all right, help with the hay and the corn and the tobacco, *when* he's of a mind to, and if there's somebody right with him. But Barney has always come and went as he pleased. He's a grown man now, but I've not ever tried to put reins on him. It just makes him mad and he commences screeching and everything gets in an uproar and always ends up with him running off and hiding out in the woods. Less trouble just to give him his head. "Barney don't have to work out," I said, "he is provided for."

"Of course he is," Sudley said, "but you will be doing him a disfavor if you keep him off this draw, Frony. You will be keeping him from getting something that is rightfully his. It wouldn't lay easy on my conscience if it was me, Frony."

"I'll take care of my conscience," I said. "Do I have to sign him a pauper idiot?"

"No, you don't," Sudley said. "All we got to do is carry him over to town and have a doctor examine him. The doctor will write out the papers. You have to sign that you're his guardeen and that's all. The checks will come in his name, but you would be entitled to the use of them for his care. It would help you out a lot, Frony."

"I can manage," I said. But it had always worried me what would become of Barney when I was gone. He would have the place, but he could easy be cheated out of that. "Would they keep on paying this after I'm dead and gone?" I said.

Sudley bobbed his head up and down. "They sure would.

You could rest easy about Barney. The state has got this up for boys like Barney. I don't know," he said, "but what it would be almost a sin for you to keep him off this draw."

"If I don't have to sign him an idiot," I said.

"The doctor will put down what's wrong with his mind, Frony. And there *is* something wrong with Barney's mind. You have got to admit it, Frony. He ain't just exactly right. You've done awful good with him, but you can be easy about him knowing he'll have something regular coming in when you're gone."

They paid good, a lot more than I expected, and it was the biggest load off my mind. I didn't have to lay awake nights wondering who'd take the care of him and how he'd get along. He could pay his own way at a nursing home or live with somebody and pay. I appreciated it the most, Sudley getting us on that draw.

When the checks began coming they came the first of every month like clockwork. Never missed and never late more than a day or two. It was the biggest comfort. "Oh, these giveaways is just like a gold mine," Sudley said. "I'll get you on the Old-Age when you're sixty-five, Frony."

"That'll be next Decoration Day," I said, "if the Lord's willing and nothing don't happen."

"Tell me then," he said, "and I'll see to it."

"Sudley," I said, "you are a good man."

"I try to take care of my own," he said. "I wonder, Frony, I wonder just how many of us I have got the giveaways for."

"We can soon find out," I said. I got a pencil and paper and he began naming them off. "Count everybody," I said. "The cousins and uncles and in-laws and all."

"I will," he said.

We had one page full and had started on another when the preacher drove up. "Now, I'll get all mixed up," Sudley said. But he was polite. He told the preacher to get out and come in and take a chair. "Would you mind to just set a minute, Preacher," he said, then. "Me and Frony are making a list of all them I've got the giveaways for. In the Fowler bunch, that is. It won't take us long."

"Not at all," the preacher said. "I would be interested to know, myself."

We went back to naming them. When we got finished we added them up and there were thirty-seven of them. It made Sudley's eyes bug a little. "I never knowed," he said, "I had helped so many. It makes me feel real good, Frony."

"Wouldn't it have been more help," the preacher said, "if they were working? If you had helped them get jobs?"

"Oh, I didn't count the ones I've got jobs for, Preacher. With my influence. Why, there's two Fowlers working at the state barn — for the highway department. There's two driving school buses. One is a maintenance man at the high school. Two of the girls are cooking in the school cafeteria . . . I just don't know how many I've got jobs for. But work is seasonal, Preacher, and politics change things. Here today and gone tomorrow. These giveaways *last*." He got out his plug of tobacco and cut him off a piece. "I don't know, Frony, but what I am prouder of getting giveaways for thirty-seven Fowlers than of anything I have ever done in my life. It has kept me working hard, but I've been glad to do it."

"Where I come from, Sudley," the preacher said, "*we* take pride in hard work. We take pride in doing a good day's work for pay. In holding down our jobs and giving our money's worth."

"Oh, these all work. Ain't a living one of 'em," Sudley says, "don't tend something — little tobacco and wheat and corn. They take a heap of pride in their land and their crops, Preacher. What's to be proud of, doing public work? It's all hand-to-mouth. If a man has a little scope of land and tends some kind of crops, that's work to take pride in. And we do."

"Where I come from," the preacher said, "we think it a shame to take welfare and relief. We don't do it unless we have to."

Sudley sort of grinned. "I wouldn't say this, Preacher, if you hadn't brought it up and I don't mean it unkindly. But ain't preaching for pay taking public relief? Way we look at it around here, it's the biggest kind of welfare there is."

That preacher was the worst got of anybody I ever saw. He couldn't open his mouth, he was so flabbergasted. Then him and Sudley got into a argument over what the Bible says. There can't anybody outquote Sudley on the Bible. That preacher didn't have a leg to stand on when Sudley got through with him. He proved up one side and down the other that preaching was a grace and a man wasn't supposed to take pay for it. Finally the preacher gave in and commenced laughing. He said, "No use arguing with you, Sudley. What I came for was to tell you there's a job over in town open — working at a filling station. I thought maybe one of your Fowlers might want it."

Sudley thought about it, then he shook his head. "It wouldn't be lasty. I wouldn't want to see one of them that I had got set up with a giveaway take it. The public assistance folks would take him off the draw and I'd have a time getting him back on. It don't pay to trade a good check for a job that might not last."

"What's Tate doing?" the preacher said.

"He's making out . . . some way," Sudley said. "I don't rightly know how. But Tate wouldn't do public work, though I thank you for thinking of him."

"Too proud to work," the preacher said, laughing a little, "but he's not too proud to take Food Stamps."

"Why, Preacher," Sudley said, "them Food Stamps is like finding money in the road. There they are — just waiting. A man would be a fool not to take 'em if he could. Like passing up silver dollars in the road."

The preacher raised his hands, sort of outdone like. "I don't believe," he said, "I ever will understand you people."

Sudley laughed, then. "Don't even try, Preacher. Just leave us be. If we go foolish to you, you go foolisher to us."

The preacher laughed, too. "Did you know the new postmaster wants to move the post office?"

"Mansel does? From the crossroads?" Sudley said. "Where?"

"To his store, on the pike," the preacher said.

Sudley shook his head. "The people are not going to like that."

"Sylvester Cahoon has got up a petition to keep him from moving it, already," the preacher said. "And Mansel is getting up a petition to move it."

Sudley laughed till he shook. "Now, that is a foolish thing for them men to do. I'd have thought they'd know better than that. They'd better of tossed a coin."

"Why?" the preacher said. "Whichever gets the most signatures wins. It will be settled peaceably."

"Was it you named that to 'em, Preacher?" Sudley said.

"Why, yes. I thought in the interest of harmony . . ."

"Harmony!" Sudley said. "You've stirred up a hornet's nest, Preacher. But it'll settle down."

"I don't understand . . ."

"Wait and see," Sudley said. "Just wait and see the way it's settled."

When the preacher left, Sudley and me had a good laugh about it. "Everybody will sign both petitions," Sudley said.

"Of course, they will," I said. "They couldn't hardly not. It don't pay to take sides amongst neighbors."

That was the way it come out and the preacher was the worst outdone. He just flatly said the people of the Broke Neck settlement were dishonest — signing two petitions that way. But we know best how to do things here. When Mansel and Sylvester had got their feathers smoothed down, they did what was sensible and tossed a coin. Mansel took heads and Sylvester took tails and it come up tails. So the post office stayed at the crossroad and nobody had any hard feelings. Why, there would have been people not speaking to each other for ten years if one of them petitions had had more names than the other. We don't like that kind of thing, so we took care to see it didn't happen.

4

THERE WAS a while, though, when I unappreciated getting those Totally and Permanently Disabled checks and wished I had never given my consent to signing up for Barney. When I wished I had never heard of that draw.

It was several months after the checks had begun coming regular. I don't remember now exactly how long, but I know it was the squirrel season and hot, as August always is, and Barney was out hunting every day, as he always is during squirrel season. He loves to hunt and he nearly always killed and kept me in plenty for the table.

I was used to him being gone all day every day during any hunting season. Commonly, he came home of an evening, sometimes early, sometimes late, but every once in a while he would stay out in the woods all night. I didn't to say enjoy it when he did so, but I didn't worry about him either. He was of a restless disposition, liked to traipse, and long as I had some general notion of where he was, and what he was up to, I didn't lie awake and fret about him. My land, I would have spent half my time worrying about Barney if it had been my nature.

But that year it got so he hardly ever did come home before dark, and where he always used to chatter about where he'd been and all he'd seen, and tell, down to the least little thing, where he'd found the squirrels and how he shot them, he was uncommonly quiet. He would come in, throw his squirrels on the bench, eat something, mumble to himself a while, and go to bed. It bothered me, but I thought he was just sulled up about something. People like Barney get their feelings hurt over the least little things. Say Boo to them and they get mad. When Barney acted sully, I generally just let him alone. He always got over it in time.

But one day he came in about sundown and started flinging things about. He pulled the feather tick off his bed, folded it up and tied it, and he carried it out and set it down beside the road. He went to the smokehouse and got a box full of old fruit jars and set them out by the side of the road. Then, bless my soul if he didn't commence unloading the old pie safe. Butter, bread, bowl of beans, jelly, jam, half a custard pie — just stacked them on the table hit or miss and mostly miss.

I was so astonished I couldn't say a word for a minute, but when I found my tongue I let him have it. "Barney Sadler," I said, "what has come over you? What do you think you're doing?" He was tugging and hauling at the pie safe by then. "You leave that safe alone and you put back in it what you took out of it. Right this minute. And you go out there and bring that feather tick in and put it back on your bed. I do declare," I said, "I believe you have lost what senses you've got."

"They're mine," he said, "they're mine." And he went right on shoving that pie safe around till he got it out on the roadside, too. Then he went to the barn and put a rope around the old piedy cow's neck and led her out and tethered her to the persimmon tree.

I followed on when he had sat down on the bank. He just set there. "Barney," I said, "have you went plumb stark crazy? Now, quit acting this way. I don't know what has got into you, but I'm not having any more of this foolishness. Now, come on, and let's put these things back. It's nearly milking time and I've got the night work to do up. Come on and help me."

He just set there and he mumbled and mumbled and I couldn't make heads or tails of what he was saying. Finally I made out something about him moving. When he was a little fellow and he got real mad about something he would yell and scream and say he was going to move if we didn't treat him different. But he hadn't had such a fit in a long time, not for years, and I had almost forgot about them. I allowed, though, some of us had hurt his feelings in some way. I said, "I don't know what you're mad about, Barney, but there wouldn't a one of us, not any of Sudley's, or me, say or do a thing to hurt your feelings on purpose. Whatever it is we've done, it was purely by accident. It wasn't by intention. And just put it out of your mind. There ain't no sense holding a grudge. Now, come on and let's put your things back inside and get the work done up and then I'll make you some apple dumplings for supper."

That pleased him. He does love apple dumplings. Quiet as a lamb he helped me gather up his things and put them back. I thought that would be the last of it, though when I told them up at Sudley's next day we all puzzled what we could have said or done to upset him so.

Well, it wasn't more than a week till I came home from Sudley's one afternoon and there set Barney on the roadside again, all his things set out, the old cow haltered again. "Barney," I said, "you are carrying this too far. If you'll tell me what's the matter I'll try to do something about it. But you are being plain wearisome, setting these things out and setting 'em back in and catching up the cow and making her stand here in the hot sun. She's wanting a drink of water right now. It ain't good for a cow to stand tethered in the sun."

He mumbled around some more and said again he was moving.

"Moving where?" I said. "There ain't no place for you to move *to!*"

He bobbed his head up and down. "There is," he said, "there is, too."

"Where?" I said. "Just tell me where? Who would bother to tend you the way I do?"

He said he wasn't going to tell. Said he wasn't supposed to tell. "Well, don't then," I said, "but I don't call the road bank moving very far. And that cow is not yours to be moving. I'm taking her back to the barn lot this minute."

That made him start howling. "She *is* my cow! She is. Pa said so. Pa said I was to have the cow. You know he said so!"

"Oh, God's little britches," I said, "of course he said you was to have a cow. But cows get old and die and you got to keep raising up another one. That is not the same cow." I started in to try to explain to him how I had split the money from selling yearlings with him and that when I died whatever cow was on the place would be his . . . but I might as well saved my breath. He didn't pay me a bit of mind. Just set his jaw and kept a tight hold on the rope and worked his mouth. I have seen his father look like that many a time when he had got his head set. "Pa give me the cow," was all Barney would say.

I went in the house, frazzled plumb out with him. When I looked out next he was heading down the road, leading the cow. I yelled at him but he didn't answer. Just led her on. I went for Sudley then and Sudley went after him. We watched from the porch and we could tell Sudley was arguing and pleading with him. Directly Barney gave over the rope and Sudley come on back with the cow. But Barney kept going. "Where is he heading?" I said.

"He won't say," Sudley said. "Just says he is moving out. I talked him into leaving the cow. Said he could get somebody to come after her with a truck when he got settled. He mortally is upset about something, Frony. Ain't you got no idea what?"

"No, I've not," I said. "If I did, don't you think I'd of done something about it by now? I don't enjoy having him act this way no more than you do. But something is really bothering him. He's not been like this since he was a little boy, and not ever this bad. Maybe we ought to follow him, Sudley."

"You can," Sudley said, "if you're a mind to. I'm wore out. Me and Witchie has been working in the tobacco all day. And needed Barney. He won't come to no harm, Frony. Like he always does when he gets up in the night and wanders, he'll bed down some place. He'll come home in the morning, hungry, wanting his breakfast in a hurry."

There was enough truth in it to be sensible. One of the burdens of caring for him has been that sometimes he would take restless spells and get up while I was asleep and roam around. Mostly on bright moony nights. The people were good to see to him . . . bring him home if he went very far. They were used to him.

We moved his things back inside and I fed and watered and milked the cow and night settled down. Next morning I looked for him, but he didn't come, so when I'd done my work I went over to Sudley's. I hadn't much more than got there when here come the preacher and he had Barney in the car with him. My, I was the gladdest to see him and I went rushing out to say so. "I am sure obliged to you, Preacher," I said, "for bringing him home. I was real upset about him. Where'd you find him?"

"Under my house," the preacher said. "He spent the night there."

I was surprised. "He don't commonly choose a house to sleep under," I said. "Mostly he likes haystacks or barn lofts. It must of been cool under your house."

The preacher looked at me kind of quare. "Does he just wander around, Miz Sadler? Sleep wherever he wants to?"

"Well, not commonly," I said. "Not real often, Preacher. But when he has a traipsing night, he does. He don't do no harm. He wouldn't hurt a fly. He just gets restless, sometimes, and likes to roam. Mostly on moony nights."

"There's no moon right now," the preacher said.

"No," I said, "there ain't. I may as well tell you, Preacher, something is bothering him. We don't know what it is. But it'll likely blow over in a day or two."

"I hope so," the preacher said. "He scared us very badly last night, Miz Sadler."

My heart flopped up in my throat. One time Barney did

set a man's corn crib on fire. Didn't burn it down. Just a
little corner, and he didn't *aim* to set it. He had just got hold
of a box of matches somehow and he just liked to strike them
and see them burn. But I thought for a minute maybe he
had got hold of some more matches and set the preacher's
house.

"What did he do?" I said.

"He didn't actually *do* anything, Miz Sadler," the preacher
said, "but a man under the floor . . . We heard something
scratching around under the floor early in the evening, but
we thought it was a coon or some other wild animal. But
after we were in bed and asleep we were awakened by singing.
Very loud singing, Miz Sadler."

I laughed. "That goes like him. He loves to sing."

The preacher looked like he hadn't loved it. He said, "We
thought at first it was someone passing on the road, but it
went on and on and finally we got up and looked out the
windows on all sides of the house. We couldn't see anybody.
Then the singing quit."

"He likely got tired," I said. "He does that when he sings.
Drops off to sleep. He likely sung himself to sleep."

"*We* didn't sleep much," the preacher said. "He sang
off and on all night long."

"Why didn't you go out and find him and tell him to hush
up," I said.

"Go out!" the preacher said. "Miz Sadler, there are some
very rough characters in this community. Men who drink too
much and cause a disturbance. I didn't know it was Barney.
I didn't know but what it was some drunk under the house. I
thought it best to leave him alone. Let him sleep it off."

"Preacher," I said, "there ain't a man in the settlement,

drunk *or* sober, can't be bluffed with a good length of cook-wood. Next time just grab you up a club of hickory and lay with it."

He looked at me as if I had lost my senses, but he went chickenhearted to me. "I'm sorry you lost your sleep," I said, "but Barney didn't mean no harm."

"I know he didn't," he said, "but it was upsetting. Some-one under the house all night singing. Do you think you could make him understand he's not to wander down to the mission again, Miz Sadler? My wife is . . ."

"I know," I said, "she's expecting again. I'll try, Preacher, but I can't promise you total success. Watching Barney is a little like watching a flea. Hop and he's gone."

The very next morning when I got up, Barney was gone again. "Lord," I told Sudley, "I do hope he's not went down to the preacher's again."

But he had. Along about ten o'clock here come the preacher bringing him home — him and his feather tick. There set Barney in the back seat of that little compact, that old feather tick bulging and billowing all around him. He was having the best time with it. He'd punch it down on one side and it would fly up on the other. Then he'd punch it down on that side and it would fly up on the other. He was having the most fun. Some of the feathers had commenced to fly, though. He had feathers in his hair and sticking out his ears and all down his neck. The preacher had a few in his hair, too. They didn't become him. He wasn't to say built for feathers.

I said, "Preacher, I am the sorriest. He went to bed same as usual last night, but he was gone when I got up this morning. I hate for him to pester you folks so."

"I would have brought him sooner, Miz Sadler," the preacher said, "but I had to take my wife to the doctor."

"Is she puny?" I said.

"She wasn't," he said, "till she found Barney asleep on the kitchen floor this morning. She was so upset then I thought it best for her to see the doctor. The fact is, Miz Sadler, she had hysterics."

"Oh, them," I said. "Well, they'll not make her lose the young one, Preacher. It takes a lot more than a fright and the hysterics to lose a young one. Now, if she had had a fall, or . . ."

"Miz Sadler," he said, "you really must keep Barney at home. I can't have him wandering into my home, or under it. It not only frightens my wife, it frightens the children. Believe me, it is not something to treat lightly. You people may be used to Barney wandering about in the middle of the night, but my family aren't. Now, I must ask you to . . ."

"I'll lock him in tonight," I said. "I don't want him bothering you no more than you want him bothering."

It worked for several nights, but there came a night when Barney just cut the screen out the window and got loose. Next morning the preacher brought him back and unloaded him. *This* time he had taken his box of old fruit jars. And he had slept in the garage. The next time, he loaded the pie safe onto a wheelbarrow and took it. Slept on the back porch. It looked like Barney was trying to move to the preacher's. "Expect the cow next," I told the man.

He shuddered, like the very thoughts of it made him sick to his stomach.

I tried everything I knew to keep Barney at home. I put on new screens, locked the doors, even tried tying him to his bed.

But locks and ropes were never any bar to Barney. He always found a way to get out. It was the most unsettling time I ever went through with him. And I can't tell you how many times that preacher brought him home next morning. Or sent for us to come after him.

All that time we never found out what was unsettling him or why he was acting so. The fruit jars got broken, we threw them away, he took mine, and when they got broken he commenced taking Sudley's. The old feather tick busted a seam and left a trail of feathers from my house to the mission that looked like a hundred ducks had been picked. The pie safe got so creened the doors wouldn't shut. I tried giving him some spoons and a dish to pack around with him, but he knew they weren't his. It was something of his own he had to take with him and was wearing plumb out.

The one thing his mind hadn't lit on yet to take was the cow and I gave thanks he hadn't, but every time he lit out, don't think I didn't look to see if he'd taken her this time. The preacher was ga'nted down the way it was and I figured the cow would be the last straw. What I was afraid of was, he would have the law carry Barney off to the asylum.

Sudley said, "Whyn't you threaten Barney just a little with it? Tell him you'll have him carried off if he don't settle down and behave. It might work, Frony."

"It would be the cruelest thing I ever heard of," I said. "It would scare him to death. They used to tease him that way in school — what little he went. He would run off home and hide under the bed. I wouldn't do such for the world."

But I can tell you I was mortally at my wit's ends, so distracted I didn't know whether I was coming or going, when things finally began to head up.

5

THE PREACHER had brought Barney home one more time. "I
didn't bring his fruit jars," he said. "They're nothing but
broken bits now. Since he's determined to move them down
to my place they may as well stay there. He won't have to
haul them around any more."

Barney had got to where he figured the preacher's car was
part his, he rode in it so much. He would get out and walk
around it and pat it and rub the dust off the sides with his
shirttail. He was doing so, now, when Sudley came windmill-
ing into the yard from the barn lot. He was agitated as I ever
saw him, arms flying about, legs pumping, his breath coming
fast. He didn't pay the least attention to the preacher, not
even to say howdy. "Come on, Frony," he yelled at me, "we
got to go help Witchie. Tish and him have got into it again
and she's run him off. He's hid under the culbert down on
the pike. She's got a pistol. We got to help him or she'll kill
him, sure!"

I ran to the porch and grabbed my bonnet. "How do you
know he's hid under the culbert?" I said.

"The biggest boy has come and told me. Benjy said they
had an awful fight and he seen Witchie hide out under the

culbert," Sudley said. "He said Tish was the maddest he ever seen and had a pistol hunting for Witchie."

"What did they get into it about?" I said.

"I never asked. Come on, we got to hurry," he said.

"If you're waiting on me," I said, "you're losing time. I'm ready."

He went flying in the house and came back with his shotgun. "Them McKittredges have put Tish up to this," he said. "She don't go flourishing a pistol around commonly. When her and Witchie fight, they always fistfight. Or maybe she takes a hickory limb to him. It's them brothers of hers has put her up to this. And no McKittredge is going to shoot my boy if I can help it."

Darkus and Lissie had come outside, the babies on their hips. Darkus, of a sudden, handed little Junior to Lissie. "I'm going," she said. "Them McKittredges have got Pap outnumbered."

Lissie's face puckered up. "I'm not going to stay here by myself," she said. "One of them McKittredges might come prowling around here and what would I do? Just me and two babies! Sudley, don't let Darkus go!"

Sudley stopped in his tracks. "I never thought of that," he said. "They might do that. I wouldn't put it past 'em. No, Darkus, you stay here, too. Run down and get Frony's gun and keep it right by you. Lock the doors and if any of them McKittredges come prowling about, let 'em have it!"

Darkus scampered off to get the gun and Barney went tearing out after her. "He wouldn't be of much help," I said, "but it might make the girls feel better if *something* with pants on was with 'em."

"He can shoot," Sudley said. "He's a dead shot. If Darkus ain't sure she can get off a good shot, Barney can. He'd about as soon shoot a McKittredge as a squirrel, I reckon."

There came a kind of squeaking sound from the corner of the porch and I looked around. I declare, I had plumb forgot the preacher. "Are you choking, Preacher?" I said. "I'll pound you on the back."

He shook his head and swallowed a time or two, then he went scuttling off and crawled in his little compact. We got in Sudley's car. It had a flat tire. Sudley swore a terrible oath. "Someday," he said, "I'm going to get out of patience with Darkus." He got out and run over to the preacher's car. "I'll have to borry your car, Preacher," he said, "we got a flat."

"No," the preacher said, gripping the wheel tight, "no, I won't loan you my car to go on this death's errand."

I was afraid of what Sudley might do, he was so worked up. I would have hated to see him point his gun at a preacher. I ran over quick and said, "Preacher, Witchie might be killed. He's hid under that culbert down there, with a woman with a gun looking for him. If we don't get down there she's liable to shoot him. You want *that* on your conscience?"

"Oh, Lord," the preacher said, groaning, "how did I get mixed up in this?"

"Because you was here," I said.

He was white as a ghost and shaking all over. "If you'll promise me you won't shoot," he said. "If you'll promise me there'll be no bloodshed . . . it's no way to settle anything, with guns. You'll have to promise me."

"I promise I won't shoot first," Sudley said, "and that's as far as I can go, Preacher. I won't commence it. But if a Mc-

Kittredge fires on me, or my boy, I have got to fire back. That's as good as I can give you."

"Get in," the preacher said, in a weak and fainty voice. "I think I'm having a nightmare. Things like this don't happen! Not in real life. Nor that lunatic boy moving featherbeds and fruit jars and pie safes back and forth. That doesn't happen, either. Not in a civilized world!"

"This ain't the civilized world, Preacher," Sudley said, "this is Broke Neck, Kentucky. If it *can* happen, around here it does."

We sailed down the hill, but when we got to the bottom and across the creek and past Ethan Green's house, the preacher slowed up. "Sudley," he said, "why don't you let me drive you into town and get the police? They're the ones to handle this, not you."

Sudley shook his head. "No, Preacher, they ain't. A man don't have the law in a family mix-up like this. I got to handle this myself."

"Sudley," I said, remembering something all at once, "you reckon Tish and Witchie could have got into it over a new youngun? You recollect Witchie told us one time if they had any more Tish was going to make him help out. On account of the Aid to Dependent Children don't pay but for five. Reckon that could be it?"

"With a McKittredge," Sudley said, "it could."

The preacher was going real slow. "Is your son drawing for five dependent children, Sudley?"

"He ain't," Sudley said. "Tish is. Witchie don't see a dime of that money. Tish gets it all."

"That's his wife?" the preacher said.

"She is his woman. They ain't married. They can't afford to get married. Tish would lose her check if they did," Sudley said.

"I have heard," the preacher said, shaking his head, "I have heard of such things . . . but I didn't really believe it. They have five children. They don't deny it. They consort together, openly, but they won't get married because they would lose their government check."

"Well, now, Preacher," Sudley said, "I wouldn't say they consort *openly*. A body *don't*, you know. But you about got the straight of it, yes. They can't afford to get married."

"You make a regular profession of getting government aid, don't you?" the preacher said.

Sudley was modest at the praise. "I have put a considerable amount of my time on it, Preacher. And if I do say so myself, I've not done too bad at it. I figger if they're giving it away, a man would be a fool not to get all he could."

"Why doesn't your son marry that woman and go to work and support those children?" the preacher said. "It would be far more self-respecting."

"Ain't nothing wrong with Witchie's self-respect," Sudley said. "You can't eat it, though, Preacher. Where would he work and make as much as Tish is drawing? It's best to be on the safe side. But if Tish is fixing to have another one, I'll have to see if I can't find him something so he can help out a little. Get down, Frony, we're coming nigh the culbert. That clump of willows this side is a good place for a McKittredge to hide."

I scrooched down a little, but not much. I aimed to see if anybody was going to take a pot shot at us. The preacher slowed down till we were barely moving. He was bent over the wheel as low as he could get and his shoulders were twitching. It came over me that never in his life had that man had a gun fired at him. "Was you in the war, Preacher?" I said.

He shook his head.

"4-F?" I said.

He shook his head again. "I was deferred. I was a ministerial student."

"Well," I said, "I reckon there was enough Fowler boys in the army to do your fighting for you, too."

We edged up towards the willow clump, just creeping. It was still as the grave. Nothing made a sound. Nothing moved. Finally Sudley heaved a sigh. "Stop here," he said, "I'll get out and nose around a little. Looks like there ain't no McKittredges here, though."

"You ain't going nowhere without me," I said, scrambling out the back, "just wait up."

We left the preacher in the car and we took the ditch for a little protection and eased up on the culbert. When we got close enough Sudley said, "Witchie?" in a kind of loud whisper. "It's me, Witchie. Pap. You all right, boy?"

Not a sound.

Sudley tried again. There still wasn't any answer. Sudley stood up. "Either they have kilt him or he ain't here. You go see, Frony. I've not got the heart."

There wasn't anything in the culbert at all. Not a thing. It was strictly empty. But somebody *had* been there. There were tracks scrabbling around in the mud. I called Sudley and he came to see. "He's been and gone," he said. "Well, at least he's not dead. I wish we could foller them tracks, but they run out in the grass."

We looked around, trying to trace the tracks, see if he had hit the road some place, but we couldn't find a thing. The grass was too thick. We went back to the car. The preacher was wiping his face. "Get in," he said, tired-like, "and let's go home, Sudley. I should have known it was a lot of smoke and no fire. You have aged me ten years, though."

"If you don't mind, Preacher," Sudley said, "I'd like to go down the road a piece . . . to the McKittredges'. It ain't far . . . just around the bend. I ain't satisfied in my mind yet that Witchie is all right."

"No," the preacher said, "I won't do that. You walk to the McKittredges'. I'll wait right here for you."

We took care, coming up to the place, but far as we could tell everything was as common. Tish was hanging out clothes. Miz McKittredge was working in her garden patch. The young ones were playing around in the back yard. Wasn't none of the menfolks at the house. Not even Witchie. "Let me do the talking," I said to Sudley.

"I wish you would," he said. "If the men was here, I would, but seeing they ain't . . ."

We went up and I spoke to Tish and she spoke back, pleasant as could be. The young ones went flocking around Sudley, glad as they always were to see him. He made over them, the way he does over all the young ones in the family. I said, "Where's Witchie, Tish?"

"He's out looking for Benjy," she said. "Him and Benjy got into it the worst way this morning and Witchie went to whup him and Benjy run off. Witchie went chasing down the road after him. I'd of thought he'd found him by now. It's been a couple of hours."

"It wasn't you and Witchie got into it?" I said.

She laughed. "Why no? Me and Witchie ain't fit since the first of the month. Over my check, like common. No, we ain't had no trouble. But Benjy is getting too big for his britches these days. He's going on fourteen and thinks he's a grown man. Witchie told him to go to the spring and get my wash water for me and Benjy said you make me and Witchie said By God don't think I can't and Benjy said you and who else and Witchie cut him a appletree limb and started for Benjy. Benjy lit out like a scared rabbit, Witchie right behind him. I was the worst outdone. Me and the girls had to get up every drop of the wash water ourselves. What did you want with Witchie? I'll tell him when he comes back."

I said, thinking quick, "Sudley's car has got a flat tire. We thought maybe Witchie could take us to town."

"I'll tell him to come right on," she said. "And I just may go with you, if I get done washing in time. There's several things I need from over there."

If Tish was in the family way it wasn't showing, but I wasn't yet satisfied she was telling all the truth. I said, "You going to the doctor, maybe?"

She laughed. "You know I don't doctor in town, Frony. I want to get some piece goods to make the girls some dresses, is what I need to go for."

I thought I'd just as well come out flat-footed with it. "You ain't fixing to have another young one?"

"I wouldn't go to no doctor for such as that," she said. "How'd you find out? Not from Witchie, for I've not told him yet and he's too unnoticing to guess."

I blurted out the whole thing — how Benjy had come tearing up to Sudley's, what he had told, and what we had reckoned might lie behind it. Tish laughed. "There ain't a word of truth in it, Frony. Benjy has made the whole thing up. But it's liable to be, when I get around to setting a fire to Witchie. And you got one thing right. This is one over the limit and Witchie is going to have to give me anyway as much as the law does for it. Or Sudley will have to get Job Rigdon to stretch the law a little."

"Them are state funds, Tish," Sudley said. "Job can't stretch 'em."

"Then you better commence thinking of some way for Witchie to make some money," she said.

We headed on back towards where the preacher was wait- ing. Didn't either one of us say anything for a spell. "What do you make of it, Frony?" Sudley said, finally.

"I make just what you make of it," I said. "Tish was telling the truth and we got a liar in the family. Benjy."

"I do hate to believe it," Sudley said, "but it sure does look like it. A lie don't serve either end, good or bad. See all the commotion Benjy has caused us today."

"Keep it in mind," I said, "from now on. And put a grain of salt on anything Benjy tells."

"And I got to put my mind on something for Witchie," Sudley said, "Tish won't give him a minute's peace if I don't." He commenced smiling. "But it'll be nice to have another little un in the family, won't it? Our Whitley is get- ting up too big for a baby. We'll have to start bringing him up soon. I do dread the day, Frony, when there's not any little chaps in the family."

"It's not likely to happen," I said, "you have done provided against it. Time your oldest boys and girls quit bearing, Na- thaniel and Whitley will be old enough to commence. You needn't worry about such, Sudley."

We didn't tell the preacher. We felt too ashamed of Benjy. We just said everything was all right. And no harm done. "Except to my nerves," he said. "I don't believe I'll ever be the same again."

We turned around and started back and when we got close to the mission Sudley said, "There's no use you driving us up the hill, Preacher. We'll just get out at your place and walk the rest of the way."

The preacher didn't raise any objections. He just said, "If you don't mind, Sudley. I think I'm going to lie down a while."

6

He had to wait, though.

When we turned in his driveway his woman and young ones were all hanging out the upstairs windows yelling and carrying on, motioning to him and screaming at him, and making the worst racket about something. He jumped out of the car, me and Sudley following, and went running towards them. "What is it?" he yelled, "what's the matter?"

His woman had to get the children quietened down before she could tell him. "That crazy man is in the house," she said, "and he's got a cow with him! He's trying to bring that cow upstairs! *Do something*, Thomas! Do something before we're all killed!"

I thought the preacher was going to collapse. He shrunk up right before our eyes. "No," he sort of moaned, "oh, no!"

"Stay right where you're at, Preacher," I said, soon as what the woman said had sunk in, "it's Barney. I'll take care of him and that cow."

I took a good grip on that piece of stovewood and marched in the house. I was so outdone with Barney I wouldn't cared in the least to hit him a few licks with it. What I saw when I got inside put it out of my mind, though. Have you got any idea what happens when a cow gets wedged in the bend of a stairway? Gentlemen, a tarpolian ought to be spread first! It gives them the scours, worse than any drench you could pour down 'em.

My land, there was my old piedy cow, stuck tighter than a fly in a molasses trap, her head going around the bend and her rump trying to follow. She was bawling her head off and she had kicked out all the stair banisters but two, and one hind leg was caught between them. The other one was slipping and sliding and plunging around in the mess.

When the preacher saw it and smelled it he just went over and set down on the sofa and hid his head in his hands. Sudley said, "Good gracious, Frony, a body wouldn't think one cow could make that big of a mess, would they? She's in a tight fix, ain't she? How'll we get her out?"

I was looking around for Barney, but he wasn't anywhere to be seen. Lost interest and gone off some place, I knew. I got a chair and stood on it and commenced rubbing the cow and talking to her and got her to quit twitching around and making so much fuss. "See if the preacher has got a saw and a axe," I said. "We'll have to cut her loose."

The preacher roused up. "You'll ruin the stairway!"

"How could we?" I said, "It's done ruint. All we got to do is cut them last two banisters out, Preacher, and the railing, and then she'll come free. Them bannisters and that railing is what has got her wedged in. We'll fix it back for you."

"Oh, no," he said, real quick, "no, indeed! When you get that cow loose just take her on home, Miz Sadler. I'll have the stairs mended." He went out with Sudley to hunt the saw and axe.

The woman and children had come to the top of the stairs

when the cow got quiet and they were sitting there looking on. The woman was kind of rocking back and forth, groaning now and then. "Maybe you better lie down," I said.

"I'm not sick," she said. "It's just . . . oh, my pretty stairs. My pretty stairs! Just look at them! Oh, it's so dreadful . . ."

"Don't give it another thought," I said, "I'll clean it up spotless. You'll never know a cow was in here when I get done."

We got her loose finally, but not without some trouble. It made her nervous hearing the saw and axe and she got to plunging around and kicked a hole in the plaster wall. We led her outside and tied her and then me and Sudley pitched in and cleaned and scrubbed and scoured. When we had got through, Sudley said, "Preacher, I aim to fix you a fine stairway. I have got some good seasoned wood . . ."

The preacher sort of waved his hands around. "Sudley, will you just go. Just, *please,* go!"

We did, taking it easy climbing the hill on account of the cow. She was plumb done up. It had been hard on her, wedged in that little tight corner. I was afraid it would make her skittery for life.

We talked, some, about how easy upset the preacher and all his family were. "They appear," Sudley said, "to be an awful nervous lot, don't they, Frony? All of 'em . . . him *and* his woman and all the kids."

"I never seen anybody yet from off," I said, "that wasn't. They are all just one jump ahead of a fit. If the rest of the United States is in the same jangle the preacher and his family are in, the country is in a sorry state."

7

DARKUS saw us coming down the road and met us at the gate. "Where have you all been?" she said. "All this time, us not knowing but what Pap and you had been killed? To say nothing of Witchie. If we've not had a time!"

I started to tell her, but she said, "Oh, it don't matter now that you're home. I done the best I could to stall him off, Frony, but he had a paper that showed the law was on his side so I had to give in."

"Who?" I said. "Give in to who? And what paper are you talking about?"

She waved her arms around like a windmill. "Tate, that's who! My brother, Tate Fowler. He has took Barney down to that old place in Coon Den Holler. Him and all his old things. Tate come after him in the truck and carried him off!"

I was astonished enough to have sat flat down in the dust. "How could he of?" I said. "How come Barney to go with him?"

"Oh, Barney was in the biggest way of going," she said. "He said he had been trying to move in with Tate a long

time. Said he never could find him. He said Tate told him
you had been cheating him of his draw — just giving five dollars out of his check. Said Tate told him he'd give him ten. If
he'd move in with him, that is."

"So *that's* the way of it," I said. "That's what lies behind
Barney being so unsettled all this time. That's where Barney
has been trying to move. You hear that, Sudley? Tate has
been luring Barney off, to get his hands on that Totally and
Permanently Disabled check! Why, I'll go right down to that
old holler and give Tate Fowler a piece of my mind! Right
this minute I'll go. I'll tell *him* who shook the bush! And
bring my boy back home where he belongs."

Sudley's face had got red and he was commencing to shuffle
his feet. He said, "Wait a minute, Frony, let's hear it all.
What was that about the law and a paper, Darkus?"

She said, "He had a paper. Tate did. It said he was Barney's guardeen. I seen it. He wouldn't let me touch it, but
he showed it to me and with my own eyes I seen it."

"That does it," I said. "Do you aim to stand here, Sudley,
and let Tate Fowler take over the guardeenship of my boy?"

"No," he said, "I don't. He has went too far, Frony. He
has done a foolish thing. I don't know how he has worked it
to get hisself named Barney's guardeen, but it don't go like
the law to me. We got to see Job Rigdon. Get ready, Frony."

"And leave Barney down in that old holler?" I said. "Why,
Tate won't get him no supper. And Barney's not going to
like down there. Tate'll talk rough to him, likely, and get
him all stirred up."

"For now, Frony," Sudley said, "you got to leave him. If
Tate has got a paper made out by the law, you ain't got no
rights to take Barney away."

"What is Job Rigdon thinking of," I said, "to let a mother's own boy be took away from her?"

"That's what we aim to find out," Sudley said.

He had to fix the flat before we could go, but when we started he floorboarded that old Lincoln all the way to town. I hung on and hoped nobody's dogs or chickens got in the way. If they had, it would have been thump and goodbye. I don't know as we ever made the trip to town faster.

Job's office was closed when we got there, it being dusky dark by then, but we went to his house. I never saw a man so surprised at what we told him. "Why, Sudley," he said, "I can't hardly believe what I'm hearing. How could Tate have got such a paper? I wish it was county funds. I could have stopped it right here. But you wait a minute. I'll call the public assistance and get the straight of this."

He got on the telephone to the public assistance. All we could hear was one side, but it was mortally worth hearing. "No," he said, "she ain't mentally incompetent, but somebody in yore office is. Believing that fool, Tate Fowler. I don't care what lawyer made out the papers, I've knowed Frony Sadler all her life and she is wittier than you and that lawyer and Tate Fowler all put together. You have been took in, mister, and you better commence making it right." He talked on some more and then hung up. He said, "I'll take care of it, Sudley. It'll be all right, now. Go get your boy, Frony." He shook his head. "That public assistance feller is new and he's from off and he's not got the hang of things here yet. He didn't know Frony. And Tate had went to that jackleg lawyer, that sot drunkard McKittredge, and he had swore she was mentally incompetent. I don't know what things are coming to, I swear I don't."

"I ort to knowed," Sudley said, "a McKittredge was back of it. They have got a mean streak a mile wide in 'em. Besides not having sense enough to tell a June day from December. I declare, I'd just as soon be pecked to death by a duck as to have any dealings with 'em."

"There ain't no need," Job said. "I'll see to it for you."

"Well, I'm obliged to you, Job," Sudley said. We stood up to go. "I really am obliged to you. If there's ever anything I can do for you, just name it. You know I'll be proud to."

Job leaned back in his chair and grinned a little at Sudley. "Well," he said, "there is something you can do, Sudley. We got a school board election coming up this fall." He reached in his pocket and pulled out a little card. "Wish you'd use your influence to elect this man. It's your district got a new board member coming up."

Sudley looked at the card. "Pink Cowley, eh?" He squinched up his eyes and studied a minute. "I know him. Be a good man for us. A real good man." He studied the card some more, then he put it in his pocket. "I tell you, Job. You know you can count on *me*. I've not ever let you down. But if you want my *influence*, I kind of think it's worth a little more than helping Frony."

"I allowed you would feel that way," Job said. He squinched up his eyes. "What did you have in mind, Sudley?"

"My boy, Witchie, needs some work," Sudley said. "His woman is expecting again."

"I see," Job said. He laughed. "Over the limit, eh?"

"Right spang over the limit," Sudley said.

"Well," Job said, "I wouldn't be surprised if there's not some changes made in the school bus drivers. Usually is after an election. 'Twouldn't surprise me one bit if there wouldn't be one or two new drivers — *if* Pink Cowley is elected."

Sudley nodded his head. "He likely will be, Job."

Job got up and slapped Sudley on the back. "Fine," he said. "Anything you need for the campaign, Sudley, let me know."

We edged out the door, Job following us onto the porch. "Ain't it a nice night?" he said. "That rain sure did cool things off."

"I'm obliged, Job," Sudley said.

"Anytime," Job said, "anytime, Sudley. Glad to do a favor for an old friend."

On the way home I said to Sudley, "Why does he want Pink Cowley elected? He don't strike me as being smart enough to be on the school board."

"He don't want him for his smartness, Frony," Sudley said. "They are aiming to pack the school board and name a new superintendent. It is a job with a heap of power. A heap of power, and a lot of patronage. It don't pay to let that job get out of hand."

"Oh," I said. "Wonder who he's got in mind for it."

"I don't know," Sudley said. "But it'll be somebody does what Job wants. You seen how quick he traded with me. He's got it all worked out."

"You aim to vote us all for Pink?" I said.

"Why, sure," he said, "what else? We traded — right in front of your eyes, Frony."

"Well, I appreciated him getting that public assistance straightened out enough I'd of been willing to vote for him without no trade," I said.

"That ain't the way you do it," Sudley said. "I appreciate

all Job has done, too. But I have done something for him for every one of them favors. That's the way politics works. He knowed he was collecting on a old favor when he helped us about Barney. He knowed when he asked me to use my influence to elect Pink Cowley, *he* was going to have to favor me. So we come to the agreement."

"And Witchie'll be a school bus driver," I said. "I don't know as I would have been that clever."

"You're not called on to be," he said. "Just leave the politicking to me, Frony."

The very next day the public assistance came out and we got things straight about Barney and that night Barney was at home and glad to be there. "I didn't like at Tate's," he said, "I'd ruther to be here."

"Of course you would, honey," I said. I hated to do it but I had to make him understand he couldn't go moving about again, so I said, "The law says you got to stay here, honey. Don't matter what Tate or anybody else tells you. It's the law says you got to live here with me."

"I'd ruther," he said. He smiled at me as sweet as an angel. "Apple dumplings?" he said.

"Apple dumplings," I said, "soon as I can make 'em."

That was the last of our trouble with Tate over Barney. It wasn't the last of our trouble with Tate. Not by a long sight. But he didn't bother us trying to get Barney's Totally and Permanently Disabled check anymore.

The preacher got Stape Cartwright from over at the Mill to fix his stairs. Put in new banisters and plastered up the holes. It was a middling job. Sudley could have done it better. Sudley would have used some of his fine black walnut that's been seasoning for ten years in the barn. He would have turned them banisters on his hand lathe and spindled them down fine and then he would have rubbed them with pumice and linseed oil and beeswax until they were smooth as butter.

A master at carpentering, Sudley is. He built his own house. Not a board in it bought. All his own timber. Fine red beech floors. Good hard maple doors and window frames. Whole house sheeted with chestnut and ash and poplar. All framed with oak. That house'll stand till Judgment Day — unless the atom bomb goes off first.

But the preacher was satisfied with bought stair rails, like he put in to begin with. Cheap, flimsy things. If Sudley had built that stairway in the beginning my old piedy cow couldn't have kicked the railings out. She would have broken a hind leg first. Both of them, likely.

But the preacher was an educated fool. There's a lot of them in the world. Education don't do a thing for them except unfit them for their natural life. Makes them foolish and nervous and uncertain. That kind is going to blow us all right off the face of the earth some day.

8

ELECTION TIME is always exciting around here. The state goes
Democrat most of the time, so every four years when it's time
to elect another governor the Democrats are out working like
a hive of bees — swarming. It's not a time us Republicans get
in much of a sweat, though. The Democrats get all the barn
jobs — the state highway jobs — so we aren't in much of a
fever in the governor's election. Generally they fight it out
amongst themselves, and gentlemen, you've not seen a fight
until you've seen Democrats fighting amongst themselves.
They mortally do cut each other into little pieces.

When *we* lay with it is when the county or district elections
come up. This is a Republican county and all the jobs go to
Republicans. We got a good Republican courthouse. So
what we work up a sweat over is the district magistrate, the
County Clerk or County Judge or County Attorney, the High
Sheriff, and the school board.

Sudley laid him in a bunch of cards and buttons and car
stickers and began handing them out. He commenced talking up Pink Cowley wherever he run into the people, crossroads, church, or swapping work. But the heat don't really

start in a campaign till the first of October — the last four
weeks. That's when you're on the go all day every day, leaving no stone unturned. All summer Sudley was talking and
handing out buttons and cards and stickers, but there wasn't
any use floorboarding the gas yet. "I got plenty of time to go
to the meetings and help get in the tobacco," Sudley said.

In this country the summer is when the congregations have
their protracted meetings — revivals, some call them. Far
and wide, just one after another all summer long, there is a
protracted meeting going on. If you're willing to drive a little distance there's not a night in the whole enduring summer
when there's not a meeting to attend.

We always attended as much as we could. We didn't always
hold with what they believed, but you don't have to to enjoy
a good revival. The singing is good, even if you don't appreciate the preaching. But if you get a preacher with the power,
who does some good old-fashioned pulpit pounding and
sweating and laboring, put him with some good, strong song
leading, the kind that makes you get goose-bumps on your
arms and shivers down your back, the kind that makes you
feel your wings sprouting, it gives you a good idea of what
heaven is going to be like. I do love a fine protracted meeting.

In our meetinghouse here on Broke Neck Ridge we didn't
commonly get in the running during the summer. We have
meetings any season. The meetinghouse is open to any and
all the year round. If any man feels moved by the spirit to
hold a revival, all he has to do is see the custodian across the
road. He will open the building for him, sweep it out, build
the fires, the word will be passed around, and we will all at-

tend and uphold and support him. Unless he commences to preach the denominations. We generally walk out on him, then. But as long as he sticks to the Bible and don't add *to* the Bible, he's welcome.

You would be surprised how tricky the denominationers can be, though. One time a fellow came driving through and said he'd like to hold a revival in the meetinghouse. We said fine, we'd be proud for him to. We turned out good crowds for him. Everybody enjoyed him. He had the real power and spirit in him — for a while. The meeting had been going on for about a week, the people coming from all the settlements around, when one night he passed out paper and pencils and asked everybody to sign their names. Said he wanted it to keep in touch. For a mailing list.

Sudley rose right up on his feet and said, "Nope. You're aiming to get up a church roll. You're aiming to put our names on a church list. I'm not signing. I don't hold with such. And I'm leaving this meeting right now." He walked out the door and one by one everybody else in the building filed out right behind him. Left the building totally empty except for the preacher and his song leader. It broke up the meeting, and the preacher left the country that night. It was good he did. If he hadn't, he would have been asked to next day. We don't appreciate being so abused in our own meetinghouse.

Commonly the congregation at the mission, just a little handful of people, maybe two dozen altogether nowadays, didn't hold a revival in the summer, either. It was a denomination didn't run to protracted meetings much — sort of a stiff-necked denomination. So we were a little astonished when the preacher came by one day early in August and said the mission was going to hold a meeting commencing on the fifteenth. We were sitting out in the yard under the big maple tree eating watermelon and the preacher was enjoying a big slice.

Sudley spit out a mouthful of seeds and said, "Well, I'm proud to hear you're aiming to hold a meeting. It'll do your folks good. Be a real spiritual refreshment for 'em. But you can't hold it the last two weeks in August, Preacher. That's when the colored folks across the river always hold their meeting. The August meeting. They always begin on the seventeenth of August, no matter what day of the week, or the weather, and they hold till the last Sunday. Then they break up with an all-day meeting and dinner on the ground. You'll have to pick another time."

"Well, Sudley," the preacher said, "there's no real conflict, is there? They're on the other side of the river . . . and it's a colored folks' meeting . . ."

I was shocked. Time out of mind the colored folks in the settlement had held their August meeting. Nobody, not even the oldest people in the settlement remember when they began it. My father said he went when he was a little boy and he reckoned his father went before him. Nobody would ever think of holding a revival during their meeting. We all went to the August meeting. Why, you'd as soon miss the opening day of the hunting season or the County Fair. The August meeting is something to look forward to from one year to the next. My land, just to hear old Aunt Dilly Byers sing, "Come, Come, Angel Band," is something none of us would think of missing. And her ninety years old and liable not to sing it another year!

And the all-day meeting and dinner on the ground! We

take our best. You never saw such cakes and pies and fried
chicken and baked ham and pickles and slaw and potato salad
— hot *and* cold — and the men save their best watermelons
and mushmelons and have them nice and cold from laying in
the spring. Oh, it's the finest time of the year — the August
meeting.

"Preacher," Sudley said, "I don't like to appear to be going
against you. I like to be agreeable with any man. But it
would go against my conscience not to tell you it would be a
mistake to hold your revival while the August meeting is
going on."

The preacher wiped the watermelon off his hands. "I'm
afraid it's settled, Sudley. I was very anxious for the bishop
himself to conduct this meeting and I wrote him several
months ago. His schedule is quite heavy, so naturally I told
him any time during the summer that was convenient for him
would suit us. I don't believe I can ask him to change now."

"It would of been better," Sudley said, "if you had told him
any time in the summer *except* the last two weeks in August."

"I think you're exaggerating the importance of this conflict
in dates, Sudley," the preacher said. "I don't see how it can
make all that difference. At any rate, we are committed now.
And I want you and your family to promise me to come to
our meeting. I want you to see for yourself, Sudley, something of the dignity of a genuinely worshipful service . . .
hear some of the fine, noble old hymns of the church . . ."

"You think we don't worship right, Preacher?" Sudley said,
roused up all at once.

"Well," the preacher said, sort of laughing, "you people are
very emotional in your services, Sudley. You certainly make
more noise . . ."

"It's a joyful noise," Sudley said. "It says in the Bible, 'Come unto the Lord and make a joyful noise.' We make it, Preacher. Singing and preaching and shouting . . . we get happy in our religion, Preacher."

"I know that's what you call it," the preacher said, "but I don't know that I would put it that way. Sudley, this half-superstitious . . ."

Sudley squinched up his eyes. He was getting agitated. He said, "Preacher, let me tell you how I was saved. I reckon you would call *that* superstition, too, but I call it the hand of the Lord. I had been wrestling with the devil all one summer. I had been going to the meetings regular and I knowed I was a sinner and bound straight for hell if I couldn't break through and see the light. But I couldn't. I just purely couldn't. It just wouldn't come through for me. I prayed and I prayed and I wrestled and wrestled. But I couldn't get no clear leading of the spirit. It was a great burden to me.

"Then one day me and Frony, here, and her boy was out sang digging. We come home through her boundary of timber and all at once we run onto the raining tree. Just a common old blackgum tree . . . no different from a hundred others in the woods. Except it was raining. It was raining pure rain, Preacher. Clear, pure water. The ground was wet all under it. We stood under it and got our heads wet and our hands and faces and our clothes. It was raining such a steady mizzle of water that it was dripping from the leaves, and the limbs and trunk of the tree were glisteny with the water.

"It was a miracle, Preacher, for you know that goes against nature. God blinded Saul of Tarsus with a bright light on the road to Damascus. He made a tree rain to wash my sins away and to baptize me with his grace. Just this one tree.

Not another gum tree, nor any other kind, was raining. But this was a sign to me, to a lost lamb and a sinner. Instead of blinding me with a light, the Lord opened my eyes and I broke through and seen the light.

"I sent around for all the people to come and witness and I repented right there, washed by the water of that tree, God's pure water. I made my confession before the people under that tree. And we opened a meeting that held as long as the tree rained. We had a season of joyful songs and prayer and thanksgiving that lasted five days. Till the tree quit raining. That was the sign for us to break up. I have been a Christian ever since, Preacher."

"Oh, Sudley, Sudley," the preacher said, "I have heard about your raining tree. My people still talk about it . . ."

"And I bet they believe in it, if you get right down to it," Sudley said. "It caused several souls to be saved, besides me."

"There was some perfectly normal reason why that tree gave off moisture, Sudley," the preacher said. "God does not set aside the laws of nature. The tree had stored up moisture, probably. For some natural reason it began to exude the moisture through its leaves and limbs."

"Preacher, let me ask you," Sudley said. "You believe in the Bible, don't you?"

"Of course I do," he said.

"You believe in the miracles in the Bible?" Sudley said.

"Yes, but . . ."

"God set aside the laws of nature to speak to Moses from the burning bush, Preacher," Sudley said. "And to part the waves of the sea for the children of Israel to pass. And for Jesus to heal the lame and the halt and to make the blind see and to raise the dead. One touch, and they were healed. You could say the laws of nature was set aside there, too."

"I'm not so sure, Sudley," the preacher said, "perhaps nature was working . . ."

"You think God couldn't pass a miracle nowadays? Is that what you think, Preacher?" Sudley said.

"No . . . yes, of course He could. But He doesn't . . ." the preacher said.

"How do you know He doesn't?" Sudley said.

"But, Sudley . . ."

"No buts about it, Preacher. The *Bible* says it! If you have been educated out of believing what the Bible says, I feel sorry for you." Sudley said. "That's the trouble with you educated preachers. You have done explained away all the miracle of the Bible and you've not got nothing to put in its place. Your religion is all brain and no heart." He grabbed up another piece of watermelon. "Here, eat another slice before I lose my temper."

The preacher laughed. "No, I've had plenty, and I must go. Will you and your family come to our meeting, Sudley?"

Sudley set his mouth. "We'll come the first two nights. But when the August meeting commences on the seventeenth we can't come no more. I wouldn't flout old Aunt Dilly Byers's feelings for nothing in this world, to say nothing of Stanley and Exie and Agnus and some of the others. We always go to the August meeting and we give as much as we can spare because they count on what the white folks give to tide 'em through the year. That's the best I can do, Preacher."

"Well, no hard feelings," the preacher said. "Come the first two nights."

We did, but it was the quarest revival I ever attended. They had men at the door to hand out little printed programs. Had "Order of Service" wrote across the top. It gave out the song numbers and when to stand and when to set and something called a "litany" written out. Adding *to* the Bible, if I ever saw it. We laid the programs down and let them lie and we stood and set when the others did. We didn't know their songs so we couldn't join in the singing.

The evangelist — I reckon he was their bishop — wore his collar turned backwards. He didn't even once feel the power. Didn't pound the pulpit or raise his voice or even begin to work up a sweat. And *he* added to the Bible. Took a notebook into the pulpit with him and preached from it. Just read one Scripture from the Bible and then used his notebook. Then he set down and the preacher pronounced the benediction and that was all there was to it. I was glad we didn't have to go but two nights.

My, how grand the August meeting was beside it. Such singing as I never hope to hear again. They had the guitars hooked up to the electric, and two tambourines, and Exie banged the cymbals the way she always does. She's not any bigger than a mosquito and the cymbals are about as big as she is, but she mortally can make them ring. And Aunt Dilly looked the nicest in her long white satin robe. Her and the song starters always wear white satin robes with long sleeves that look like angel wings. They had her up front on the platform and her hair was white and hung in long curls and her sweet old face looked the happiest. It did your heart good just to look at her.

I don't know as I ever heard her sing "Angel Band" any sweeter. She sang the verses by herself but when she come to the chorus everybody joined in — "Come, come, angel band. Come and around me stand. Bear me away on your snowy wings, to my eternal home." Aunt Dilly would lift her long white satin sleeves and they looked just like snowy wings and you could almost feel them lifting you up and bearing you home. It had everybody crying, it was so sweet. They had a fine meeting, the colored folks did, and reaped the harvest well.

We heard about the mission meeting. They didn't save a soul in the whole two weeks of their meeting. The people said the church was nearly empty every night after the August meeting commenced. Everybody went across the river. But the preacher told Sudley, "We had a good meeting."

"By their fruits ye shall know them," Sudley said. "There was ten souls saved at the August meeting, Preacher. I hear you didn't save none."

"We have different purposes, Sudley," he said. "Different aims and goals. Our meeting was fruitful. It was a time of great encouragement to our people."

Sudley laughed. "That goes like an excuse, Preacher. You're a good man and I like you, but you don't know much about religion, Preacher. There's not but one aim and one purpose. To save souls. If you don't do that you just as well to close your doors."

That made the preacher mad and he went away sort of huffy. Like to overset his little compact turning around in the lane. "Maybe you was too hard on him," I said.

"He'll get over it," Sudley said. "I feel sorry for that man, Frony. He ain't got much of a handle to hang nothing on, has he?"

9

WITH THE MEETINGS over and September at hand, it was time to begin cutting the tobacco.

We had two crops — mine and Sudley's — and when cutting time comes it takes us all. The cutting is not so bad. It's the hauling to the barn and housing it. Hanging all those heavy sticks of tobacco on all those tiers clean to the top of the barn is enough to break your arms and your back and your legs, to say nothing of giving you the wheezes from the dust and turning your head from dizziness. It wears the strongest out.

We had about worn out — me and Sudley and Witchie and Barney and Darkus. Darkus wasn't as good a hand as common. She appeared to have something on her mind — and did, as we found out — and she lagged along and kept behind and held up whoever was paired with her till we all lost patience. "I declare," I said to her one morning, "you ain't much more help this year than Lissie would be. Go on to the house and help her, or else quit your woolgathering and pitch in and work."

"I will, Frony," she said, "I will."

She didn't. Six sticks later and I had to punch her to get her to move on.

Next morning, and us with half the crop yet to haul in, Sudley said, "I believe I'll see if Tate would come help us out. He always was a good hand in the barn."

"Now, Pap," Witchie said, "you promised you wouldn't give Tate no part of the tobacco."

"And I'll keep my word," Sudley said. "All I aim to do is see if he'll work. I'll pay him for his time."

"Don't let him talk you into trading no other way," Witchie said.

"I'll not," Sudley said. He saddled the mule to ride over, being his back was so stiff it hurt him to walk.

He was gone a time and a time. We kept on working, but finally we got real uneasy. "Reckon what could of happened to him?" Darkus said. "Reckon old Dander could of throwed him?"

"I a little doubt it," I said, "I a little doubt that mule could throw as much as a shoe, much less Sudley."

We worked on, but I was beginning to have second thoughts. Finally I said, "Dander might of stepped in a hole and broke his leg. *That* would go just like him. One of us better go see, I reckon, Darkus."

"It best be you," she said, "for I'm so stove up I don't believe I could walk that far."

It was a good thing it was me that went, for I don't know as Darkus could have kept her head. She flies to pieces when it would serve her better to keep cool. If Darkus had gone, she would have been down in that holler to this day, going in circles.

When I got down where the old cabin was there wasn't a sign of Tate or of Sudley, or of old Dander for that matter. I went inside the house and looked around. It was the first time I'd been since Tate moved there and I felt curious about it. It was about what I'd expected. Bed, a chair, an old cookstove, a wash bench. As little as he could put together and make out with. It was cleaner and tidier than I'd thought, though.

The cabin is built on a kind of bench about halfway down in the holler, on account of the spring, and there's a little pasture to one side and an old barn. I traipsed over the whole place. Not a sign of anybody. I hated in the worst way to crawl down into that steep old holler but if what I feared had come to pass, there wasn't anything else to do. I was afraid Dander had made a misstep and slid off the edge of the path and rolled him and Sudley both to the bottom. I took off down the path, hollering every few steps. About halfway down Sudley yelled back, "Hooooo-eeeee, Frony! Come on down and see what I've found!"

Clean down at the bottom of that dark old holler was where he was. And what he had found up a little side holler was Tate's still. It fairly took my breath away. It was the prettiest still I ever saw and it was set up the best. The boiler was the finest copper and so was the worm. He had a good thumpkeg and barrels for his mash. It was all tidy and big and handsome. "My land," I said, "ain't that the prettiest layout you ever saw?"

"It is, for a fact," Sudley said, "it mortally is. I don't know as I ever saw a handsomer one."

Time was when we all made our own corn whiskey here.

I've never held with the notion that using whiskey is a sin. Used right, it's good for a body. A dram before breakfast gives you an appetite and makes your food set easy. A dram before going to bed makes you sleep better. Mixed with honey and spring water it makes the best cough syrup there is. And a hot toddy when you're chilled or feverish is a good, soothing medicine. I don't hold with overdrinking, mind, but whiskey has got its uses. Our people have known that down through the generations and always made their own. My father used to make several barrels every year. So I know what a handsome still looks like, and Tate had a handsome one.

"Fire's cold," Sudley said. "He likely bottled a run yesterday. Wonder where it's at, Frony. I wouldn't mind having a little dram right now."

"Me neither," I said.

We looked around some but couldn't find where he kept it. "Up at the house or barn, probably," Sudley said. "Be handier to sell. He wouldn't want many to know where this still is at."

"Couldn't nobody find this still," I said, "except by accident. It is the best hid. How come you to find it, Sudley?"

He rubbed his chin and squinched up his eyes. "You recollect the Camerons used to still down this cove? Thirty year ago or more?"

"I had clean forgot," I said, "but they did, didn't they?"

"Yes, and never got snooped out, either," Sudley said. "They quit because bootlegging commenced to cut into their operations. Well, it come to me the other day that Tate knew about this little cove and knew about the Camerons stilling here. I allowed I knew, then, the reason he wanted this old place. To do the same. Made up my mind I'd find out, first good chance I got."

"Upon my word and honor," I said. "I ort to thought of it, myself. Why, Witchie knew. He even hinted at it one day. Wouldn't you know it would be Tate to remember and foller along? But it's risky, Sudley. Awful risky, nowadays, ain't it?"

"My opinion," Sudley said, "it's costing him pretty heavy to be let alone. He's paying out, regular, and a lot." He nosed around some more. "But you know, Frony, there's times I downright envy Tate. If God ever made a free man it's Tate Fowler. Don't nobody tell him what to do. He hunts and fishes to suit himself, when it suits him, where it suits him. Don't never buy a license. Hunts with e'er kind of gun he likes. Traps. Sets out fish baskets in the river. He don't actually need nothing or nobody. He can shoot and trap what he needs to eat, run off a batch of white lightning when he wants some spending money, and don't have to work except when he feels like it. Don't owe nobody a blessed thing. Garden of Eden must of been like that, Frony, wasn't it?"

"Tate don't have no Eve," I said.

"Her," Sudley said, "we could of done without. She was the cause of us losing it."

"No," I said, "it was the serpent was the cause of us losing it and that was a boy snake. It says so in the Bible."

I had been poking around a little, and besides his mash barrels Tate had three more set over against the bank. "I wish I had me one of these for a rain barrel," I said. "Reckon Tate would sell me one? He don't need 'em all."

"He likely would," Sudley said coming over. "They're nice, ain't they? He's went up to the distillery and got 'em. They don't use 'em but once. They age out one batch and then just stack the barrels some place to sell or burn up." He tilted one up on its side. "I do believe," he said, "there's some left in here, Frony. I believe I heard it slosh. Enough, maybe, for us a dram a piece."

We sloshed the barrel around but couldn't actually tell. "Well," Sudley said, "there's one way to find out. I'll just strike a match and peer down the bunghole."

He done so.

Do you know what happens when you stick a lighted match down the bunghole of a whiskey barrel? Well, gentlemen, I'm here to tell you there's an explosion. Like the atom bomb had went off. Whooooosh! Bang! Before you could say Round the barn that barrel exploded into little pieces and staves went flying in all directions at once. Me and Sudley was blown off our feet and next thing I knew I was flat on my back on the ground and fireworks was whizzing and rocketing around in my head. I'm not sure I didn't see some kinds that have not yet been invented — even for the fourth of July.

When I got the stars quiled down and the sky settled back in one piece, I set up and looked around. Sudley was sitting alongside of me. He looked like death warmed over. Face black. Hair swinged. Eyebrows plumb gone. Eyes bugged out. Mouth caved in. I said, "Sudley, are you kilt?"

He swallowed two or three times. "No," he said finally, "but I ain't sure but what I'd ruther be. Frony, I've swallered my teeth."

"Surely you ain't," I said, scrambling over towards him.

"They're gone," he said, "both plates." He laid his hand

on his stummick. "I think I feel 'em grinding around inside me already."

"My land," I said, and I commenced pounding him on the back.

He coughed a time or two and then he said, "Quit. You ain't going to jolt them teeth back up now."

A little reason had come to me. I said, "Sudley, you've not swallered them teeth. They would have choked you going down. They have been blowed out of your mouth, is what."

"Swallered or blowed," he said, "up, down or out, I ain't got even a piece of a plate left in my mouth."

"I'll look around," I said, and I began searching about on my hands and knees. I found the lower plate, finally, about twenty feet away. Sunk in the bole of a little sapling like they'd aimed to take a bite.

We never did find the upper plate, though. Had to write it off as a dead loss. Sudley tried to collect on his insurance for it but they wouldn't pay. Said they didn't have any provisions for such. Sudley threatened to cancel his policy and take his business someplace else. Rufus Quaile told him, "Go ahead, Sudley, but I a little doubt you'll find e'er other company that covers losing your upper plate from sticking a lighted match down the bunghole of a whiskey barrel."

Sudley left it lie, but to this day he's not give up on finding that upper plate. Every time he's down in that cove he searches around some more. He says they have got to be there some place and he'll be dogged if he's going to let an upper plate lick him.

The explosion scared the mule and I had to hunt for him, but he couldn't run far and I finally found him. With me

shoving and Sudley hauling we got him on the mule's back
and I led him home. He complained considerably about his
ribs and I didn't know but what he'd cracked a few, so I
bound him up good and tight and we kept him in bed several
days. It nearly drove us crazy — waiting on him. A man in
bed is worse than any two little ones for waiting on.

Tate couldn't figure *what* had happened to that barrel, to
bust it in such little pieces, but when he heard Sudley was in
the bed he stopped by to see him and learned the truth. He
laughed till his sides hurt. I never saw anybody laugh harder.
He thought it was the funniest thing he ever heard. He got
Sudley all riled up with his laughing. "You'll see, boy," Sudley said, sucking in his mouth, "you'll see. No good will come
of that still. What's got over the devil's back is eat under his
belly."

Tate wiped his eyes and snorted and said, "I'm eating too
good to give it a thought, Pap. You just leave me to take care
of the devil."

He sold me a rain barrel, though. Fifty cents. There were
times when Tate could be right obliging.

It was while Sudley was in the bed with his cracked ribs
that we found out what Darkus had been studying about.
Sudley was always a great hand to pick a guitar, or banjo, or
anything else with strings. All the Fowlers have always liked
to make music. But he couldn't be picking and making music
all day every day he was laid by. Time got to hanging heavy
on his hands and he commenced to fret, so I cast around for
something to pacify him. There were some magazines in the
back room where Darkus slept. One morning I went in there

and picked up a stack and took them to him and said, "Here. Now look at these and keep quiet a while and let us get the work done up."

"I ain't no hand to read, Frony," he said, "you know that. It makes my head go quare."

"You don't have to," I said, "just look at the pictures."

He started fluttering the pages, flouncy like a little young one that has been put aside. Me and Darkus were both working in the room, me mopping the floor, Darkus dusting. Out of the corner of my eye I saw Sudley pick up a magazine that was open and folded back — one of those gray-looking magazines that the paper is so rough it's barely good for starting a fire.

We went on with the work but all at once Sudley started laughing. "Look at this," he said. "Come here, Frony, and take a look. Here's a page in this paper called Lonely Hearts and it's got all kinds of ads from people wanting 'pen pals,' 'friendly connections' and the like. Just look at 'em, Frony. Did you ever see the like?"

He handed me the paper and I slid my glasses down off my head and run my eyes over the page. "My land," I said, "there must be a hundred of 'em. Who would of thought there was that many lonesome people laying loose? Here's one signed Widower. Two or three signed Bachelor. Object matrimony. That means he wants to get married, don't it?"

"You'd think it wouldn't be hard to do," Sudley said. "All a man's got to do is tetch 'n take. Now, what woman would be foolish enough to answer one of them ads? Be like putting your hand in a barrel of apples, blind, just as like to come up with a knotty, wormy one as a good one."

Darkus made a little squeaky sound, like a pullet learning to squawk, and we both looked at her. Darkus had a face that was like an open book to read. She couldn't ever hide a thing. Never in her life could she tell a lie. Her face always gave her away. She looked flustered, now, and ducked her head to one side and slid her eyes around the room as wild as a hunted deer. Sudley looked at me and I looked at him and I reckon it hit us both at the same time Darkus was exactly foolish enough to answer some of those ads. Object Matrimony. That would suit Darkus fine. She hadn't had any object but matrimony for fifteen years. My heart sunk.

Darkus suddenly went dashing around, dusting so fierce she raised more than she settled, and then all at once she went skittering out of the room. Sudley picked up the paper again. "Widowers," he said. "Bachelors. Fellers laid on the shelf, likely, hamstrung and passed by. Good prospects, they say, which I a little doubt. This one has got a farm. Probably rock and cedar. This one has his own business. Fruit stand on the courthouse square, likely. This one is a teacher. Wants a educated woman to share his life." He threw the paper down. "What would they be doing lonesome, Frony? I ain't ever been lonesome a day in my life."

"Not everybody," I said, "has been as blessed as us in this country. Not everybody has got family and friends and neighbors like we have. There's lonesome people, Sudley. We see 'em on the TV all the time."

"Well, let 'em stay there," he said. "I don't want 'em mixed and mingled with any of mine. You talk to Darkus, Frony. She needs a mother to talk to her, not a old dried-up pappy like me. Why, Frony, if she was lucky and got hold of a good feller, he'd likely want to take her off some place. Don't she know that?"

I studied a minute how best to warn him. "It could be," I said, "Darkus would like that. To get off."

"Well, *I* wouldn't," he said. "I have got all my young ones around me, close by, where I can see to 'em, and I aim to keep it that way. I would perish away, to have one of mine off. You tell her so, Frony." He laid back against the pillows. "Hand me my gittar, Frony. I can think better, picking."

I handed it to him and went out. He tuned up and directly I heard him singing. He was singing "Jordan's Stormy Banks," and I felt the sorriest for him.

But I felt sorry for Darkus, too. There hadn't anybody talked to her since the road-grader except Cleon Dillon and he was a widower with six young ones and lived so slatternly you couldn't stand him for the smell. She would be hard put ever to find a man around here. And being a woman I knew how her heart was aching for a man of her own and a place to keep and things of her own to tend. She had a home and it was a good one, and a good father who didn't deny her any-thing it was in his power to give her. But it wasn't like it was her own. A woman is not made to be satisfied with such. She wants *her* house and her dishes and her cow and chickens, and she wants *her* man and her young ones. I declare, I felt the worst torn in two. I hated to see Sudley bothered. But I felt for Darkus, I really did.

When I'm upset I fly into baking a pie or cake. It keeps my hands busy while my mind is sorting things out. It keeps me from pacing the floor or stewing around. So I built up a fire and opened up the meal chest and set in to make Sudley a stack cake. I was just sifting out the flour, though, when Darkus stuck her head in the kitchen and went, "Ps-s-st, Frony! Come here."

I went across the hall to the back room. "What is it?" I said.

"Did he catch on?" she said.

"He ain't no fool, Darkus," I said, "and neither am I. We both caught on. You been answering them ads."

"What did he say?" she said.

"He don't like it," I said. "He don't want you to do it no more."

She went over and stood by the back window and looked out. "I got to, Frony," she said. "I have just got to. It's the only chance I've got."

"How many have you wrote to?" I said.

"Four," she said. "I picked out the four likeliest. I got the prettiest paper to write on. Here, I'll show you."

She opened Zilpah's blanket chest — the prettiest chest I ever saw, made of walnut and cedar by Zilpah's pa when her and Sudley got married — and got out a box of writing paper. It was pink. With bluebirds across the top. All smelled up with perfume. "Ain't it nice?" she said. "I got the best. I wanted to make a good impression."

I said the paper ought to do it. "These four you have wrote to," I said, "where are they from?"

"My land, Frony, how would I know?" she said, putting the paper away. "They don't give where they live. You write to 'em care of that Lonely Hearts and they give the letters to 'em."

"You don't know if there's any close by," I said.

"No, and I don't care," she said. "Truth is, Frony, the further off they're from, the better I'd like it."

"That," I said, "is what is mostly bothering Sudley."

"I know it," she said. "I knowed it would, when he found out. And I knowed he would find out. You can't keep nothing like that very long. If I ever get an answer from one of them men, he'll likely read it before I do, way he meets the mail at the box all the time. I been studying on that. I dislike to bother him, Frony. But Pap just don't realize there's other places in the world as good as Broke Neck — and maybe better. He thinks God made Broke Neck first and then used the leftovers to make the rest of the world."

"I have got some leanings in that direction myself," I said.

She stuck her chin up. "Well, I don't. I have read magazines and papers and I have watched the TV. Broke Neck, Kentucky, ain't the whole world."

"It is to some of us," I said. "Have any of them four you wrote to answered?"

"Not yet," she said. "It took me a time and a time to get up the nerve to write. I just mailed off the letters last week. I hate to go against Pap, Frony, but this time I have got to. Try to pacify him. Try to get him to see my side."

"He won't do that," I said, "not if it would take you off. He is not ever going to give his consent for that."

"Then I'll just have to do without it," she said. "I aim to finish what I have begun."

I had no doubts of it. Darkus could be as stubborn as Sudley when it suited her and she had set her head. "Is it your intentions," I said, "to write to more of 'em, or just these four you have already wrote to?"

"I'll wait and see what comes of it with these four," she said. "I allow four at one time is all I can handle."

I allowed it might be four more than she could handle, but I didn't say so. "Which four did you write to?" I said, "if you don't mind telling."

"Oh, I don't mind," she said. "I wrote to Anxious and Texas Ranger and Lonesome and Brokenhearted. They all had something to go on," she said. "Some property. I wouldn't want somebody lives hand-to-mouth."

"No," I said, "it wouldn't pay you to."

I had to tell Sudley. "But take hope," I said, "she's not wrote to but four and ain't aiming to write no more till she sees what comes of these and maybe nothing will. Maybe they won't even answer back."

He didn't raise as much fuss as I expected. Just said, "how sharper than a serpent's tooth is a thankless child, Frony."

I said, "Darkus is not thankless, Sudley. But she's past thirty and she wants to get married."

A day or two later I knew why he hadn't stirred up any more fuss than he had. He was at the mailbox waiting every morning. Nobody else stood a chance to get their hands on the mail but him. He meant to see Darkus didn't get a letter from any of those men. What puzzled me was it didn't appear to bother Darkus. I would have thought she would have screeched her head off. But she acted like she didn't even notice.

We went on and got the tobacco cut and in the barn. Sudley would help till time for the mail, then he would go meet it, then come on back and do his work the rest of the day. Day after day went like that and not one thing come in that mail except what we were used to — box-holder and ads and the weekly paper and the *Progressive Farmer*. It went on like that through September and Sudley let down a little. He said, "They ain't interested, it appears. Or else that whole Lonely Hearts is a fraud. Wonder if she had to pay 'em anything?"

"Yes," I said, for she had told me, "she sent 'em a dollar. For handling the mail. She said it was a service charge."

"She can kiss it goodbye," he said. "They are out to cheat people like her. No wonder she's not heard. They likely throwed her letters in the wastebasket. She ought to sue 'em."

"For a dollar?" I said.

"For misrepresenting and defrauding the mails," he said. "People like that ought to be in jail."

He felt eased enough to send Lissie or Nathaniel to meet the mail some days, instead of going himself. "It was a storm in a teacup," he said, "and I ought to knowed nothing would come of it."

It was October now and time for Sudley to begin campaigning hard for Pink Cowley. From now on he would be hitting the roads, all day every day. "Frony," he said, "you're a good hand to talk with the women and I aim to take you with me some."

"Who'll make the apple butter?" I said.

"Would it be a sin not to make it one year?" he said.

"Waste not, want not," I said.

"Then let the girls make it for once," he said. "If there is aught a man can do to help his boy, he is beholden to. We got to get Witchie that school bus job."

10

THE TRUTH is, it suited me very well to go politicking. It does
a body good to get out once in a while, away from the house
and the chores, and go traipsing, looking at a different part of
the country, and talking with people you wouldn't commonly
see for years on end. I always enjoyed campaigning with Sudley, though it was wearing.

He knew every ridge and every holler, every house and
every family, and when he was campaigning he crisscrossed
the country like old Nebuchadnezzar following out a trail.
There wasn't a place too hard for him to get to — off up some
dark old holler, or out some rock and cedar spur. "They got
four votes," he would say, and take to the creek bed for a
road, or leave the car and set out on foot up a cowpath.
"Don't never pass anybody by, Frony," he said. "One man's
vote is as good as another's. In the ballot box, nobody is better than anybody else. You pass a man by and he hears you
been to see his neighbor and his feelings are hurt. He feels
belittled and he is liable to vote the other way. It's untelling
how many elections have been lost because a candidate got
careless that way. He didn't want to drive his car up some

creek bed, or walk a mile across a broom sedge pasture, because he was hot and tired and didn't think that old house off
at the end of nowhere would count. Everybody counts on
election day. And it don't pay to leave anybody feeling belittled. Of course a candidate can't see everybody hisself. He
just can't divide hisself up that much. But if he's smart he'll
make sure some of his boys do. It makes people feel good. It
makes 'em feel important to be singled out. It makes 'em feel
like they *count*. And they do.

"Listen to 'em *after* an election. Down at the crossroads
store. You'll hear 'em tell, 'Well, on the start I liked that
feller pretty good. I allowed I'd vote for him. But he never
did come around. Nor any of his boys. Never set foot on my
place, nor said howdy nor boo. I allowed he didn't think my
vote counted, so I just cast it for the other feller.' " Sudley
shook his head. "We don't want any slip-ups for Pink that
way."

There are four precincts in our district. We can carry
Broke Neck with our Fowler votes. It's in the other three we
have to work hard. Sudley always got a little cash money from
Job Rigdon, in small bills commonly, and put it in his pocket.
We would drive out a ridge, way the other side of nowhere,
and haul up in front of a place. "This is Saul Herron's
place," he would say. "That's him out there sawing wood.
He has got fifteen votes, Frony. And he's got a sick boy needs
doctoring. You go in and talk to his woman and see if there's
anything you can do for the boy."

Sudley never did want me to name politics. He took care
of that. I just set and talked to the women, the way women
talk. Usually there would something come up they were hav-

ing trouble with — like this sick boy, or their apple butter, or
their chickens not laying, or a sour place turning up in their
garden patch. Whatever it was, I could tell my remedies, and
if they were pushed with their work, I could lend a hand. I
washed that sick boy's face and hands that day and said maybe
some snakeroot tea would help break his fever. The woman
said she had clean forgot about snakeroot tea and she would
gather some roots that very afternoon.

I knew what Sudley was doing out in the wood lot. Talking crops and weather and the best warehouse to take the tobacco to sell. What to do for a cow with the hollow-tail.
When he'd covered all that he would ease into the campaign.
Talk a little, but not pushing, about Pink and how he could
serve the county. That would be all till time to go. Then
Sudley would reach in his pocket and pull out maybe ten dollars. He would say, "Take your boy to the doctor, Saul."

If Saul took it, Pink Cowley had fifteen votes.

Next place maybe it would be a mudhole where the man's
driveway turned off the county road. "The boys'll put some
rock in there for you, Fred," Sudley would say.

"I'd be obliged, Sudley."

Next place maybe a tile was needed. Sudley would promise
it. He never promised much. No more than Job Rigdon and
the Fiscal Court and the county highway could do. But it was
a little here and a little there, and it added up into a lot of
votes.

Some places we didn't stay long, just long enough to pass
the time of day and for Sudley to hand out Pink Cowley's
card. "Floaters," Sudley would say. "They'll cost us a half-
pint of likker and two dollars apiece on election day."

"Wait'll they've drunk the half-pint," I said, "and you can save yourself the two dollars. You can lead 'em in, then."

Sudley said, "I've did that and don't think I've not." He began laughing. "Frony, you remember back long years ago when me and my pap and your pap and the others used to outdo one another riding hell-for-leather to see who could vote the most times? I could nearly always beat 'em. I had me that fast little mare, remember? I'd commence when the polls opened at Broke Neck. Vote and hit the leather for the down end of the county. Lord, I have voted in every precinct in the county and every name you can think of! It was as much as a man's life was worth to challenge in them days. Sometimes a whole bunch of us would come down together at one voting place. Clerk wouldn't even bat an eye when he seen it was Fowlers."

"And sometimes," I said, "you have come home cut up pretty bad."

"I sent more home cut than ever cut me," he said.

"Yes," I said, "I reckon that's so. You were handy with a knife. But I used to wonder sometimes, Sudley, if you wouldn't be left for dead one day. You come home with nine gashes in you one time me and Zilpah had to bind up."

He laughed. "I remember. Didn't either one of you say a word. Just went to work and washed out them cuts and bound me up. Good blood, Frony. We got good blood in us." He sighed. "It ain't like that nowadays. Oh, the boys still fistfight around some on election day. But law and order and the voting machines have made a difference. It ain't as rugged as it used to be." He sighed again. "Ain't as much fun, either."

Some places we stopped just for Sudley to pass the time of day. The men were solid on our side. Needing nothing or wanting nothing, yet they would vote right. All it would take was some whiskey on election day to make them know the candidate appreciated their votes.

Sudley always got in a good supply of whiskey. Job Rigdon used to say, "Don't be saving on the whiskey, Sudley. Get plenty and pass it out openhanded." Some floaters will vote for a pint of whiskey, though they commonly want a little cash, too. Some men carry their own bottles on election day. But if you want to *win* in this country, plenty of free whiskey has got to be passing around. It's remembered who had the openest hand with it.

I know a candidate that was a teetotaler. It got around he wasn't going to pass any whiskey. Wouldn't stand for it. He got three votes in Broke Neck. His, his woman's, and his boy's.

All the Fowlers were helping with the campaign. Witchie was helping and even Tate was doing a little, and all the in-law boys and grandsons. Whatever kind of a quarrel might be going on amongst the Fowlers, when it came to an election we stood solid. We backed Sudley all the way. He was the head of the family and nobody went against him. When Sudley said we vote this way, that was the way it was. I don't remember a Fowler ever breaking away. If he had, it would have gone hard with him. To be outlawed by your own family is about the worst that can happen to you.

Every night when Sudley came in he spread out the voting lists for the precincts on the kitchen table and went over and over them, tallying up his sure votes, his likely votes, those that needed more work on them, and the floaters that could go either way. "I believe," he said, "we are doing real good. Pigeon Roost is shaping up all right. Nothing don't happen we ought to carry it. We got more work to do at the Mill. And we'll have to fight for Lo and Behold. It looks, right now, though, about as I expected it to."

"The boys at the courthouse," I said, "ought to be real pleased, Sudley."

"Frony," he said, looking at me over the top of his spectacles, "we don't say 'the boys' no more. We say 'the establishment.' And we don't call it the 'courthouse' no more. We call it the 'power structure.'"

"Fiddlesticks," I said, "you can call it the power structure if you want to. But when I go over to pay my taxes to the high sheriff *I* go to the courthouse."

He turned his eyes up to heaven, like he had given up on me and went back to studying his lists. He was worried, he said, about peaking too soon. "Doing what too soon?" I said.

"Peaking! Peaking!" he shouted at me.

"I didn't know you aimed to at all," I said, "and it don't sound to me like a thing a decent man would want to do. What do you aim to go around peeking for? You think they hide votes under the bed, maybe?"

"Frony," he said, "when a body don't know what they're talking about, it's best for 'em to keep their mouths shut."

He got out the calendar and studied and studied it. The first Tuesday in November came on the sixth that year. He finally made up his mind. "I aim," he said, "to peak the first week in November."

*

When Sudley first had to be gone all the time campaigning, he still kept Darkus and the Lonely Hearts in mind a little. He told Lissie to meet the mail. But as the time went on and Lissie shook her head every night and the campaign got hotter and hotter, it gradually seeped out of his mind. He didn't have time or thought for anything but the campaign.

At first Darkus was as bright and peart as common, but by the end of October she was looking pretty droopy. I never said a word to her but it was plain she was giving up hopes of getting a letter.

Then one morning she came flying down the path to my house. It was a fine day and I was outside keeping a sulphur fire going smoking some apples. Sudley was just about to peak and he was going like one of these satellites in orbit. The time for a woman to be of use to him was past, so I was catching up on my work.

The minute she saw me, Darkus started waving an envelope. "They've wrote," she yelled, "they've wrote. I got a letter. From Georgia!" She sank down on the wash bench. "My, but I'm pleased. Frony, I had just about give up."

"I allowed you had," I said. I sat down beside her. "How do you know it's from Georgia? You've not opened it yet."

"It says so," she says, "right here. On the postmark, see?"

I looked at the envelope. The fellow had used gray paper and put an airmail stamp on it. Which is a waste of money, for what good does airmail do back here in the hills? If an airplane tried to stop here to let off the mail it would wreck itself. Clee Osborn used to deliver the mail by muleback. Then he bought a jeep. Now an ordinary car will do, but the day hasn't yet come that an airplane could make it. The man had written in red ink and he had drawn a picture of a heart on the back with an arrow through it and dripping down red drops. "My," I said, "he can draw good, can't he? I never could draw a heart. Always got 'em one-sided. Why don't you open it and see what he says?"

Darkus just looked at the envelope and then she looked up at me. "I'm scared to, Frony," she said. "What if he didn't like my letter?"

Poor child. I felt the sorriest for her. I do believe it was right then, that minute, when I went over on her side. When I saw how much it meant to her. Sudley was wrong to try to keep her from whatever chances she had. "Would he be writing if he hadn't?" I said. "Would he be drawing red hearts?"

"That's right," she said, giggling like a little girl. She tore the end off the envelope and started reading. Then she drew in her breath. "Oh, my," she said, "oh, my, Frony, but he does write the most stylish . . . just listen to this . . ."

I don't now recollect all that he said, but he started by saying he liked her name. Said it was a good old Bible name and he knew in reason she must be a fine, old-fashioned girl, like he was looking for. It went on several pages and told how lonesome he was since his wife had died and how a man was purely lost without a woman and he was hoping to find one soon and maybe he had now that she had written so kindly and did she like children for he had several. Didn't say how many. Said he lived on a farm. Didn't say if he owned it or rented. Said he wished she would write again and send him her picture. He signed his name at the bottom, but I have now forgotten it, and he put a lot of those little "x" marks that mean kisses. "It's my first love letter," she said, "the first one I ever got in my life." She folded it up and put it in her bosom.

"Which one is he?" I said.

"Which one?" she said. "Why, you seen his name."

"But which one . . . Anxious or Brokenhearted or Lonesome or who?" I said.

"Oh, I don't know," she said. "The ads don't tell where they live or what their names are. But I have got the ads here. I tore the page off the magazine. Maybe we can figure it out."

We looked the page over. "These are the ones I wrote to," she said. "I made a pencil mark by 'em."

The first one went: "High class gentleman with means, forty-five, wishes to correspond with high class lady. Bachelor. Object matrimony. Address, Lonesome, care of the Lonely Hearts."

"It ain't him," I said, "he's a bachelor."

"The next one said: "Are you lonely? Write Texas Ranger. Man of forty, well-off, unattached, wishes to make a friend. Object matrimony. Write Texas Ranger, care of the Lonely Hearts."

"It *could* be him," I said. "He don't say *how* he's unattached. It could be he's been attached but ain't no more."

We studied on it but couldn't come to any conclusion. It went pretty farfetched to think the Texas Ranger lived in Georgia, though.

The next one said: "Single man, good job, forty-seven, wants to correspond with young lady. Looking for a wife. Can offer the right woman a good home and living. Address Looking, care of the Lonely Hearts."

"It's not him," I said, "for he says plain out he's single. The one that wrote has had *one* wife, anyway."

The last one she had answered went: "Honest man, with property, fifty, lost and lonely without his mate. Address Brokenhearted, care of the Lonely Hearts."

"That's him," I said, "it's Brokenhearted that has wrote. Bound to be. He has lost his mate."

Darkus thought so, too. "He didn't sound very broken-hearted in the letter, though, did he?"

"Maybe he has got over the first pangs," I said. "You made sure they all had object matrimony, didn't you, Darkus?"

She laughed. "There wasn't any use me wasting money writing to somebody just wanting a pen pal, Frony. I'm look-ing for a man to marry and I don't make any bones about it. My, but I'm pleased one of 'em has wrote. I had got plumb down in the dumps over not hearing. Thought I had just threw my dollar away."

That reminded me of Sudley. "Did Lissie see you get this letter out of the box?" I said. "Sudley has got her watching."

Darkus shook her head. "It won't do him any good. I told Clee a long time ago to put my letters in your box, if I got any. You don't go to the box more'n once a week and I knew in reason I could beat you to it."

"It was witty of you to figure that out," I said, "but you took a chance. If I had found a letter I might have took it to Sudley's. You ought to told me, Darkus."

"I was aiming to. *If* a letter come. And I have told you, very first letter I got." She looked at me straight. "Frony, are you on my side or not?"

"I don't know for sure, yet," I said. "But I've got leanings that way. I'll go this far, Darkus. I won't give you away. I can't help but think you ought to have an even chance."

She laughed. "I almost knew that's what you'd say. I believed I could put my dependence in you. What do you reckon it's like in Georgia, Frony?"

"Lord, how would I know?" I said. "I don't even know where it's at."

"You got a geography book?" she said.

"There might be Lissie's old one here," I said, "Why?"

"We could look and see," she said, "how far away it is."

I rummaged around and found the geography book. Georgia wasn't but an inch away. In miles it was right far, though. Too far to suit Sudley, I knew.

"I wish," Darkus said, when we'd finished looking, "he had said how many of the younguns there is. I a little doubt I'd like tending a house full."

"Just come plain out and ask him when you answer," I told her. "You got a right to know. Maybe there's not so many. They're all kind of old, ain't they Darkus? The men, I mean. Lonesome is forty-five and the Texas Ranger is forty. Anxious is forty-seven and this one is fifty."

"You wouldn't expect 'em not to be, would you?" she said. "A young feller can get him a woman without running an ad, Frony. I don't look for no movie star. I'm not any great catch myself, and I know it. I don't begretch 'em their years. I'd take any one of 'em so long as they do the right thing."

She looked so pitiful my heart just went right out to her. Say what you will about Darkus — I know she's scatter-brained and flighty — but there never was a better-turned girl in the world. She would give you the dress right off her back if you needed it and not expect it to be paid back. I knew she might not make a man the *best* wife in the world,

but she wouldn't make him the worst one, either. I thought
it was a pity and a shame she hadn't had the chance.

"I wish you well," I said, "I hope you have good luck with
one of 'em. If I was you, though, Darkus," I said, "I wouldn't
make up my mind too soon. If this one has wrote, some of the
others likely will. Take your time, and take your pick."

"I aim to," she said. "I aim to take the best that's offered."

I couldn't help wondering how good that would be, but I
didn't say so. I didn't want to damp her spirits.

In working the precinct backwards and forwards Sudley
naturally stopped and talked with the preacher several times.
That was how he learned that the preacher was registered
as an Independent. "Just a high-class floater," Sudley said,
"that's what an Independent is. Usually takes a little more
than a half pint of whiskey to buy 'em. Some kind of issue
will do it. Civil rights or labor or education. They always
tell you they vote for the man not the party. It's a wonder they wouldn't find out that the man *without* the party
wouldn't ever get nominated."

He didn't give up on the preacher. He kept on talking the
Republican party and Pink Cowley to him. One evening just
a few days before the election two cars pulled up in front of
Sudley's. It was the preacher and some visiting church people
from up north. I never saw such a denomination to visit.
That poor woman of the preacher's was always having to
make down beds and cook for visitors — bishops and preachers and their families from off. It was sure a denomination on
the go.

The preacher introduced the folks around and said they

were just fixing to leave and wanted to buy a bushel of apples to take with them. Sudley said, "I wouldn't sell you an apple for all the money in all the banks, but you're welcome to just go help yourselves."

"We'll pay for them," the people said.

"They're not for sale," Sudley said. "Just go on out to the orchard and pick what you want."

The men took a bushel basket and went out to the orchard, Sudley going with them to help. The women said they wouldn't come inside. They walked around in the yard and looked at the house and talked together. Then one of them said, "Tell me. This is my third trip to Kentucky and I just love it, but why do all your houses have two front doors? It's such a quaint custom."

People from off always want to know why we have two front doors. And maybe it was quaint. It was real handy, too. If a family is big enough there's got to be a bed in every room but the kitchen, you don't relish the idea of anybody that has to go outside in the night stumbling through half the house before he gets there. It makes sense to make it easier for him. But I didn't think that would be a very nice thing to say to the ladies. So I just said I didn't know. "We've just always built that way," I said.

She raised her eyebrows and said, "You people place a lot of emphasis on the way things have always been, don't you?"

You can count on such folks being unmannerly and while it riled me up, I kept my temper. "Yes, ma'am," I said, "we do. Until something new proves out better than what we've had, we hold onto the old."

"It makes it very difficult for those of us who come in here to help you," she said.

I wasn't able to let that go by. "It depends," I said, "on what you call help. Maybe it goes like butting in to us."

One of the other women pulled at her sleeve, then, and said, "Gertrude . . ." So she didn't say any more. Just cleared her throat. Then the other woman said what a nice day it had been and wondered what was keeping the men and they sort of wandered on out to their car.

When the men came back, not with one but with two bushel baskets of apples, they all piled in and drove off, except the preacher. He came in the house with us.

"Draw you up a cheer, Preacher," Sudley said, "you've not been in a time and a time."

It was chilly enough for a little blaze in the fireplace and the preacher drew up a chair and stretched out his toes. "Sometimes," he said, "I wish we had a fireplace in the parsonage. Few things are as cheerful as an open fire."

"I don't know how you make out without one," Sudley said. "I'd as lief live in a barn as a house without a fireplace."

They talked on and in time it got around to politics. Bound to, that near election. The preacher said he had finally made up his mind. "I'm going to vote for your man, Sudley," he said. "I don't honestly think either man is fully qualified, but I believe Pink Cowley knows the issues a little better. I talked with him recently and he is in favor of a bigger budget for the school library system, which is very dear to my heart, as you know. He was in full agreement with most of my proposals. He said he had given it a lot of thought and would work for it if elected. I know we can't expect miracles, but every little bit helps. A man committed to higher educational standards must be my choice."

Sudley didn't flicker an eyelash. His head just went up and

down agreeing with the preacher, the way Pink Cowley's had done, likely. I a little doubt Pink Cowley even knew what a library was. Sudley said, "Yes, sir, you have got the right of it now, Preacher. I am proud to hear you say so. Them were exactly my reasons for coming out for Pink Cowley myself. You have chose well, Preacher. Pink will lay with it when he gets on the school board. He will do," Sudley said, "a *states- manlike* job."

Witchie had been studying the ceiling. He puckered up his mouth now and commenced to whistle, real soft. I saw the back of Sudley's neck stiffen a little, but that was the only sign he gave that he heard Witchie. Darkus and Lissie cut their eyes at me, and Lissie sort of sucked in her breath. I thought if the preacher caught on, maybe I could start some kind of commotion — pretend I saw a mouse or heard something out- side. But I needn't have worried. He was too full of himself to catch on. He never even noticed Witchie whistling, much less caught on *what* he was whistling. That fool boy was double-noting, "Jesus, Lead Me Home." The preacher just went on expounding his views.

Sudley walked him out to the car and when he came back he really lit into Witchie. "You cut that one too near the bone, boy. How come you to do such a thing?"

Witchie was doubled up laughing. "Aw, Pap, I couldn't help it. The *way* you was leading him home. 'Them is ex- actly the reasons I picked Pink Cowley, myself, Preacher.' 'Yes, sir, Preacher, Pink Cowley will do a real statesmanlike job.' God's little britches, Pap, that's about the thickest I ever heard you lay it on."

"Witchie," I said, "keep a civil tongue in your head. It's your father you're speaking to."

"Never mind about me," Sudley said. "What I want to know is how come you to forget your raising so. To be so unmannerly and make fun of a man when he's visiting under my roof. I was so mortified if I'd had a chunk handy I'd of throwed it at you!"

"Aw, Pap," Whitchie said, "he never caught on."

"That don't matter," Sudley said. "He might of. The man ain't *all* fool. But that ain't here nor there. What I'm getting at is, I won't have one of mine being unpolite to somebody visiting. You was taught to be agreeable and pleasant to all, Witchie. When somebody comes to visit, no matter how curious and quare he goes, you don't let on. You *know* that, boy. You was brought up right. And if you ever forget it again, Witchie, big as you are, I aim to cut me a hickory limb and wear it plumb out on you. I'll not have you shaming us that way, you hear?"

"Yes, sir," Witchie said. He was still grinning, but he reached over and patted Sudley's knee. "I'll keep it in mind, Pap. You won't have no call to take me to task again."

"I hope not," Sudley said. He ran his fingers through his hair and made it stand up like a rooster's comb. "I declare," he said, "sometimes I believe this generation has just plain went to the dogs."

Witchie stood up and stretched and gave a big yawn. "Well," he said, "I better be getting on down and see if Tish is all right."

"Is she puny?" Sudley said.

"Not to say puny," Witchie said. "But she don't feel her dead level best. Getting a little heavy on her feet, mostly. Says she's tired all the time."

"You make her take care, Witchie," Sudley said. "Make the chaps help her more."

When Witchie had left, Lissie stood up to carry Whitley to bed. He had gone to sleep in her lap. He was a big armful. Nearly four and as chunky and fat as a little pig. Passing Sudley she stopped for him to give the boy a goodnight kiss. Sudley brushed his hair back. "Ain't he the sweetest little feller," he said. "I don't know but he's the nicest boy I ever had."

"You've said that," I said, "about every one of 'em — boy *or* girl."

"And meant it," he said. "Every least one is the best one. You be sure and put him over to the back side, Lissie, where he can't fall out and make sure he's covered good. Which bed did he aim to sleep in tonight?"

"He never said," Lissie said. "The preacher being here took his mind off it and he dropped off without taking his pick."

"Better put him in mine, then," Sudley said. "He slept with you last night."

When Whitley was born Sudley had put up another bed in their room and he took Nathaniel in bed with him. Lissie kept Whitley with her. But the last year or two Whitley had got notional and every night said where he aimed to sleep — with Sudley or with Lissie. Sometimes he took an hour making up his mind, changing it two or three times. It took a lot of patience to get him settled down at night. Nathaniel was good-natured about it, taking wherever Whitley left him. It's our way here to give up to the baby.

Lissie didn't come back and we knew she had laid down,

too. Darkus gathered up Junior and led him off to bed and I was fixing to wake Barney and go home myself. Sudley said, "Frony, the preacher is going to haul votes for us election day."

I could tell he was proud of it. I said, "Sudley, it wouldn't surprise me one bit if you don't talk him around into registering Republican in time. It wouldn't surprise me one bit."

"I don't know as I would go that far," he said. "Independents is slippery. You can't count 'em in the bag till you close it on 'em. They do go the quarest. Talk so high-minded and pure. All full of ideals and good causes." He laughed. "Give an educated Independent a good cause to sink his teeth into and away he goes, headed for the peapatch." He shook his head. "Ain't even got one foot on the ground. Don't know that first thing about politics and power and patronage. Give 'em a good cause and you can feed 'em cream puffs and they'll think it's beefsteaks."

He had been whittling on a sliver of cedar all evening. He stood up of a sudden and snapped his old Barlow to and laid it on the mantel. "It's as plain as eating and sleeping, Frony. From the President to Pink Cowley, from the Rockefellers to you and me, everybody pulls the quilt over on his side." He swept the shavings into the fire with his foot. "Take care nigh the spring, Frony. I seen a copperhead snake there a few days ago."

I snapped on my flashlight to show him I had a light. "I'll take care," I said.

II

THE VOTING PLACE for Broke Neck precinct is in the warehouse of Ethan Green's store at the crossroads. Big, barny old concrete block building with a concrete floor. So drafty that just to open a door starts a cyclone blowing through. Built by some people that came into the settlement one time with more money than sense and thought Broke Neck was ready for a roller skating rink and bowling alley.

They were bowled right out of the settlement. Roller skating and bowling are both revelings and go against what the Apostle Paul says in the Bible. As plain as day it says, in Galatians 5:19-21, what the works of the flesh are, and along with idolatry and hatred and variance and emulations and wrath and strife, it puts revelings. And it says they which do such things shall not inherit the kingdom of God.

Anyway, Ethan Green bought that barny old building for a little of nothing and began using it for a storeroom. He kept fertilizer and seed and feed and tools and such in it. You couldn't begin to fill it up so there was plenty of room for the voting place. The only thing is, it's cold. It doesn't matter in the primaries, in May, but any time you are an official in the

November elections, you mortally do earn your day's pay.

I have chilblains that still make me walk with a limp from the time I was Clerk. Try sitting from six in the morning till six in the evening, with the thermometer down to thirty, in a building as big as my lower pasture and as drafty, and not even a hot brick for heat. That is guaranteed to separate the men from the boys.

It was blowing a blizzard that day and snowing. Me and Lizzie McKittredge, who was the Judge, had both worn all the clothes we could pile on, but by ten o'clock there wasn't a bit of feeling left in our limbs, from the waist down, and my hands were so frozen I couldn't even hold the pencil much less write down a voter's name.

Ethan brought over an oil stove and we set it under the table and Sallie brought over some quilts and we draped them around and it worked fine till Lydie Cameron caught on fire. What happened was that Lizzie has got allergies. Smoke or fumes of any kind make her break out with hives as big as bee stings. We had got those quilts tucked around the table good and tight and didn't either one of us think the fumes from the oil stove could reach up where she breathed. And they didn't. But her limbs got hot from the fire and broke the hives out and she started itching. When she commenced itching, she began fanning the quilt around. Next thing we knew Lydie Cameron was just writing down her name in the voting book and I was making out her ballot when she let out a scream and commenced beating out the blaze on her dress tail.

Me and Lizzie and Lydie could have put her out without much fuss but Joe John Pierce was just casting his vote. Joe John is a man who acts as quick as he thinks, and sometimes before. He saw the blaze and he saw a fire extinguisher and he put two and two together and grabbed up the fire extinguisher. He upended it and got it to squirting and he came charging up and gentlemen, I mean to tell you, he was a master squirter. He mortally did douse that fire. He didn't quit squirting till the tank of that thing was empty. Lydie was as wet as the day she was baptized, hair, face, clothes, shoes, and me and Lizzie were pretty damp around the edges. When the tank ran dry, Joe John peered past it and said, "Lydie, are you out?"

Out? My land, she was drowned! She couldn't say a word. Just stood there and blew bubbles. "Go put that thing up, Joe," I said, "and don't never lay your hand on one again. Let the Volunteer Fire Department put out the fires from now on. They do less damage."

Her man took Lydie home and Sallie came and got her quilts and hung them on the line to dry. She was right provoked. Said she didn't think when she loaned them to us we'd try to burn 'em up and then squirt 'em with chemical. Said she wouldn't be surprised if the colors didn't run and she didn't know if they'd ever quit smelling. As if we had done it all on purpose!

The men thought it was the best joke they ever heard. Said that was what come of having women election officials. Said it was the hottest election ever held in Broke Neck. Sudley threatened to have me purged from the voting list.

But last year November was as pretty a month as you ever saw. Fine weather, the days sunny and warm and very little rain, and no killing frost till after Thanksgiving. Election day couldn't have been finer. We all stirred soon. Truth is, I

don't guess Sudley slept more than a few winks. I know I
didn't. I was tired of the bed by four o'clock and just got up
and built a fire and set on the coffee pot. Sudley saw the
smoke and came over to have a cup with me. "Going to be
pretty," he said. "Clear as a bell. Some frost, but not much.
It'll warm up with the sun. There'll be a big turnout, Frony.
A heavy vote."

"You nervous?" I said.

"No," he said, "not to say nervous. I got the tingles,
though." He poured out some more coffee in his saucer and
blew on it. "Frony, if they don't have elections in heaven,
I'm not sure I want to go. There just ain't nothing more
exciting."

"Not even," I said, teasing him, "when old Nebuchadnezzar gets up a coon?"

He studied a minute, then he laughed. "You know, there is
something about 'em alike. Coon hunting and electioneer-
ing. They're both races, to see who's best. See who'll come
out on top. They both get me worked up about the same
way. Like I had electricity in my veins. I'm glad I don't have
to choose between 'em. I'd hate to do without either one."

He went on, to be there when the polls opened. He didn't
like for us women to come over to vote early. The early
voters were generally people who worked in town, on public
works. Sudley didn't like for them to be crowded or have to
wait in line long. He said it made them ill and cross, for they
already had the clock on their minds, having to be at their
jobs by a certain time. Usually the first two hours after the
polls opened was a rush with them. Then there was a little
slowdown until the people from all over began to come in.

He didn't mind us coming over then, but he liked best for us to come right after dinner in the slackest time of all. The Fowler women kind of took up the slack.

Sometimes we were too worked up to wait that long. Election day is a good time for visiting. After you vote it's nice to go around from one store to another and see who's there and sit and talk and exchange news. If you've been in the campaign you can't help but watch the votes come in, either. You'll see this one you talked with, and that one, and you speak, and you wonder if you've done any good with them.

I liked to watch Sudley, too. He had his boys staked out all around. Some of the Fowler men were at the other precincts, but he always ran things himself at Broke Neck. For the Republicans, that is. Sudley was the man to see. He carried the money. He had got the liquor in and hid it away and tolled off the ones to handle it. He was the one sent the haulers out. He watched every voter come in. But you never saw him handle a voting list. He didn't have to. He had it in his mind. All four hundred names on the Republican list. He knew who to expect, what time of day, who was still out and why, and when to send for them. He knew ahead of time if the least thing was going awry. He never missed a trick. For thirty years, that had been Sudley's job every election.

What tickled me was, a stranger couldn't have told it. He looked just like all the other old men loafing around, a little shabbier, maybe, than some. Leaning up against a car or the side of a building, whittling on a piece of cedar, spitting his tobacco juice, talking slow and easy to whoever stopped. Not too close to the polls, but not too far away either. His own boys used to tease Sudley about his whittling. Said it took a whole cedar tree to keep him in whittling wood on election day. He shaved down a lot of chunks, no two ways about it.

You never saw the money leave his pockets. You never saw where the men went for their bottles. You never saw a bottle tipped. If a man got drunk a little too soon in the day and commenced being troublesome, Sudley just looked at somebody and he was carried away. You never saw a hauler get directions. Cars went out empty and came back loaded and it was like they worked on a track. Commonly, that is. This time it went a little different.

I told the girls that on account of Sudley was looking for a heavy turnout, we ought to try and wait until after dinner to go vote. "How'll we pass the time?" Darkus said. "I do hate to set and wait when I know I'm going some place."

"You *could,*" I said, "piece on a quilt. Or you could write some more Lonely Hearts letters."

"I've done answered the one I got," she said. "Until I get some more there's none to write. I'll just watch the TV. Me and Lissie."

"I'm going to cook," I said. "I'm going to make Sudley a stack cake and I'm going to fry some apple pies and make some sweet cakes. That'll keep me busy."

We put in the morning, then Darkus drove us down to the crossroads. The minute I saw Sudley I knew he was fussed up about something. Maybe nobody but us in the family could have told it, for he was leaning against the side of the post office building whittling. Nothing out of the ordinary. But that old Barlow knife was really flashing and he wasn't taking pains with his shavings. Not peeling them off thin and slivered at all. He was a master whittler and carver and commonly took the greatest pains. Something was bothering him.

I voted and then walked up towards Ethan Green's store. Witchie was angling across from the garage and I caught up with him. "What's gone wrong?" I said. "Are the Democrats paying more for votes?"

"No," he said, "we got plenty of money. The boys weren't scarce with it this time. No, we're paying ahead. How'd you know anything was going wrong?"

"Your father," I said. "He's making kindling wood out of that cedar chunk."

Witchie laughed. "You're noticing, Frony. It's that preacher."

"I might of knowed it," I said. "What's he done?"

"What ain't he done?" Witchie said. "I reckon you know he's hauling for us today."

"Sudley told me he was going to," I said.

"Well, first several loads he went where he was sent and brought back who he was supposed to. But the next thing Pap knowed he was going out on his own, anywhere and everywhere, and bringing back anybody he wanted to. Since dinner he's brought in two cars full of solid Democrats. Not a Republican vote in the bunch, not even a floater. Cahoons and Harbins, and they're hard-core real Confederate Democrats and been so since time out of mind."

"Well!" I said, "What in cat hair has got into him? Don't he know that every Democrat brought in is a vote against Pink Cowley? And us paying him ten dollars for the day's work! Why don't Sudley put a stop to it?"

"He's not been able to catch him," Witchie said. "You know how Pap runs things. Smooth and easy. He's tried to get the preacher's eye, but the preacher don't even look his way. Don't ask where next, or what. He just scuttles that little compact in with a load, then scuttles it out. You can't put your finger on him."

I studied a minute. "The Cahoons," I said, "are up-the-holler people. Live on up the creek past the mission. But I reckon you could call 'em neighbors. The Harbins belong to his church. I believe I know what the man is doing, Witchie."

"I do, too," he said. "Making Pap mad enough to bust a gut."

"He is seeing to it everybody is doing their civic duty. I have heard him say that it's everybody's civic duty to exercise their franchise. He's not counting votes. Democrat or Republican don't matter to him. He's just helping folks exercise their franchise."

"*We* would ruther," Witchie said, "not too many Democrats would. How he got out of hand, I can't figure. But I a little doubt Pap will pay him."

"He oughtn't," I said. "He don't deserve it."

I kept an eye on the man. The rest of the afternoon he scuttled backwards and forwards busier than all the rest of the haulers put together. Commonly a hauler makes a trip, then there's maybe a little spell of waiting till he's told where to go next. Sudley knows just when to send for the people — when they like best to come in, and why. Maybe a man can't get loose from his work till, say, dinner time. Or maybe a whole family has got to gather in front the hollers to one place and it takes till two or three o'clock, then several cars have to pick them up. You have to keep watch and you have to know and have cars handy, for there's always the chance somebody extra will call in and if you're caught without a car the Democrats are liable to get there ahead of you. But the preacher was paying no mind. He had the bit in his teeth and was headed for the peapatch.

I visited all the stores, did a little trading, drank more pop than was good for me, and caught up on the news and talk with the other women. About an hour before the polls closed I thought me and the girls had better go on home and set the supper out. Sudley would be ready to eat soon as the boys took the ballot box in. Then he'd want to get into town himself for the counting.

I went to find him to tell him we'd be going. Him and the preacher were standing just inside the garage. I didn't bother him, but I couldn't help hearing. "You have went out on your own most of the afternoon," Sudley was saying. "You didn't get your trips from me or any of the boys."

"Of course not," the preacher said. He laughed. "This morning I didn't seem to be very useful. Most of the people seemed to have their own transportation. I had time to go where you asked me to go. But this afternoon I found many people needing a way to the village. I didn't need to bother you at all. It's been a most rewarding experience, Sudley. I have been delighted to be of help. It must be a record vote. I myself have brought in forty or fifty people."

"And most of 'em," Sudley said, "we could of done without. If we lose this election, Preacher, we can lay it to you."

"I don't know what you mean," the man said. "Every registered voter should have an opportunity to exercise his franchise. If he has no way to the polls, it is a man's civic duty . . ."

"You can preach that from your pulpit, Preacher," Sudley said, "but I'd a little ruther you wouldn't practice it on election day. Specially when we're paying you to haul for us."

"Paying me?" he said. "Who's paying me? I wouldn't think of taking pay for doing my duty. I resent that, Sudley. I consider it an insult."

"You didn't resent it when you agreed to haul for us," Sudley said.

"I agreed to . . . yes, said I'd be happy to use my car . . . there wasn't anything said . . ." he commenced to splutter. "Do you mean to tell me that you believed I had agreed to use my car to bring voters to the polls for pay? Is that what you believed I had agreed to do?"

"Me and the whole settlement," Sudley said. "That's the way it's done, Preacher. That was your bargain when you give me your word."

"I gave you my word I would . . . I said I'd be happy . . . nothing was said . . ." He was trying to drive about three teams at once. "You and the settlement," he finally said. "Does the community believe I was hauling votes for pay?"

"*Republican* votes," Sudley said. "Naturally they do. I told 'em all . . . all the people . . . we had got you lined up right finally. Said you was going to work for us."

"You had no right!" he said.

"I don't know why not," Sudley said. "It was a bargain, far as we knowed. Of course the whole settlement knows *now* you went back on it. You're a man that'll take one man's pay and do another's work."

"They can't!" the preacher yelled. "They *can't* believe

that! I am an honorable man . . . an honest man. They surely must know that. All I was doing was . . ."

"Preacher," Sudley said, "an honest man is a man that stays bought. You didn't. That's what the settlement knows about you. Yore stock has went way down today. I a little doubt anybody will put much dependence in your word from now on. It don't matter what you was trying to do. What you did was what folks from off generally do. You made a fool of yourself. Now, if you'll excuse me, I got work to do."

He walked off and left the preacher standing there. Neither one of them saw me. The preacher stayed all slumped down for a long time, then he went and got in his car and drove off. They said he went home and went to bed for two days.

I didn't follow Sudley. Me and the girls went home and just for something extra to soothe him a little, I caught a hen and wrung her neck and stewed her and made dumplings.

We didn't lose the election and maybe we wouldn't have anyway but Sudley didn't take any chances. When he saw what the preacher was doing he commenced throwing a lot of money around. He didn't let a single floater get away and he commenced buying Democrat votes. Ten dollars a head. It was the most anybody had ever paid and the boys over at the courthouse wouldn't have liked it if Sudley hadn't pulled it off. He spent all the money they had allowed him, then collected up from the Fowlers and put in a lot of his own.

Sudley didn't mind the money. He didn't give it another thought. He helped get Pink Cowley elected and Witchie got his job. What Sudley hated was putting his trust in a man and having him prove out not worth it. "I don't know as I ever will have any confidence in that man again," he said. "In my opinion his congregation had better watch him. A man dishonest in one way is generally dishonest in most ways."

His congregation was put to shame on account of him again, I know that. Logan Crockett and some others stopped by to see Sudley. "Try to overlook it," they said. "He don't know no better."

"I would feel better about it," Sudley said, "if I thought he was ever going to learn."

Logan shook his head. "We're beginning to feel some dissatisfaction ourselves, Sudley. Now, mind, we're not going against the preacher . . . yet. But he keeps things stirred up all the time. Most of us don't like them Orders of Worship he prints up and distributes around at service. We don't see no use of 'em and it don't put us in a very good light amongst the people of the settlement."

"It don't," Sudley said. "You know the Bible as good as I do, Logan, and you know it don't only not look right, it *ain't* right. It's strictly adding *to* the Bible."

"What bothers me most right now," Rufus Pierce said, "is he keeps the young folks all agitated up. Last summer it was taking 'em all to some kind of youth camp. Mine like to pestered me to death to go, but I just couldn't get my consent to let 'em. It hardened 'em against me. Now, he's wanting to get up a bus trip for 'em. Take 'em to Frankfort and places off. Says it's so they can see how the state government works."

"Is he aiming," Sudley said, astonished, "to take 'em right in the caucus rooms?"

"I a little doubt it," Rufus said. "I a little doubt he would know a caucus room if he seen one."

"Well, my land," Sudley said, "he don't have to take 'em to Frankfort. I can just take 'em around the precinct and over to the courthouse and they can learn how the government's run. They run things in Frankfort the same way the boys at the courthouse do. And they run things in Washington the same way. Little push here, little shove there, a few heads put together, some trading and dealing. That's the way the governments are run."

"He wants 'em to see the legislature in session," Logan said.

"That is strictly no use," Sudley said. "You can't tell nothing about how the government is run going to the legislature."

Logan Crockett laughed, then he said, "The preacher don't know that, Sudley."

"Well do I know he don't," Sudley said, but he laughed too. "He ain't dry behind the ears yet in politics."

"He says he wants the young folks to have a 'wider experience,' " Rufus said.

"What of?" Sudley said.

"He don't really say."

"The preacher," Sudley said, "is a well-intentioned man. I've got no doubts of that. But I a little doubt he is a very good example of what we'd like our young ones to be, with his jangled-up nerves and his to-ing and fro-ing across the face of the earth. He don't know how to set still and just enjoy being a child of God. He don't know the difference between a redwing blackbird and a sparrow and to this day he don't know whether crow's-foot or bloodroot comes up first in the spring. Some day Old Man Death is gonna catch up with him and it won't matter where he's been. It's where he ain't been that'll count, and he ain't been at home on this earth. If he is wanting your young folks to turn out like him, I would take second thoughts if I was you."

"That's what we are commencing to wonder about," Logan said. "He has already got 'em considerably rattled up. We would hate to have them set against us."

"I would think it," Sudley said. "It would be a great grief to you."

"His woman," Rufus said, "has bought herself an automatic washing machine." Didn't anybody say anything for a minute. It wasn't Sudley's place to name what people would think of that. But after a little spell, Rufus said, "The women folks look askance at it. They say she is putting herself up better than others."

"Which don't go seemly in the preacher's wife," Logan said. He went on to say, "We are sorry about them women hurting Frony's feelings, too. That time they come and you give 'em the apples. Way they went on to Frony about the doors and us being old-timey."

"I wouldn't say they hurt her feelings so much," Sudley said, "as they riled her up. She spoke unthoughty herself. I took her to task for being as unpolite as them."

Rufus said, "Well, the long and the short of it is, Sudley, that we are about to come to the opinion it would be better if the preacher would go. Only thing is, we don't rightly know how to go about it, without hurting *his* feelings."

"He just don't suit," Logan said. "He don't seem to learn one thing about the people or the country, and he don't even seem to want to learn."

"They don't any of them," Sudley said, "not any of them from off. Them government people is like that, too. And them from that Economic office and them Vista young folks.

All them college professors that taken that survey a while back. As much traipsing and nosing around as they have done you'd think they would have learnt *something* by now. But they ain't got the least idea that we're Bible people and go by the Bible and the Bible says what we can do and what we can't do. We can't join things because they're worldly, and we don't want them community centers because they are revelings, and we don't want them low-cost housing units because they would put us up above others. And most of all we don't want them jobs off some place.

"They are all proud of their education and their ways and they keep wanting everybody and everything to be like *they're* used to and us to be like folks where *they* come from. It just don't seem to get through to them that we feel sorry for 'em — for what they are and where they're from and wouldn't have none of it as a precious gift."

"One of them college professors said our young folks ought to get a better education and have a better chance," Rufus said.

"Chance for what?" Sudley said. "To stand in front of some kind of a belt and put little jigger things into more little jigger things? A chance for one of them little boxes to live in? All crowded up amongst a lot of other little boxes? Two bathrooms? Two cars? When did that guarantee a man contentment? When would you get time to live? Where would you walk? Where would you see things grow? And where could you put your feet in living water? I sometimes do believe they are all mad at us for having so much when they have got so little. So they can't rest still till they trade us out of what we have got for a mess of their pottage."

"You have got the right of it, I'd say," Logan said. "Well, as far as the preacher goes, we have done our best to help him. It's a hard knot, I can tell you, trying to get shut of a preacher without bemeaning or belittling him. And we couldn't get our consent to do that."

"I can see you couldn't," Sudley said.

"About the best we can hope for," Rufus said, "is that next time the Assembly meets he will put in for a transfer himself."

"I would do a little praying on it if I was you," Sudley said.

They went away then, but it shows how the settlement valued Sudley's opinion that they stopped by to talk, and how well they thought of him that they didn't want him to feel too bad about the preacher.

12

It was just before Thanksgiving that Darkus began getting letters. We were finishing up the tobacco — stripping it out and bulking it down. Sudley was bearing down on all of us. He wanted to get the tobacco to the warehouse for the opening week of sales. The price is generally better opening week. Besides, the money always comes in handy for Christmas and Sudley did like to be openhanded with the little chaps in the family at Christmas. He overspent on them, to my notion, spoiled them, but he didn't think so. He said life got hard enough for them when they got to the bringing-up age and he wanted it kept bright for them as long as he could.

It was all day every day in the barns, with our noses running and our hands frozen, that Darkus commenced getting letters. And my land, did she ever begin getting letters. Somebody left the gate open and they strictly poured through.

First she got an answer from Brokenhearted, and before she could write him back here came another one from him, and then he took to writing every day. In the middle of him writing every day, there came a letter from Texas. We allowed that one was the Texas Ranger. She was trying to get him answered when there came one from Florida. That was Lonesome, for he said plain out that's who he was. What with Brokenhearted writing every day and her trying to answer the Texas Ranger and Lonesome, she had second helpings on her plate, and then Clee left a letter from Missouri. "He's bound to be Anxious," she said, "for he's the only one left."

I met the mail that day and Clee said, "Darkus is getting a heap of mail lately, ain't she?"

I knew he was hinting to find out what was going on, but I wouldn't give him any satisfaction. I said, "It looks like it, don't it?"

"It mortally does," he said. "Commenced all of a sudden, too, didn't it?"

"It does sometimes," I said. I tucked the letter in my apron pocket. "How is Malzeeny?" I said.

He knew he wasn't going to get anywhere, but he took it good-natured. "Tolerable," he said, "she's tolerable, Frony."

"That's good," I said. "Tell her I found my Star of Bethlehem quilt pattern and I'll send it by you soon as I get it traced off."

It distracted Darkus to get so many letters all at once. "I don't know how I'll ever get 'em all wrote," she said. "You've got no idea, Frony, how long it takes to write a letter. And so many all at once. It gives a body the quarest feeling — like having to run to keep up. Way you feel when you get behind with your work."

"Just take 'em one at a time," I said. "First come, first served."

"I would," she said, "but Brokenhearted writes every day! I just can't keep up with *him!*"

"Don't even try," I said. "Write him once in a while. What does he find to write about? Every day. Looks like he'd run dry."

Darkus giggled. "The same thing. Over and over. Just love letters, Frony. Love letters don't say anything new very often, I reckon. You say it once and there's not much of a way to say it any more that's different. But if the others commence writing every day, I am going to be hard put to keep my senses."

"Discourage 'em from it," I said. "Tell 'em you've not got the time."

"No," she said, "I wouldn't want to do that. My goodness, Frony, it's took me long enough to get 'em started. I don't want 'em to stop. I would just like 'em not to be so all-at-oncey. The worst is," she said, "I don't have any good place to write. I ought to be writing on them letters every day, but I can't get away from the rest. And Pap is fussing already about the light being on in my room so much. Says I am running up the light bill too much and what am I doing reading so late and don't I know I'll put my eyes out."

"I can see you would need to take care," I said. "What are you doing with all these letters you're getting?"

"I've got 'em in a shoebox," she said, "hid in Mam's blanket chest."

"Just redd out the whole chest," I said, "for you'll be needing all of it if these letters keep coming."

It wasn't long until she was hearing from all four of those men regular — several times a week for Lonesome and Anxious and the Texas Ranger, and still every day from Broken-hearted. "You better commence weeding 'em out," I told her. "You have surely got some idea by now which one you like the best."

"Not till I get their pictures," she said. "They are all aiming to send me one. I can tell better when I've seen what they look like."

"I can see how it would help," I said.

"They're beseeching me to send mine," she said.

"All four of 'em?" I said.

"All four of 'em," she said.

"I don't know as I would," I said. "If it was me, I believe I'd pick me one and just send him a picture. Looks to me you'd just be wasting three pictures sending all four of 'em one."

"I've not made up my mind yet," she said.

In time their pictures began to come. Lonesome, from Florida, was a big man, heavy-set though not fat. He was beginning to go bald but he had taken care to brush what hair he had across his bald spot. He wore glasses but they didn't hide that he was a little bit cross-eyed. He had a pleasant face, though. Looked to be a good-natured man.

Brokenhearted was thin and on the spindling side. Long-faced, like a horse. He had his picture taken standing by a table with his hand on the Bible. He was the one that had lost his mate. Darkus thought maybe he had got thin since she passed on. It looked to me more like his food soured on his stummick.

She was disappointed in his looks, though, I could tell. "He writes nice letters," she said, "but he does look awful scrawny, don't he?"

"That one," I said, "is pickled in his own juice. I hope you don't feel drawn to him."

She studied his picture a long time. "No," she said, laying it aside, "I believe he would be my last choice. He don't have much to offer, anyhow. A farm and a bunch of younguns is about all."

"Has he ever said how many?" I said.

"He avoids against telling me," she said. "I've asked him several times but he just skips over my questions."

"He's got a house full," I said. "Just throw his picture and his letters out and put him out of your mind. He's looking for somebody to do his drudge work and raise his young ones."

Anxious was just an ordinary looking fellow. We couldn't tell too much about him because he sent a kodak picture and it wasn't real clear. He was standing by a gas pump in a filling station and had on a uniform of some kind, so we guessed he worked there. He was the one from Missouri.

It was when the picture came from the Texas Ranger I knew which one Darkus was going to pick. It impressed her. He had on fancy cowboy clothes, boots, spurs, guns, ten-gallon hat and all. I reckon he aimed to look like Matt Dillon's brother, but he wasn't exactly the build for it. The clothes looked too big for him. "Does he foller cowboying for a living, Darkus?" I said. "I thought he was a Texas Ranger."

"That is just a name he made up for the ad," she said. "He's got a ranch in Texas, Frony. I reckon he has to herd cows on it."

"Not in them clothes, he don't," I said, "they're too fancy. Look at that shirt. All over embroidery. Looks like he stepped right off the stage of the Grand Ole Opry to me."

"They're probably his Sunday clothes," she said. "Don't he look elegant? I like that one, Frony."

"I can tell you do," I said. "Texas is a long way from Broke Neck, Darkus."

"I know it," she said, "that don't bother me. But Texas . . . I kind of wish he was from somewhere else. From what I've seen of Texas on the TV it looks to be scarce of hills and trees."

"And water," I said. "Wasn't it Texas where the wagon train like to perished in that desert? On the TV last winter?"

"That was Death Valley," she said.

"Well, it's out there some place," I said. "When that show was over I mortally did give thanks for my good spring. What folks want to leave a good country for and go wandering off out there is more than I can understand."

"It's not all like that," she said, gathering up her pictures. "You've saw the Rocky Mountains on the TV and them big falls and trees and the ocean."

"Not in Texas," I said. "I don't much believe any of that country is very civilized yet, Darkus. I would take second thoughts, if I was you."

"I've not said goodbye yet," she said. "Frony, lend me ten dollars till I get my check."

"What for?" I said.

"So I can have some pictures made," she said. "I can get six for ten dollars at the Supertone Studio."

"What do they charge for one?" I said.

"They don't make 'em that way," she said. "The fewest they'll make is six. I have done asked about it, Frony."

I don't have as much put by as some say I have, but I don't

spend much either, so the old coffee can hid in the meal chest which is where I keep my cash till I get to the bank, stays pretty full. My land, a body *couldn't* spend it all, the way the checks come in so regular. I buy what I need, and sometimes things I don't need, but as fast as I spend more comes in. You take fifty dollars every month of the world and it soon mounts up.

William Petry, over at Cartwright's Mill, that gets the biggest war pension of anybody around because he was shell-shocked and shot up too, says he has banked at both banks in town beyond the government insurance and has had to start on the building and loan. William lives plain, I admit. He's not ever married and stays on where he heired and was raised. Lives mostly in one room of the old house and don't even have the electric. Too crippled to drive a car so he rides horseback where he goes.

William went in town one day to buy a chain saw. He was so shabby the clerk didn't pay him much mind. I reckon he thought William would be buying on the installment and would be hard credit. It tickled William. On purpose he carries a roll of bills would choke a horse. He dickered with the man and traded him down to a rock-bottom price, then pulled out that wad of money and paid cash. Said the man's eyes like to popped out of his head. My goodness, William could buy three or four of those hardware stores, lock, stock and barrel, and still have money left over. It don't pay to judge people by their looks.

I gave Darkus the ten dollars and she had her pictures made. Six. Three by five. And they turned out real nice. She said the man put a lot of lipstick on her mouth and painted her face all over and he had her to go in a little room and take off her waist. Gave her a piece of black velvet to put around her shoulders. She came as close to being pretty in that picture as I ever saw her. She was awfully well pleased and said she believed, after all, she would send one to all four of those men. "I can't help wishing," she said, "for 'em to see who they've been writing to."

She wrote on the pictures, just like the movie stars. Same thing on every one. She said they were going to different men and what did it matter. What she wrote was, "My heart beats for you."

13

CHRISTMAS came and went and it was one of the best we ever had. All of us here except the boys in Vietnam.

We went to the school exercises, and Nathaniel and Junior both spoke a piece. They looked the sweetest and did the best. Sudley had got both of them new suits and shirts and shoes and they did look nice. I was in a sweat for fear one of them would forget his piece, but they didn't. They said them right off, just the way they had practiced at home.

Christmas Eve we went to the colored folks' sacrificial feast. They hold it every year and it goes as far back as the August meeting and draws as big a crowd. It wouldn't be Christmas without the sacrificial feast.

They decorate the church with red and white. The red is a symbol of the blood of Jesus shed upon the Cross and the white is a symbol of his peace. All around the walls they hang red cloth and around the top it's scalloped in white. In front of the altar they put a long table. It reaches almost across the church and it's covered with white tablecloths. At the ends they make arches covered with fresh cedar boughs. You can't hardly see the white tablecloths because of the cakes. The table is loaded down with cakes. The rest of the supper is in the back room, but the cakes they put before the Lord's altar. We all make one and take it. They have to be white, or white and red. For the red we nearly all used those little red-hot cinnamon drops.

The colored women always wear red dresses with white yokes and the men wear a red sash draped across one shoulder over their white shirts, and a red cap trimmed with white.

On Christmas Eve the women are in charge and after the singing the sermon is preached by a woman . . . on account of it is Mary the Mother of Jesus's night. Aunt Dilly used to preach it mostly, but she's too old now, so Exie, her girl has taken over.

When she got through preaching we had the march around. The women go first, all around the church, then outside and all around, with the men following, everybody singing, "Lead Me, Jesus, Lead Me, Everywhere I Go." When we came inside again we stood until the supper was blessed, then we went to the feast in the back room. It was a happy time, to be all together, singing praises, and remembering Our Lord.

The next day, Christmas, the whole family came to Sudley's for dinner. We had been cooking for two weeks, all the women, and we had to set the tables out in the hall there were so many of us . . . fifty-two Fowlers, which is just a drop in the bucket to all the Fowlers, but these were Sudley's. We counted Andrew and James and John though they were in Vietnam for Sudley put their pictures, in their uniforms, on the table. And he prayed the prettiest prayer for them. None of us had a dry eye when he said Amen.

The children shot off their firecrackers and torpedoes and

cherry-stones and lit their sparklers and Roman candles. The biggest grandboys always think it's a joke to throw at least one giant firecracker in the kitchen and watch us women jump. We put up with it on Christmas. It's against the law to have fireworks in Kentucky now, but Sudley don't hold with that law. He goes down across the Tennessee line and loads up the car with all it can carry. He doesn't mean for the young ones to be deprived of any of their happiness at Christmas time.

It was a good thing we had such a happy time together, for we were heading into all that trouble had we but known it, although I still say Darkus was no more to blame for it than Sudley or Tate or any of us. How was *she* to know what those men she was writing to were going to do? And how was she to know what Sudley was going to do, or Tate? And even the preacher getting mixed into it. Of course if she hadn't been writing to the men none of it would have happened, but nobody can foretell the future.

It was in February that Sudley found out about the letters Darkus had got. Just by accident. It was a rainy day and the children were in the back room playing. Me and Sudley were in the front room. I was ironing, where I could watch the TV and Sudley was sitting there by the fire, keeping one eye on the set and the other on the axe handle he was sanding down. Junior came in all at once lugging a shoebox. Sudley said, "What you got there, boy?"

Junior said, "A box full of letters. They was in the blanket chest. Grandpa, can I have 'em?"

I looked around and saw that shoebox, some of the letters spilling out already, and nearly fainted. The fat was mortally in the fire and I knew it.

Sudley said, "Give 'em here first."

I said, "Sudley, they're none of your business . . ."

"If they're what I think they are," he said, "they are plenty of my business. Let me have 'em, Junior."

I was just glad for one thing. Darkus wasn't at home. She and Lissie had gone down to Tish's. The newest young one had come a few days before and Tish was up and stirring but not able to do all her work. They had gone to help out.

Sudley read every one of those letters, every blessed one of them. He didn't skip a one. I kept on ironing. Fact is, I like to ironed one of Sudley's shirts into the ironing board. I wouldn't know how many times I smoothed over it till I came to myself. I kept darting glances at him to see how he was taking it. He didn't say a word, but he got paler and paler and his hands went to shaking. I was scared at first of what he would say. I allowed he would be so mad he would storm around. Then I got afraid he was going to have a heart attack. I had visions of him just expiring right there and then.

He went on till he finished them and then he just rose right up and laid them all on the fire. Burned them up. I could have cried, for I knew how it would hurt Darkus. She set such store by them. But I wouldn't have opened my mouth to go against Sudley for anything in this world. It wouldn't have been right. He retched up and got his hat off the mantel. Drug it off so hard he nearly drug off the lambrequin. I did say, then, "Where are you going?"

"Down to have it out with Darkus," he said, "and I don't know but what I'll cut me a hickory limb to take with me."

"Sudley," I said, "you never laid a hand to her even when she was a little chap. You surely wouldn't now."

"Maybe that's where I made my mistake," he said. "Maybe I ought to whupped her. Maybe what I did was spare the rod and spoil the child."

"She's got the car," I said, "how'll you go?"

"I got two legs," he said.

I pulled the iron plug out. "If you're bound to go," I said, "let me saddle old Dander. It's too far for you to walk."

"I'll make better time walking," he said, "and I'd ruther. I've not figured out yet how she sneaked them letters by without me knowing it, but I will. In time, I'll get to the bottom of it." And he walked out.

I felt like I used to when I was a little girl and my father would get mad at me. There is something about having a man mad at you that makes you want to go crawl under a rock some place. I never felt the same when my mother was mad. You can put some dependence in the way a woman reasons, even when she's mad. But a angry man just don't make any kind of sense to a woman. It nearly killed me that I had had to go against Sudley in the least way, but I did believe he was in the wrong this time. I believed he ought to see Darkus's side of it. I folded up the clothes and put things away and just set down and held my hands and waited. If I'd been waiting for the Judgment Day I couldn't have felt worse.

When they came back Darkus's eyes were red, where she'd been crying and Lissie was cowed-looking and scuttled into the kitchen to be out of the way. But Sudley didn't come in. He went to the barn. Men take a lot of comfort out of a barn. It must be the quiet and the dark and it being mostly a man's place, but I never saw one that didn't do a lot of his pondering and studying in the barn.

Darkus said he was awfully mad and had bawled her out hard, but what had made her cry was him burning the letters up. She said she had known he would be mad if he ever found out, and she had made up her mind to take that. And she wasn't going to give in. But she did hate to lose her letters.

"I don't reckon," I said, "he will ever speak to me again. Letting you use my box the way I've done."

"You don't think I dragged you into it, do you?" she said. "You must have a poor opinion of me. I told him the truth, but not all of it. I said I'd been meeting the mail. He said he'd put a stop to that. He would tell Clee not to give me no more letters."

"I a little doubt he can do that," I said. "Clee can't hold up your letters. And he has got to put 'em in the box you say. Clee just delivers the mail. He don't decide *what* letters to deliver. Well," I said, "I aim to tell Sudley my part in it. In for a penny, in for a pound. I am not going to hide behind your skirts. I just as well to have it out with him and tell him that in my opinion he is doing wrong. His intentions are good, Darkus, but you are not a little child and it's not his right to decide your life for you."

He was outdone with me, but not as much as I expected. "You'll take her side against her own father?" he said.

"I wish I didn't have to," I said, "but you're being bull-headed, Sudley."

He was more sad than mad. "I never thought I'd live to see the day," he said, "when my own family lined up against me."

"Which we wouldn't," I said, "if you would only see a little daylight."

"It ain't a big enough crack," he said. "I'm not having no

more of it, Frony. I'll meet the mail at your box same as mine from now on."

Well, that was easy got around. Darkus just made her a box out of some old boards and nailed it on a fence post further up the road. She had to do some ducking and dodging to get there without Sudley catching on, but he couldn't watch her every minute. Clee was outdone a little. He said he did wish Darkus would make up her mind where she wanted her mail put and what in cat hair was going on amongst the Fowlers anyway.

It was in March she got the letter from the Texas Ranger that rattled her up so bad. He said he was coming to see her and the day he named wasn't but a week off. She went running round and round the dining table. "What'll I do? What'll I do?" she kept moaning. "I never thought about one of 'em coming!"

"How did you think you could marry one of 'em without?" I said. "It generally takes a man and a woman standing up in front of a preacher to get married, Darkus. You surely must have known you couldn't marry by mail."

"I never thought about it at all," she said. "I just never thought that far ahead. That one of 'em would come *now*. It seemed a long time off yet."

"Write and tell him not to come, then," I said.

"I can't," she said, "he has done and started."

"It's further to Texas than I thought," I said, "or else he's coming by horseback, to take a whole week."

"He's aiming to stop off in Dallas," she said. "He's coming on the bus."

"I would have thought he would be driving his car," I said.

"How will he get backwards and forwards from the hotel in town to see you? Or are you aiming to borry Sudley's car and carry him?"

"He's fixing to stay with *us,* Frony," she said. "He don't aim to stay at the hotel in town."

I set down. "Let me get the straight of this," I said. "He is fixing to stay out here? On the ridge? What gave him the idea he could do that?"

"I didn't think you'd mind," she said.

"*I* don't," I said, "but Sudley will. He is strictly going to be one jump ahead of a fit when *he* finds out. He is not going to like having one of them men visit in his house. He don't think highly of them at all. If he don't run the Texas Ranger off at the point of a gun, it'll surprise me."

She hung her head. "Not up at our house," she said, "here."

"Here?" I said. "At *my* place?"

"Now, Frony," she said, "I never exactly invited 'em to stay here. In a way, I never. But I kind of let on . . . I just said there was room . . . Frony, I never really thought any of 'em would come. I didn't think about having to go through with it, and I kind of made out . . ."

"You have wrote *all* of 'em there is room for 'em to stay? At my place? Well," I said, "you have let on more than you can make good. Just meet the bus, Darkus, and tell him things have changed and he'll have to stay in the hotel."

"It would shame me," she said, and began crying. "It would shame me the worst, Frony. I would ruther just not even see him."

I oughtn't to have done it and I wished more than once later I hadn't, for little did I know what she had told the man, but she cried so hard and I felt so sorry for her I gave in. Foolish as it was of her, my heart went out to her and I didn't want her shamed. I said, "All right. Just this once though, Darkus. Don't let none of the rest of 'em come here expecting to stay on the place. I will put this one up for you. He can have Barney's room. But don't make a practice of this, for I won't do it no more."

She dried her eyes and began to make plans. She wasn't going to let Sudley know. She would meet the bus and bring the fellow out by the old road. He wouldn't stay but a day or two, while she was looking him over, and then if she decided to marry him they could go get married and leave out together. "When I'm married to him and gone is soon enough for Pap to find out," she said.

"It's awful risky," I said. "You aiming to keep the feller under lock and key so he won't wander around and Sudley see him?"

"I'll handle that," she said. "I'll take him off in the car during the day. We can stay over at town most of the time."

"Doing what?" I said. "Walking around the square? It's one block each way. There's four department stores, six hardware stores, two drugstores . . ."

"Oh, Frony," she said, "quit worrying. If you've got a car there's plently of things to do."

"Some of which," I said, "are what brought on Junior."

"I have told you," she said, "I don't aim to do that no more. Now quit bothering around and let me think."

She thought of a new dress, which cost me twenty-five dollars, and a new pair of slippers, stockings, petticoat and a new brassiere. "I *got* to have a new brassiere," she said.

"Why?" I said.

"My old ones have been washed too much," she said. "It takes a brand new one that's not been washed to have a good uplift, Frony."

"I am glad you told me," I said. "I always thought uplift went with religion. I never knew it had anything to do with bosoms."

She bought her clothes and brought them to my house and got a home permanent for us to put in her hair. "I want to bleach it first, though," she said, "and then dye it."

It didn't turn out too good. Sudley noticed it at supper that night. He was talking and all at once he got a glimpse of Darkus and he stopped talking right in the middle of a word. He looked two or three times before he ventured to say anything. Then he said, "Darkus, if you had to buy you one of them wigs they been advertising on the TV what I want to know is why in cat hair you got a *pink* one?"

She got up from the table and left the room without answering him. "You've hurt her feelings," I said. "That ain't a wig."

"It's her own hair?" he said. "What happened to it?"

"Total disaster," I said. "A king-size bottle of White Monday clothes bleach and one package of that warm, chestnut brown hair dye that only your hairdresser knows do you or don't you."

He studied me a minute, then he said, "You feeling all right, Frony?"

"I am," I said, "Why?"

"You ain't making much sense," he said.

It rebuked me. It wasn't his fault I had got myself caught between a rock and a hard place and was feeling ill and tetchy about it. I said, "Make out your supper. I got to be going and do up my own work."

We turned out Barney's room next day and cleaned it from ceiling to floor. Darkus mourned that I didn't have one of these new waterfall-front modern bedroom suits. "This bed and dresser," she said, "are so old-timey."

"And I'm proud they are," I said. "My great-grandpa made 'em. All out of one big wild cherry tree. Turned them cannonball posts on a hand lathe."

"What did he make it so high for?" she said. "My land, a body needs a stepladder to get into it."

"So the trundle bed could slide under it," I said. "I put it in the loft room. I aim to make it up for Barney to sleep in while that man of yours is here."

In my opinion, the room looked nice enough for a king to sleep in. I took pains washing the curtains for they were frail. My great-grandma wove them — out of pure linen. The old log cabin and bar pattern. They looked like lacework. And she wove the coverlid that went on the bed. Blue and white Whig Rose. I treasured these old things that had come to me down the generations and when antique hunters came scouring through the country I wasn't ever tempted to part with them. For any price. Money is only money, but a cherry cannonball bed made by your own great-grandpa is something to love.

The big day finally came and Darkus drove off to town to meet the bus. One good thing. Sudley was openhanded with the car. Anybody in the family that could drive was welcome to use it — if there was gas in the tank and the tires were up. He was used to Darkus being off and gone in it most of the time, so he thought nothing of it when she said she was going to town.

I was nervous and I make no bones about it. I wasn't used to having company, except the family. The house was as clean as a new pin but I went over it again. I had seen on the TV where people used flowers in all their rooms, so I set my sultanas and ferns and begonia plants around to the best advantage, though I commonly keep them all in the south window to get the sun.

Then I set in and cooked the best dinner I could think of. I cooked brown beans and white, and opened half a gallon of green beans to be safe. I opened fourteen-day pickles and nine-day pickles and three-day pickles, just in case — and beet pickles and tomato preserves and corn catsup. I killed a hen and stewed her and made dumplings and cut into one of my big hams to fry. In case he didn't like home meat I got pickled bologna and canned mackerel and brine fish at the store. I made mashed potatoes and hot and cold potato salad. Made a stack cake and blackberry cobbler and bought sweet cakes if he didn't care for home baking. There was bought bread, biscuits and cornbread. Sweet milk, buttermilk and coffee. I knew folks from off liked tea, but I didn't know how to make it and thought I'd better not pick this time to learn.

I wasn't really expecting much in the man, but as poor as I thought he'd be what Darkus brought home with her was a lot worse. He was frail and drinlin' and the sorriest excuse for a man I ever saw. Came to Darkus's chin and she's not overly tall. It would have pushed him to weigh a hundred pounds with all his clothes on. They were the ones he'd had his picture made in, except he'd left off the guns and instead of a rope he carried a guitar. He had weak watery eyes and no chin to speak of and he was bowlegged. This one, I thought, is as little of nothing as I ever saw. But I made him welcome. "Draw you up a chair," I said.

He did so and then he took a good look all around the room. "Is this," he said, "your property you was speaking of in your letters? Is this the house? And is this the land?"

Darkus cut her eyes over at me and sucked in her breath. She didn't have the nerve to say anything. She just nodded her head. She was scared to death I would give her away, would say in front of him it wasn't *her* property at all, it was mine. If I hadn't been so astonished I might have. But I was caught flat-footed and could only stare at her, amazed.

"Do you mind," he said, "showing me around the place?"

"Oh, she don't mind at all," I said, getting my breath back. "Just take him around, Darkus. Show him *all* of your place. Show him the upper pasture and the lower pasture, the tobacco patch, the spring and the whole place. Don't miss the old piedy cow. She's using in the lower pasture. And the pigs and chickens. And don't forget the new heifer. *They* are all property, too."

Darkus sidled out the door, quick, not saying a word, him following, and I put dinner on the table. I felt like turning her over my knee. It's all well and good to bait a trap, I thought, but if you're going to get caught in the trap yourself, it's best not to set it. Pretending she had property might interest the men, but they'd be bound to find out the truth sooner or later, and then how it would better her to have lied I couldn't figure. Darkus's property was her check for Junior every month, which would stop when she got married, and one-twelfth of what Sudley left, *when* he left it.

They didn't stay out too long and when they came in they

ate. I needn't have worried about that man enjoying his food
or being picky and choosy. He ate anything and everything
and more of it than anybody I ever saw. I do believe he
hadn't had a square meal in a month. We take pride in setting a hearty table here, and I was proud of mine, but it could
have been poor-do and he wouldn't have known the difference the way he shoveled it in.

When he had taken the edge off his appetite, he said,
"You've got more land than I thought at first, though it lays
mighty rough. And it's further from town than I expected.
It would be unhandy in some ways."

Darkus was eating fast and pretending she didn't hear him.
"In what ways would it be unhandy, Willard?" I said. His
name was Willard Wilson.

"Well," he said, "I play the guitar over the radio. There's
a radio station in the town, I know, for I seen the tower. I
might get on to play for them."

"Oh, yes," I said, "there's a radio station in town. But
don't you foller cowboying for a living?"

"No," he said, "I'm not a cowboy." Then he turned red in
the face and laughed, sort of embarrassed. "I mean . . ." he
said, "I mean, I don't do the work myself. I have got men to
do all that kind of work on my place."

"Oh," I said, "have you got a place? In Texas?"

"Willard has got a big cattle ranch in Texas, Frony," Darkus said. "How big did you write me it was, Willard?"

He fumbled around with his collar and said, "I don't keep
a close account . . ." It was plain he had forgot what he'd
told her.

"I believe," Darkus said, "you wrote it was two thousand
acres."

I'll believe that, I thought, when Broke Neck Creek starts to run uphill. But I didn't let on. "My," I said, "that's an awful big place. I don't know as I ever saw a farm that big."

"It's not a farm, Frony," Darkus said, "it's a ranch. A cattle ranch."

"Like the ones on the TV," I said. "How many cows have you got, Willard?"

"Well, right now . . ." he started, "well, I've sold some of 'em lately . . . and right now . . ." and you could tell he didn't know as much as I did about how many cows make a herd. I have seen them on the TV. Hundreds and hundreds. Trail driving.

"There's likely so many," I said, "you can't remember."

He laughed. "Selling some off has got me confused," he said.

"I can believe it," I said. "How does it happen that with your big ranch and all them cows you foller picking the guitar on the radio for a living?"

"Oh," he said, kind of airy, "I don't have to do it for money. But a man gets tired of seeing to cows and such and likes a change."

They went in the front room, then, and I washed up the dishes. I could hear Darkus begging him to play and sing for her and he didn't need much pleading. He may not have been the worst I ever heard but he was next door to it. The way he picked and sang "North to Alaska" would have shamed Junior who is just commencing.

I hauled off and went over to Sudley's. He wanted to know where I had been all morning. "Things get in the worst mix," he said, "when Lissie has got the tending to do."

I said my head had been hurting and I was favoring it. He

said, "I've not ever heard of your head hurting you before. Are you coming down with something, Frony?"

"No," I said, "just foolishness and I don't know of any cure for that. I'm getting old, Sudley, and have not got the judgment I once had."

"The day you lose your judgment, Frony," he said, kind and sweet, and patting my arm, "they'll be putting you under the sod. I wish Darkus hadn't went off in the car. You might ought to see the doctor. But she went early this morning and said she might not be back until tomorrow. Said she might take the night with Rachel." Rachel was one of his married girls. One of his and Ordrey's.

I felt the worst, deceiving him. I would love to have just blurted it all out right then, I felt so miserable. I wasn't used to keeping things back. All I could do, though, was pitch in and set things to rights. Lissie hadn't cleaned up after dinner, or after breakfast either far as I could tell, and she had the washing machine pulled out, trying to do the wash. I was glad to have a lot to do so as to put in the rest of the day.

When I went home late in the evening Darkus and Willard had gone off in the car. Barney came in and didn't like it because his bed was changed and I couldn't get him to go up in the loft room to sleep. He couldn't understand why he couldn't sleep in his own bed. He got stubborner and stubborner and finally he said he was going up to Sudley's and sleep. "Go, then," I said, "and maybe I'll have some peace." He trailed off and I went to bed.

I don't know what time Darkus and Willard came home. They waked me standing on the porch talking and snickering and, doubtless, kissing. Finally they came on through and stood in the door of the back room. They were still carrying on. Darkus cautioned him once when he laughed out. "Sh-sh-sh," she said.

"You needn't bother to be quiet," I said, "I'm not asleep."

The way Willard scooted into the back room and banged the door you'd have thought I'd fired off a gun. Darkus came to bed with me. "What time is it?" I said.

"Two o'clock," she said, giggling.

"In the morning?" I said.

"Well, it ain't afternoon," she said.

"Where have you been all this time?" I said.

"In town, mostly," she said. "We eat supper at the Brown Jersey and then went to the drive-in movie."

"You been drinking, too," I said. "I can smell it on your breath."

"Only beer," she said.

"Beer'll addle you same as whiskey," I said.

"I only had two cans," she said. "Frony, what is your opinion of Willard?"

"I hate to tell you," I said, "it's so low."

"I think he's real nice," she said.

"You would," I said. "He's a man. Or passes for one. He wears pants. Darkus, now you listen to me. That Willard has no more got a cattle ranch than I have. He is lying to you, just plain lying to you."

"Why would he lie to me?" she said.

"For the same reason you lied to him," I said, "to show off. He is meaning to marry you and live off of you the rest of his life."

"Well," she said, "he couldn't do that, for I've got nothing he could live off."

"He don't know that," I said. "You lied to him about own-

ing a place and you led him to think you had property. He is
out to get his hands on it."

She sat straight up in bed. "Well, my land, Frony, I didn't
aim to stay here on this ridge. Mostly what I want is to get off
of it. Staying here is not according to my intentions at all!"

"You have drove your ducks to a poor market, Darkus," I
said. "That man has got no place to take you and is looking
for a place to stay himself. Now, tomorrow you own up
you've got no property and you tell Willard you are not aiming to marry him and he'd better pack his things and go."

"He's not got any things to pack," she said. "He didn't
bring nothing but his guitar."

"I knew it," I said, "I knew it the minute I laid eyes on
him. He's nothing but a radio tramp. I have read of them.
They just foller picking and singing wherever they can get a
day's work. Now, you give that man his marching orders first
thing in the morning."

She was quiet for a little bit and then she said, like a little
young one begging for a favor, "Frony, couldn't he stay one
more day? I had the best time today. I don't know when I've
had such a good time. He's a lot of fun, Frony, laughing and
joking and carrying on."

"He's a joke, all right," I said. "I'll bet if you emptied his
pockets there wouldn't be a nickel hanging to the lining."

"Oh, no," she said, "he's got plenty of money. When he
went to pay for the hamburgers he said he didn't have nothing less than a hundred-dollar bill on him and did I have
some change."

"Did you see his money?" I said.

"Well . . . no . . ." she said.

"I reckon you give him some change," I said.

"It wasn't but a dollar," she said, "and the drive-in tickets."

"Kiss it goodbye," I said, "the fool is dead broke."

She was still and then she lay back down and kind of sighed. "I don't much care, Frony. It was worth it, I had such a good time."

I tried to harden my heart but couldn't. I said, "Go to sleep. We'll talk about it some more tomorrow."

14

IT DIDN'T SEEM to me I had much more than closed my eyes till there was the unholiest yell a human being ever heard. It bounced all through the house and kept on bouncing. It came from Willard's room and brought me out of bed standing, Darkus right behind me clutching the tail of my nightgown. "What was that?" she said, quavering like a little old scritch owl.

"I don't know," I said, "but I aim to find out."

There came another yell, then, and I grabbed me up a stick of stovewood and started marching towards the door. Darkus was hanging on so tight I couldn't hardly walk. "Leave go my nightgown, Darkus," I said.

"I won't," she said, hauling back. "You're fixing to get killed. Don't go in that room, Frony. If it's Willard done and lost his mind he's liable to kill us both. Bar the door with a chair, Frony, so he can't get out and let's run over to Pap's. We don't want no maniac on the loose."

"Fiddlesticks," I said, "in his mind or out of it I'm not scared of that little runt. I've got me a stick of wood, haven't I? Leave go my nightgown! If I've got to take a swing at him, how can I with you hanging on?"

There came another yell and then it sounded like some-body was thrashing around, sort of moaning and groaning. Darkus commenced shaking. "He's having a fit," she said, "he's having a stark, raving, crazy fit, Frony! Let's get out of here!"

Well, the hair sort of stood up on *my* neck, the way he was taking on, but I took a good grip on the stovewood. "Nobody is going to run me out of my own house," I said, and I was just fixing to fling the door back and march in, when it busted open and Willard came flying through in his long underwear. It was just daylight enough to see. "Somebody's trying to kill me!" he yelled in passing. "There's a crazy man in there. He tried to get in bed with me. He pushed and shoved me around and then tried to choke me to death!" He made a long, sliding dive, then, under the bed.

I threw away my stick of wood and went in, for I knew what I'd find, and there, just as I had figured, was Barney. Lying right in the middle of his own bed, the covers pulled up under his chin, looking the peacefullest. "My bed," he said, smiling at me, patting the covers, "my bed. I'd ruther be here."

He hadn't any more tried to choke Willard than anything. Just tried to shove him over to make room. Barney don't care how *many* are in his bed as long as he can scrooch in, too. He maybe shoved a little hard, but the wonder was he didn't begin screeching when Willard didn't give. He just hadn't got mad enough, was all.

We got Willard quiled down, but he wouldn't go back in the bed with Barney. Said there wasn't money enough to pay him to. Said Barney was dangerous and he was going to stay clear of him. We got him out from under my bed and into it and he lay there and trembled until the bed shook with him. Sorriest sight I ever beheld. Pure rabbit. No more backbone than a broom straw.

It was daylight and time to get up anyway, so me and Darkus took our clothes to the kitchen and dressed and started fixing breakfast. We had the fire going and the coffee on to boil and Darkus had gone to the privy when I heard footsteps pound across the porch. "Now, what?" I said, going to see.

It was Sudley. "You'll have to come, Frony," he said. "Lonesome is over at my place. Come out early on the milk truck. Lissie is so rattled up she has burnt two skillets of meat already."

All the starch went out of my knees and I sunk down in a chair. "Lonesome?" I said, "Lonesome who?"

"That Lonesome feller Darkus was writing to," he said.

"How do you know it's him?" I said.

"Because he said so," he said. "Said his name was Clayton McCoy and he was from Florida and he'd been writing to Darkus and she sent him her picture and he liked her looks and made up his mind to come see her. Said he had wrote under the name of Lonesome. Is your coffee boiled yet? I've not had a sip."

I poured him a cup and he saucered it and blew on it and supped. "I give thanks," he said, "Darkus is not at home. I have been pondering how to get shut of that feller before she comes back. Soon as he eats, I've thought maybe I could commence easing him out. Florida, Frony! Even if wasn't so far away I wouldn't want her to live *there*. It ain't safe. It's half-way out in the Atlantic Ocean and likely some day a big tide to swaller it up. If a hurricane don't blow it away first."

"Sudley . . ." I said.

"Trouble is," he said, "he ain't too bad, for somebody from off. Friendly. Nice. The younguns have took up with him already. He had Whitley on his lap inside of ten minutes, making over him. And you know how backward Nathaniel is. Won't hardly peer at a stranger from behind Lissie's skirt. He was setting on the sofa beside this feller when I left and the feller was showing him his tattoos. He was in the Navy during the war and has got tattoos all over his arms."

"Sudley," I said, taking a firm grip on my nerve, "the fat is in the fire and you might as well to know . . ."

At that very moment Willard called out. He said, "Darkus, is that coffee I smell? Would you mind to bring me a cup here to the bed? I'm still so trembly I don't believe I can get up without I have something in my stummick."

Sudley's mouth dropped open and he stared at me. "Who," he said, "is that?"

"That," I said, "is the Texas Ranger. I was just fixing to tell you, Sudley. Darkus ain't at Rachel's. She's here. Been here all along. This one come yesterday. On the bus. That's where she went. To meet the bus. She brought him here and they've been here since."

Willard yelled again. "Darkus? Didn't you hear me? I would like a cup of coffee."

"Hold your horses," I yelled back at him. "Darkus ain't in the house right now. She'll bring you a cup soon as she comes in."

"Are they done married?" Sudley said, low so Willard wouldn't hear.

"No," I said. "It takes three days now, Sudley, since they

passed the waiting law. There's not been time for 'em to get married."

"They could have went across the line to Tennessee," he said.

"I a little doubt they did," I said. "Darkus slept with me last night."

"Then what's he doing expecting her to wait on him?" he said.

"He don't know no better. And Barney scared him. Come home in the middle of the night and crawled in bed with him. Willard has had the weak trembles ever since. His name is Willard Wilson. He is strictly a polecat, Sudley. The sooner we get shut of him, the better it will be."

"He oughtn't ever to come," Sudley said. "How come him to?"

"She sent him a picture, too, and he liked her looks, too. But mostly this one has come to get his hands on her property which she's not got but he thinks she has," I said.

"I am getting more rattled up all the time," Sudley said. "Why would he think such a thing?"

"Because she lied to him, Sudley. She let on my place was hers. He is one of them radio cowboys, Sudley. Not got a nickel to his name," I said.

Sudley groaned. "Two of 'em," he said. "Two at oncet. How come Darkus to bring him *here?* How come you to get mixed up in this, Frony?"

"Has there aught ever happened to yours I've *not* got mixed up in?" I said. "I've got no excuses, Sudley. Foolish of me or not, I felt sorry for Darkus and let her talk me into it. She was afraid you would run him off."

"Which I likely would," he said. "But two of 'em! I was puzzling how to get rid of one. I don't know as I can grapple with two."

I had made sure Sudley would take me to task but he appeared more beset than anything else. "I wish I hadn't, now," I said. "I have repented of it."

"And well you might," he said, "deceiving me." But his heart wasn't in it. He was still a little dazed. "But, Frony, she's not had no more letters since I burnt them. How did all this come about? And what is all this about her sending pictures? I've not seen e'er picture of her."

I told him the whole thing and got the picture she had given me. She had two left over was why she gave me one. Big tears came in his eyes when he looked at it. "I wish she would give me one," he said. "Ain't she pretty, Frony? Look how big and pretty her eyes are."

It went straight to my heart and pierced it. Sudley was the only one that ever thought Darkus was pretty. I said, "You can have that one, Sudley."

He put it in his pocket. "I'll get a frame for it," he said, "next time I'm in town. Where is Darkus at now, Frony?"

"Out," I said, "but I hear her coming."

She came in and shut the door and then she saw Sudley and said, "Oh, my Lord . . ." and covered her face with her hands.

Sudley worked up enough temper to give her a good scolding, but he didn't really cut loose because of Willard in the next room. He wouldn't have wanted a stranger to hear family troubles. He kept his voice down when he said, "How many of them men have you wrote to come, Darkus? Lonesome is over at the house and the Texas Ranger is here. I reckon we can expect Anxious and Brokenhearted any minute."

Darkus had sunk in a chair. "Pap," she said, "I'm so rattled up I don't know. But I give you my word and honor I never told but Willard he could come. If any more comes, it's on their own independence."

Sudley told her this was what came of her deceitfulness and it was a fine kettle of fish and now we were into it what were we going to do. All Darkus could think of was to flutter her hands. "My land," she said, "imagine two of 'em coming. Frony, would you have thought it?"

"I would ruther," I said, "not tell you what I am thinking. Now, you take Willard a cup of coffee. Me and Sudley will commence making plans."

With her out of the room, I said, "It might be best if they don't meet, Sudley — these two men. It could cause trouble. A fistfight at the least, if not knives or guns?"

"Ain't this Willard too chickenhearted to fight?" he said.

"By the ordinary, I would say so," I said, "but a man courting can rouse up enough jealousy to forget his fears."

"But how'll we keep 'em apart?" Sudley said. "It ain't far from your place to mine and with all the passing we do, they'll be bound to run into each other. We got to shift 'em out in a hurry, Frony." He pulled at his chin. "Trouble is, Lonesome is not going to leave till he's talked to Darkus. He has done said so. Said that's what he come for. And if she'll have him, he aims to take her off with him. Frony," he said, "I'm not used to having my children fixing to go away. It gives me a pain — right here," and he laid a hand on his bosom. "It mixes me up in my mind. I can't figure out nothing. I feel sick to my stummick." His chin started to quivering.

"Sudley," I said, "now don't you start worrying. What you need is a little dram. I'll fix you one."

I fixed him a good strong hot toddy and he supped on it. "Now," I said, "you take Darkus on home with you. She's steadier than Lissie and she can cook breakfast for you. I'll wait on this one and make some kind of arrangements for him. Then I'll come on over."

"I wish you would," he said, "till I get hold of myself."

It suited Darkus to go with Sudley. Her mind had already left Willard behind and she was anxious to see what Lonesome looked like. And I needn't have worried about the arrangements for Willard. He figured out his day for himself. Said he didn't feel up to getting out of bed and would it be all right if he just laid up. I told him to lay as long as he pleased. He wanted to know where Barney was and I told him he had gone off already. He said he could rest easy, then. I left him with his guitar, propped up on my pillow, in the middle of my bed.

Lonesome was a fine figure of a man. Big, brown from being outside in the Florida sun, stout but not fat. He looked just like his picture, only nicer. He was hearty and what I'd call handsome. He was going bald, but that was to be expected at his age. Not that he was old, but he had weathered some. His eye didn't appear to be as crossed as the picture showed it, either. And he was turned the friendliest. Laughing and talking with all of us as if he'd known us all his life. Just plain pleasant. I couldn't help but take to him and wish

he was from nigh us some place. I thought what a good man
he would make Darkus if only he wasn't from off.

He didn't let on he had a lot of money and property, either.
He said right out he didn't have much. "You have a right to
know," he said to Sudley, "seeing as you're her father, that I
don't have much. I have a little place and I built my house
myself. I get a small pension from the war. I was in the Seabees and got hurt a little. That's why I get a pension. It's not
very big, but I'm a carpenter by trade and I get enough work
by the day to make out. I couldn't promise Darkus any luxu-
ries, but she wouldn't ever want."

He didn't ask about how Darkus was fixed. I thought
maybe she had lied to him the way she had to Willard, but
apparently right from the start she had taken to that cowboy
and put most of her eggs in his basket. It seemed as if Clayton
— that was his name, Clayton McCoy — wanted to marry
her and take her back with him and *he* would make the living. I kept *wishing* he wasn't from off and aiming to take
Darkus away.

After we had spent some time in the front room talking, I
went in the kitchen to start dinner. In a little while Darkus
came in and said her and Clayton were going to town. "Did
Sudley say so?" I said.

"I've not asked him," she said.

"Then ask," I said, "this time I'm not helping you go behind his back."

I marched into the front room with her and stood there
until she asked if it would be all right if her and Clayton took
the car and went to town. Sudley said the tires were too bad
and they would likely have a flat, or if they didn't she was

such a poor driver she would likely run them into a culbert and kill both of them. But he was halfhearted about it. He didn't make near the commotion I expected. And Clayton didn't turn a hair. He just laughed and said he would do the driving, and if they had a flat he would fix it. He said he had a cranky old car at home and was used to such. Said that was why he came on the bus. Said he wanted to make sure he got here.

Sudley made no more objections and they drove off together. "Well," I said, "that gets *him* out from underfoot. Now, if Willard comes wandering around they won't run into each other."

"Frony," Sudley said, "it is worse than I thought. Clayton wasn't born and raised in Florida. He's not been living there except since the war. Clayton was born and raised in Pike County, Frony."

"There, now," I said, "I *knowed* he was too homey and friendly to be from that far off. Why, Sudley," I said, "that's real nice . . . him being from Kentucky. Pike County is not very far away at all. Maybe he'd just as soon go back there. Instead of Florida. If he would take Darkus there . . ."

"Frony," Sudley said, "he is a *McCoy*. From Pike County."

"You needn't to keep telling me," I said, "I heard you the first time. So he's a McCoy . . . from Pike County . . ." And then the light commenced to dawn. You might say it came broad daylight all at once. "He surely ain't one of *them* McCoys," I said.

I was getting used to my legs going limber, but I wished they wouldn't. It gave me the quarest sinking-down feeling.

"If he's from Pike County," Sudley said, "he's bound to be.

They are as thick as flies in a molasses trap over there to this good day."

I had to fan myself with my apron a minute, then I took heart. "That old war has been over for forty years or more, Sudley. There's not a Hatfield or a McCoy shot at one another for a time and a time. Besides, we are not connected with either one of 'em. Not that I know of."

"Have you forgot that Grandpap's youngest sister married a Hatfield?" he said, "And he taken her the other side of the Tug to live in West Virginny?"

I just made for the door.

"Where you going?" Sudley said.

"For the whiskey," I said, "I allow we *both* need a dram right now."

When it had quiled me down I felt real outdone. I said, "It beats me how Darkus could of retched in the barrel and come up with a McCoy. If she tried, she couldn't of done it in a hundred years."

"Well," Sudley said, "that's what she's done. And without even trying. It was trouble enough without him turning out to be a McCoy."

I studied a while and began to see a little reason. "Well, that was three generations ago, Sudley. Clayton has likely never heard of the connection. The Hatfields, like us, were a mighty big family. That Hatfield Aunt Suse married might have been a distant connection."

"They don't come too distant for Hatfields and McCoys not to know about," he said. "I don't recollect now who it was they said she married. Except he was a Hatfield. He come through the country — seems like Pap said he was buying timber — and she just got on his horse and rode off with him. It was the last anybody heard of her. She never wrote home or ever come back."

"Well, there now," I said, "how would they ever know she was connected? Much less Clayton, down through the generations."

Sudley got up and went to his room and came back with his old over-and-under. "What are you going to do with that gun?" I said.

"Make sure it's loaded," he said.

"Put it up," I said, "and don't start the war all over again. You're not called on to fight the McCoys on account of old Aunt Suse."

"I don't aim to," he said, "but I'll feel better if I'm ready." He stood the gun in the chimney corner where it would be handy.

"Well," I said, "we might as well be doing something that's better paying. I'm out of feed. Why don't we grind some corn in the hand mill?"

We went to the barn and shelled off several bushels, Barney helping. Barney loves everything about grinding corn, but what he specially loves is turning the handle of the mill. We got along so good I finally left them with it and went to the house. There was a little dab of ironing to do.

Sudley had just got back to the house, along the middle of the afternoon, when a car drove up out front. He peered out, "He's strange," he said.

I looked for myself. He was a tall man, gangling and awfully thin. He was what we call fox-faced — sharp nose, sharp chin, narrow, thin mouth. But he was kind of bulldog-jawed.

I had the awfullest feeling he was Brokenhearted, from Georgia. I said, "If he is another of them Lonely Hearts, Sudley, he'll have to sleep with Clayton. I've not got room for him at my place."

The man blew his horn, then, and Sudley fixed to go out. "I'll tell him we're crowded," he said, "and maybe it will discourage him."

The fellow got out of his car and came towards the gate and Sudley went to meet him. "Which one are you?" he said. "Anxious or Brokenhearted? The Texas Ranger and Lonesome have done come, so you're bound to be one or the other."

The man stopped walking. "I beg your pardon?" he said.

Sudley said, "I am Darkus's pa. And I may as well tell you plain, for there'll be no hiding it now, you're the third one that has come and I don't know what your chances will be. There is Willard — he's the Texas Ranger, down at Frony's place, and there's Clayton McCoy — he's Lonesome, staying here. And we're a leetle bit crowded. If you don't snore or pull cover too bad, maybe Clayton will let you sleep with him. When Darkus answered them Lonely Hearts she ought to made it clear that one at a time was all we have room for, but apparently she never, for you're all showing up at once. Which one did you say you was?"

"I didn't say," the man said.

"Well," Sudley said, "there's just two left. She never wrote to but four. Where you from?"

"Missouri," the man said.

"Then you're Anxious, ain't you?" Sudley said.

"Yes, sir," the man said, "I would say I am. Right now. I *thought* I was lost. I wanted to ask where I was . . ."

"Oh, you ain't lost," Sudley said. "You've hit it right on the nose. You have come to the right place, all right. Come on in the house."

"I don't believe I'd better," the fellow said. "If you'll just tell me where . . ."

Sudley took him by the arm. "This is it. This is the place. Just come on inside and make yourself at home. Darkus is not here right now. Her and Clayton have went some place, but she'll be back before night."

He led the man inside. "Frony," he said, "this here is Anxious — from Missouri. Get you a chair and draw up to the fire."

The fellow looked like he would rather go back outside, so Sudley pulled him a chair around to the hearth. "What is your real name?" he said. "I know it's not Anxious. That's just the way you signed the ad. My name is Sudley Fowler. It's my girl that has wrote all of you men."

"Oh," the fellow said, and he took a seat all of a sudden. It was like, when he heard Sudley's name, he came unsprung inside and sort of let down. "So you're Sudley Fowler. My name is John Singleton. I have heard of you."

"Well," Sudley said, astonished, "I knowed I was well-known hereabouts, but I wouldn't of thought my name had spread to Missouri."

Mr. Singleton laughed. "As far as I know it hasn't," he said. "I was speaking of your county seat."

"Oh," Sudley said, "yes. Well, the boys over there think pretty well of me, I reckon."

The man had nice manners. I stayed long enough to be polite before I went to the kitchen to get supper. He was friendly and ready to talk about anything Sudley brought up.

They talked about the weather and crops and politics and the War in Vietnam and the War on Poverty, and when I left them to it Sudley was telling him all about his family and how much comfort they were to him. He told him about Darkus writing to the Lonely Hearts. "It's not my wish," he said, "for Darkus to go away, but with so many of you turning up at oncet I believe I'd better just wash my hands of the whole thing and be as consoled as I can with the ones left nigh me."

I ought to have known better right then. Sudley don't wash his hands of matters that easy. But at the time I only felt sorry for him and believed he had a change of heart and meant for Darkus to have her chance. It pleased me he would be so reasonable. Whilst I fried the meat I wondered which one Darkus would take, Clayton or Mr. Singleton. I didn't even include Willard in the running. He was a long shot too far back to count.

We needn't have feared where to put Mr. Singleton for the night. He wouldn't stay. Said he had already made arrangements in town and he wouldn't trouble us. We thought it was real thoughty of him. He stayed for supper, though, and ate hearty.

Darkus and Clayton came back just in time to eat. I wondered if when Clayton saw Mr. Singleton it might make him mad and there might be trouble. I felt real nervous about their meeting. But Clayton shook hands with the man as pleasant as you please and sat down to talk with him and Sudley as if it didn't bother him one whit to have another one come courting.

I allowed it would send Darkus into the fluttering fits, too, for Anxious to turn up this way, but she barely spoke to him and sailed right on into the kitchen. "Who's he?" she said, tying her apron on.

I told her and then said, "Can we expect Brokenhearted next, Darkus?"

"I wouldn't know," she said, saucy like, "and couldn't care less. Frony, I got something to tell you. Me and Clayton got our blood tests today."

I was a little taken aback. "You didn't lose no time," I said. "Now that Mr. Singleton has come, maybe you ought to waited. You might like him best."

"No," she said, "I have made my pick and there won't nothing or nobody change my mind. Mr. Singleton can go back where he come from, far as I am concerned."

"How did you get Clayton in the notion so quick?" I said.

"I didn't," she said, "he got in the notion hisself. It was his own idea. When we got over to town he asked me point-blank if I was willing to have him and how soon could we get married. He said he had a piece of work coming up next week and ought to get back for it, but he would like to take me with him. I told him we had to get the blood tests and then wait three days. He said, 'Let's get started.' And we went right to the doctor's office. Oh, Frony, ain't it just like a dream come true? Me — going to be married and live in Florida and have me a home of my own and a man of my own. I can't hardly believe it yet. Ain't being in love the *nicest* thing? He is the *best* man, Frony."

"You can tell me if you still think it when you've been married to him a few years," I said. But I was glad for her. McCoy or not, I believed he was a good man, and it didn't hardly seem she could be so lucky. "Are you going to take Junior with you?" I said. "Or did you tell him about Junior?"

"Not straight off," she said, "we'll send for him. And yes, I told him. You needn't to worry about that. Sometimes I use my head, Frony, though you don't often think so. I knew it couldn't be hid. And if it could, Junior's mine and I aim to raise him. I told him straight off. That's why I said he was such a good man. He didn't mind at all. He said everybody made mistakes. Said nobody was perfect. Said we would just have a head start on a family of our own. Said he loved kids and he wouldn't ever make any difference between Junior and his own. That's why," she said, "I wouldn't change now for Mr. Singleton or *nobody* else. I have picked Clayton and I mean to stick to him."

"It will go hard with Sudley," I said, "but I believe he has give up for you to marry one of 'em." I told her what he had said to Mr. Singleton.

"Maybe so," she said, "but I don't want to take any chances. Clayton wanted to be open about it and tell Pap, but I talked him out of it. I said Pap was witty and he might put a spoke in the wheel. I said the best thing for us to do was tell nobody but you."

"Not even Willard?" I said. "Or that Mr. Singleton? Just keep 'em both dangling, thinking they've got a chance."

"I believe it's best," she said. "I want Pap to think I've got 'em on my hands and can't decide amongst 'em. Friday the time will be up and me and Clayton will go over to town and get the license and get married and catch the bus to Florida. I believe that's best, Frony. You can tell Pap Friday night, or

I'll write him a letter. But if I get shut of Willard and this one, Pap will know I've picked Clayton and he'll take measures. I just know he will, Frony. This will be the last thing I ever ask you to do for me."

"Have I got to have Willard on my hands three more days?" I said.

She studied a minute. "To sleep, I don't see any way out of it. But he just as well come and go, hadn't he? Now that this one has showed up from Missouri, I don't see it would hurt for Willard to mix and mingle."

"Then you go down there and haul him out of my bed right now," I said, "and if he's still feeling too weak to stand tell him if he's fixing to eat tonight he'll have to get his strength back. I don't mean to fix supper here and fix for him there."

She went for him and he came, teetering along in his high-heeled boots and his guitar strung around his neck. If that guitar had been solid gold he wouldn't have valued it higher. Sudley hadn't seen Willard before, but if he shocked him, he didn't show it. He was pleasant to him.

We were still at the supper table when Tate stopped by and I offered to set him a plate but he said he had eaten. Sudley made him acquainted with the men. "They are here," he said, "for Darkus to take her pick. They are Lonely Hearts men." Mr. Singleton swallowed his buttermilk the wrong way and strangled and sputtered. Clayton shook hands with Tate, and Willard nodded his head at him and went on eating.

When they had finished their supper and gone in the front room, Sudley and Willard started tuning up their guitars. I hoped Sudley could bear it when Willard cut loose. Tate stayed in the kitchen a minute or two. He thought Darkus's Lonely Hearts was the funniest thing he ever heard of. He wouldn't pass up the chance to tease her and make fun of her. "The whole settlement is talking," he said, "about all these men coming. The people are buzzing like bees swarming. And Clee Osborn has told around about all the letters you've got and how you've changed your mailbox around. They've all got pretty nigh the truth, too."

"It makes me no difference," Darkus said. "It's my business and none of theirs. They're welcome to talk. I won't be here long to hear it."

"You mean one of 'em is actually going to marry you?" Tate said.

"That's for me to know and you to find out," she said.

"Well," he said, "all I've got to say is the Lord ain't quit making fools yet."

"Now that you've said it," I said, "get on out of the way. Me and Darkus have got to redd up the dishes."

He went outside but directly he came in again with two half-gallon fruit jars of moonshine. "Here," he said, setting them beside the wash bench, "is something for Pap's nerves. I allow they'll be so rattled up by morning he'll need something to quile him down." He went on home, then.

To this good day I don't know why he was so openhanded with it. Commonly we had to buy, same as anybody else. But there's nobody doesn't have a few good points in their favor, and whilst Tate grieved Sudley a lot, sometimes he acted the way a boy ought to act towards his father.

I made a chance to tell Sudley about the corn likker and he

nodded. He said, "It was real thoughty of Tate. If we pick and sing much tonight it'll be good to have something to wet our whistles with."

I told Darkus I was going on home. I said I was too worn out to enjoy listening. "When you and Willard come in," I said, "show him the stairs. I don't mean to misput Barney from his bed no more and I don't aim for Willard to have mine. He'll have to take the trundle bed in the loft room."

Darkus was so worked up I didn't know whether she heard me or not, but she nodded her head. Then I couldn't find Barney. He had come in for supper, with his eyes all bugged out at the strange men, not eating as much as common and scooting out as quick as he'd finished. I looked in the barn and in the corn crib, where I'd left him and Sudley grinding corn in the afternoon. I thought maybe he had went back to play turning the handle. But he wasn't there. I gave up and went on home, hoping I'd find him there, and I did. In bed. He was scrooched down so far he had his head covered up. I said, "Barney, you'll smother yourself. Don't cover up your head that way."

"Have they gone?" he said.

"Has who gone?" I said.

"Them men," he said.

"No," I said, "they've not gone, but they will be in a few days."

"I don't like 'em," he said.

"Why, they won't hurt you," I said, smoothing down his hair, "they've come to see Darkus."

"I don't like 'em," he said. "I don't like 'em. I want 'em to go away."

"They will," I said, "pretty soon. You go on to sleep now. You don't have to be with 'em if you don't want to."

That pacified him and he turned on his side and I switched off the light.

I was so tired I went to sleep the minute my head hit the pillow, but the next thing I knew Darkus was shaking me. "Frony," she said, "Willard won't sleep in the loft room. He's afraid there's mice up there. Where'll he sleep?"

"Not in my bed," I said. "You tell him it'll have to be with Barney or the kitchen floor."

He took the floor. We spread him a pallet and to make it as soft as we could I got Barney's new feather tick, which I'd made for him when he wore out his old one hauling it backwards and forwards to the preacher's. Barney didn't want to part with it. He kept tugging on it and saying, "Mine. It's mine."

I had to pry him loose from it. "I know it's yours, honey," I said, "I just want to borry it. The man is not going to hurt it. He's just going to sleep on it. You can have it back in the morning."

We finally got all bedded down and I, anyway, got a good night's rest for a change. I wouldn't know about Willard. Some time during the night Barney sneaked in and slid the feather tick out from under him. Next morning when I went in to start the fire, Willard was lying under the table rolled up in a quilt. I wished it would make him leave the country.

15

THAT DAY started off with a scare about Junior.

Witchie came fogging over just after I had got up, white as a sheet and heaving for breath, for he had run every step of the way. "Frony," he said, between heaves, "come on quick! Junior has drunk coal oil!"

I grabbed my bonnet. Willard rolled over and opened his eyes and sort of groaned. "Is everybody on this ridge crazy?"

"When you got here," I said, "you made the total lunatic population." And I slammed the door behind me.

Then I thought — coal oil! I grabbed Witchie's coattail. "Go down by the spring and gather me some elm bark. Don't lose no time. I'll get on over to Sudley's."

He slid off down the hill and I took the foot path and made tracks. When I got there Sudley was sitting in the rocking chair holding the boy, rocking him backwards and forwards, the tears running down his face. Lissie was running around crying, too. Clayton was trying to get Sudley to bundle him up and take him to the hospital. I said, "How bad is he?"

"Mighty bad," Sudley said, "he's been puking, pore little

feller." He smoothed the boy's head back. "He's mighty sick, Frony."

"What have you done for him?" I said.

Lissie put in, "Bathed his hands and face. That's all Sudley would let us do till you got here. He's been holding him ever since. We can't get him to put him down."

"If he's going," Sudley said, all fierce and hurt and hugging the boy tighter, "I aim to be holding him. I don't want him skeered."

I felt of the boy's face. It wasn't hot. He looked a little white, but he was quiet and his eyes weren't rolled back. "How much did he drink?" I said.

"Oh, it's untelling," Sudley said. "The girls hadn't used out of the jar but very little. It was nearly full. He might of drunk a full quart."

Clayton looked at me and I looked back at him and then he went in the kitchen and came back with the jar. It was still nearly full. He set it on the hearth. I said, "Junior, I don't want any lies, now. How much did you drink?"

He sat up in Sudley's lap. "I didn't swaller none," he said. "It made my mouth burn. I spit it out."

"How come you to puke?" I said.

"I couldn't help it," he said. "Grandpap grabbed me up and run his finger down my throat."

"I wanted him to get up all he could," Sudley said.

"You done the right thing," I said. "But there's naught to be worried about, Sudley. He didn't swaller any. Let me look in your mouth, Junior."

He opened wide and I looked and he'd spit it out so fast it hadn't even burned. "Does it hurt?" I said.

"No," he said. "Just feels kind of quare and puckery."

Witchie came in then with the elm bark and handed it to me. I said, "I'll make some slippery elm tea, Sudley, and have him to rinse his mouth with it off and on through the day. You just get yourself quiled down. He's come to no harm and he'll not. The slippery elm will be soothing to his mouth, but I a little doubt it will even be sore."

Sudley hugged the boy hard and set him on his feet. "Don't go skeering your old grandpap that way, boy. You put ten years on my age and I don't need 'em any faster than the Lord intends." He stood up. "I knowed you would know what to do, Frony." He put his hand on Clayton's shoulder. "I'm obliged to you for offering to help. Though it wasn't needed, you offered. I won't forget it."

Clayton laughed and said, "It would have been more help if I had thought to look at that fruit jar sooner."

Sudley said, "I don't know why I didn't. But when one of the little chaps is in danger it appears something just locks around my heart and I can't think of aught that's sensible. I just want to comfort 'em."

When we got to the bottom of it, it turned out that Junior tried to drink the coal oil thinking it was moonshine. Not that he drinks moonshine, mind you. My land, no. Not at six years. But he had seen the men drinking it out of the fruit jars the night before and just out of curiosity, the way a young one will, thought he'd taste it. And the reason he got the coal oil by mistake was because Tish had sent up several days before by Witchie to borrow some coal oil and he said he'd just take the can, so it wouldn't leak in the car, and when he bought her a new can he'd bring it back. He poured out a

quart jar for the girls to use till he brought the can back. It
did look a lot like corn likker, I must admit.

Outside of the fright, it was a day as ordinary as any other.
Clayton and Darkus went off in the car again. Clayton was
paying for everything. He said he wanted to see the country
whilst he was here, for it might be a while before he got back.
That Mr. Singleton didn't come that day. Not at all. Which
went quare, seeing he was supposed to be courting. Commonly a man courting makes the best use he can of his time,
and here he was missing a whole day of it. Sudley said maybe
he had changed his mind and gone back to Missouri.

When I went home to see to things there, Willard said he
had had such a poor night he believed he'd rest and he
crawled in my bed and slept all morning. Barney was off
some place, with the gun. Willard came over to Sudley's for
dinner and then him and Sudley picked and sang a while.
The preacher came by, around two o'clock, and stayed for an
hour to listen. He had Sudley to sing the songs he liked best
—"Over the River to Feed My Sheep," and "Nottamun
Town," and "In Yonders Valley." Old songs Sudley got from
his Pap and him from his and on back to the olden times.

Willard didn't know them and he got restless with Sudley
doing all the singing. Some of the old songs are sorrowful and
make you feel sad, but they have got a tune, which is more
than can be said for songs nowadays. When the preacher left
Willard broke in with a real fast one that just said over and
over Hold my hand. I wished somebody *would* hold his and
keep him from picking his guitar. All he could do was chord
and even that was sloppy. "I wish," he said, "I could get me
an electric guitar. You can't get nowhere in show business
without one."

"Is that what you're hoping to do?" Sudley said. "Get in show business?"

"I have had some thoughts of it," Willard said, "but I need me an electric guitar and a good amplifier."

"What," Sudley said, "is an amplifier?"

"It's a thing that makes the music louder," Willard said. "All the big cowboy singers have 'em."

"I believe," Sudley said, "I would give it second thoughts before spending the money."

"What do cows sell for here?" Willard said.

"It depends," Sudley said. "The market is not steady. Depends how old a cow is, what breed she is, and several things. Was you thinking of driving some of your cows up here and selling 'em?"

Willard plunked an E-flat chord a lot flatter than it was supposed to be. "Not specially," he said. "I was just wondering. What would a plain old spotted cow bring?"

"A little of nothing," Sudley said. "Frony has got an old piedy cow wouldn't bring five dollars."

"Oh," Willard said. He plunked a few more chords. "A good electric guitar costs five or six hundred dollars. New. But I know where I can get a good secondhand one for two hundred."

"If you've got the two hundred," Sudley said, "that's the one you'd better get." He stood his guitar in the corner. "Well, I've enjoyed picking and singing with you, Willard, but I have got the night work to do up now."

I followed him to milk while he fed and we laughed about how awkward Willard was hinting to borrow two hundred dollars. "I believe," I said, "I would have had to put in my two cents' worth if you had fell for it."

"Oh, I seen through him," Sudley said. "I wasn't falling for it. But you better shut your cow up in the barn of a night. If he was to leave out unexpected I wouldn't put it past him to drive her to market and sell her for her hide."

"I a little doubt it," I said. "He wouldn't walk fourteen miles and drive a cow before him. Now if Darkus was to pick him and he believed he had a legal right to the cow, he might try to *haul* her to the stockyards."

"I hope Darkus is not thinking of taking him," Sudley said. "You were strictly right about that one, Frony. He is not of much account." He forked down some hay. "I reckon she'll make her pick in a day or two, won't she?"

"Have you give up hope," I said, "that she won't?"

"Oh," he said, "a body don't ever give up hope. But what can't be helped has got to be stood. Anyway, it'll all be over before long."

"And not a minute too soon to suit me," I said. "I'm commencing to feel the strain."

When I got home Barney was skinning two rabbits he had killed. "Dumplings?" he said.

"All right," I said, "I'll make you a stew and dumplings, but not tonight. I'm too tired. You go on over to Sudley's and tell Lissie to give you some supper."

"I won't," he said.

"Then you'll just have to eat a snack," I said. "I don't aim to build up a fire in the cook stove tonight. Why won't you go over there and eat?"

"Them men," he said. "They'll get me."

"Now, what makes you think that?" I said. "They don't care about you. Not the least little bit. They have come to see Darkus. I've done told you that."

"I don't like 'em," he said.

"You don't have to like 'em," I said. "You don't even have to see 'em. Just go in the kitchen and tell Lissie to give you some supper."

But he wouldn't, so I fed him cold beans and bread and a slice of cold ham and we both went to bed.

When Darkus and Willard came in, he decided he'd chance the mice in the loft room rather than take the floor in the kitchen again and he stumbled up the stairs. I told Darkus I'd appreciate it if she would stay home the next day and help with the work. "I don't want to come between you and true love," I said, "and if there is aught I can do to help, I will, but I'm not as young as I used to be and I am getting wore out."

"We aim to stay," she said, getting in the bed with me. "That Mr. Singleton turned up after you'd left. He's a quare one, ain't he, Frony?"

"Did he say where he'd been all day?" I said.

"Didn't even name it," she said. "Just drove up and come in. Set with us a while. I just wonder if he's not one of these alcoholics."

"What makes you wonder that?" I said.

"The way he likes whiskey so good," she said. "He hadn't been there half an hour till he was asking Pap if he had any in the house."

"What did Sudley say?" I said.

"Said he didn't. Said they had drunk up what Tate had brought," she said.

"What did Singleton say to that?" I said.

"He kind of hinted they could go get some more, but Pap said tomorrow would be another day," she said.

"And if we don't quit talking it'll be here too soon," I said.

Darkus turned on her side. "Well," she said, "it's none of my worry, seeing as I've not picked him, but it might not go easy for the girl that gets him. If he likes to drink heavy."

The next day was a Thursday and just one more day to go until Darkus and Clayton could get married. I thought if we could make it through that day, things would turn out all right. I don't mind admitting I was looking forward to having it over and the men gone and things back the way we were used to. It was getting on towards time to burn the tobacco beds and begin the other spring work. The willows had begun to swell and redden a little and some days a soft, easy wind was blowing. The peeper frogs were sounding on warm nights and I found a bloodroot blossom near the spring one morning going over to Sudley's. It was time all this foolishness was over and we got settled down to our own ways again.

Darkus and Clayton stayed home — most of the day. Darkus pitched in and was a big help in the kitchen and Clayton lent a hand sawing some cookwood. When he got through with that he mended a loose board in the back porch and put new hinges on the door. He showed Sudley how to rub coal oil on a piece of glass and cut it smooth and even. He made a new pane for a broken window that way. He was the handiest man around the house. It was plain to see he would make a good man for Darkus. It puzzled me why he had advertised for a woman. I'd have thought he wouldn't have any trouble finding one. I came straight out and asked him. He laughed a little. "I have always been bashful with women," he said, "and I thought it might be easier to break the ice by writing first." Well, that went reasonable enough. There are plenty who will write things they wouldn't ever bring themselves to say.

It was the prettiest, warmest day we'd had — one of those deceiving March days when you feel in your bones spring has come and it can't ever be cold again. Every year we have them. Sometimes they last three or four days, sometimes a week, and they trick people into dropping potatoes and planting early garden too soon. There's not a bit of use planting garden till you hear a whippoorwill, for more than likely you'll have it all to do over because of frost. But the warm, thawy days *do* make you hunger to work the earth.

What they made Clayton hunger for was some fish. He and Darkus dug a can of worms and after dinner they took off for the river. I didn't much count on them catching a mess, but I did get out and gather some wild greens to go with them, just in case. If there's any better eating than dry-land creases mixed with crow's-foot and shonny, I don't know of it. Bake a pone of bread, stack a platter full of crisp-fried little bluegills and red-eyes, and a king oughtn't to turn up his nose.

Darkus and Clayton caught just enough. We had supper early and because it was so pleasant and warm went to sit on the front porch after. That Mr. Singleton came about then. I offered to fix him a bite of supper, but he said he had already eaten. He was a quiet-turned man, didn't ever seem to have much to say. He would just sit and listen and sometimes ask a question. He hardly ever talked to Darkus at all, or seemed to take much notice of her. I thought to myself, if that was the way they courted in Missouri it was a wonder the state didn't die out.

It wasn't yet dark when the preacher drove by and seeing us outside stopped to visit a while. He mostly wanted to know if Sudley could spare him some seed potatoes, but he stayed on to talk. Then Willard went inside and came back out with his and Sudley's guitars and they tuned up. The preacher said, "Are you going to play and sing tonight?"

Sudley must have been feeling mighty well and in the notion, for he said, "Preacher, it's my opinion we are going to have the pickin'est and singin'est night tonight we have ever had. My fingers are limber and my supper is setting easy and I feel a singing spell coming on."

"Wait, then," the preacher said. "Just wait a minute. I want to tape it. Let me run home and get my machine. It won't take a minute."

Sudley laughed and said, "We'll just warm up a few till you get back, Preacher."

They fiddled around some while the preacher was gone without trying to get really into it — mostly just limbering up, the way all guitar pickers have to do. Mr. Singleton spoke up and said, "Seems to me what you need most is something to oil your throat."

Sudley winked at him. "Maybe you're right, Mr. Singleton, maybe you're right. And maybe we'll get something a little later on."

When the preacher came back and hooked his machine up, Sudley humored him and sang a bunch of the old songs the preacher liked best — "Foreign Lander," "Maria," "Little Maggie," "Fair Ellender." Sudley could slide his voice up and down in the old-timey quavery way exactly like our grandpap used to do. It was the way he had learned from him and he never changed it, but that's not the way the singers on the TV do.

Willard was a little outdone that Sudley was stealing the show, and he kept trying to break in, but between Sudley and the preacher they kept him out. All he could do was follow along the best he could.

"When are you going to do 'Shady Grove' for me?" the preacher said. "That's the one I want to tape. You've been promising me for a long time."

Sudley ran a long string of picked notes up the neck of his guitar. "That's a fast piece," he said, "and my fingers stumble a little nowadays. I tell you, Preacher. You've not ever heard my boy Tate pick and sing, have you?"

"No, I haven't," the preacher said, "and I have been wishing I could. They tell me he is the best in the country."

"He is," Sudley said, "even if he is my boy and I oughtn't to say. But truth is truth and Tate is the best there is. Now, he's the one to lead out on 'Shady Grove.' Whyn't we all go down to his place and get him to make some music with us?"

Mr. Singleton was the first one out of his chair. "I'm for it," he said, "let's go."

The preacher had to study a little and then he said, "Well, I told my wife it might be some time before I got back. I don't suppose she will worry. And," — and you could tell he had made up his mind — "I might never have an opportunity to tape Tate Fowler again. All right, Sudley, let me close up the machine."

I had seen Sudley wink at Mr. Singleton. I knew in reason why him and Singleton, anyway, were wanting to go to Tate's. Myself, I would have taken second thoughts before taking the preacher to Tate's, with such a mixed crew and not knowing how Clayton or Willard or Mr. Singleton carried their likker, but men follow their own notions. With Sudley, anyway, if he set his head you might as well shout in the wind as try to change him. There wasn't any use me saying one word. I don't know as I would, anyway, for I knew the preacher was going to hear music like he never heard before when Sudley and Tate Fowler had a few drinks and really commenced to lay with it. He would get a tape that as far as our kind of music went couldn't be beat. I knew our men would take care with their drinking and the preacher wouldn't even catch on. If Sudley figured the others would be polite, I allowed he had been studying them and passed his judgment.

We collected ourselves up and began piling out to the cars. Lissie said she wasn't going. She was too tired and besides somebody had to stay with the young ones. Witchie was down at Tish's. Barney was home in bed. He had been off all day again, hunting. I had got a glimpse of him two or three times during the day, slipping around in the woods.

But there was still seven of us and the guitars and the preacher's tape machine. "We can go in two cars," Sudley said, counting off. "We'll take mine and Mr. Singleton's. The preacher's is too little."

"Now, Sudley," the preacher said, trying to be folksy, "don't make fun of my car."

"I'd ruther have a wheelbarrow," Sudley said, "it'd be roomier. Anyway, we'll have to leave the cars at the head of the holler and walk down."

When we got there we all crawled out and Sudley lit the lantern and we took off down the path, him leading the way. Mr. Singleton was the last in line, with his flashlight. It seemed he was having trouble with it. It kept flickering on and off, but then he got it to working right. "This is a mighty steep old hollow," he said. "It's curious, the way it's formed, isn't it?"

"It's the Coon Den Holler," I told him. "The sides are as nigh straight up and down as makes no difference. Till you get to the bench where Tate's house is at. Then straight up and down to the bottom again. I have never liked this old holler," I said, "it's got a bad name. A lot of meanness has gone on in it and one killing that I know of."

"Is that so?" he said. "Was that recently?"

"Twenty years ago," I said. "The Camerons and the Cahoons had some trouble over a boundary fence. They shot it out. Lias Cameron got his shot off last, after he had done been hit in the shoulder, but it was a good one and he left Dudgeon Cahoon lying across a bobwire fence — right on the boundary. Deader'n four o'clock."

He didn't say anything for a minute, then he said, "Well, is that all of it? What happened next?"

"Nothing," I said. "What could of? That ended the trouble. Lias Cameron made his point. That bobwire fence was where the Camerons claimed the boundary was. The Cahoons seen the point."

"Wasn't he indicted?" he said. "Wasn't he tried?"

"In them days," I said, "there wouldn't of been a bit of use indicting Lias Cameron. Wouldn't anybody have served on a jury to try him. They'd of been scared to."

He didn't say anything again, for a little spell. Then he said, "This is quite a country, isn't it?"

"We think so," I said. "Dudge Cahoon is buried right beside the trail — down at the bottom of the cove."

It wasn't till we came up to Tate's cabin and I saw the

lamplight that I remembered and said, "My land, Tate don't have the electric. The preacher can't use his tape machine."

"Oh, yes, I can," he said. "This machine works on batteries, too. There are too many ridges and hollows around here without electricity to depend entirely on an electrically operated recorder. I'm all set for Sudley and Tate, Frony."

Tate let us in and if he was surprised to see us he didn't let on. Good raising shows up, even in a rogue like Tate. He made us welcome, helped the preacher set up his machine, and allowed he was glad we had come and he was in a fine notion of picking and singing himself.

I couldn't tell you what it was like. You'd have had to be there yourself. There are some things so fine there's no words to tell it. When Sudley and Tate feel like it, and they did, and really lay with it, and they did, they make music that will stand your hair right on end. They gave the preacher the old songs first and I thought he would go right on up to heaven, he was so excited. We sang "Foreign Lander" all together. I never can sing that song without the salt tears flowing, the way it goes about being a foreign lander, full seven long years and more. And then his dearest duel when the girl's beauty conquers him. He tells how he would live on some lonesome shore or among the rocky mountains where the wild beasts roar, if he could but be wed to her. It is a song of real, true love.

We had been singing, I reckon, about an hour and all the men but the preacher had been slipping out, one or two at a time, just now and then, not noticeable, to the back room. They took good care, but Sudley's color was highing up and his eyes were a little glisteny. Clayton stayed as steady as a

rock and Mr. Singleton showed no difference. Tate never was
much of a hand to drink, but I could tell he was tippling
enough to feel good. Willard was the only I thought might
prove out to have no head. I hoped if he didn't he would just
pass out peaceful and make nobody any trouble.

Sudley said, of a sudden, "Tate, the preacher wants us to do
'Shady Grove.' You take the lead and I'll second you."

Tate grinned and flung one hand high, then he busted into
it hotter than I knew it could be picked. We commenced
clapping, then stomping, then singing:

> Cheeks as red as the reddest rose,
>   Eyes of deepest brown,
> You're the darlin' of my heart,
>   Stay till the sun goes down.
>
> Shady Grove, my little love,
>   Shady Grove, my darlin',
> Shady Grove, my little love,
>   Stay till the sun goes down.
>
> Wisht I had a big fine hog,
>   Corn to feed him on,
> And a pretty little wife to stay at home,
>   And feed him when I'm gone.
>
> Shady Grove, my little love,
>   Shady Grove I say,
> Shady Grove, my little love,
>   Stay till the judgment Day.

It goes on and on, a dozen verses or you can make up new
ones if you're clever. We might have, but Tate shifted to his
fiddle about then and commenced scraping up the fox and

hounds, Sudley following right along, casting the hounds and baying on the stops. It was pure delight.

When they got through with that, Tate flung into "Bile Them Cabbage Down," and gentlemen, I mean to tell you, they mortally biled 'em down! It went to Clayton's feet and he began to clog a little, then he swept Darkus up and commenced a reel. Then, bless my soul if Mr. Singleton didn't haul me up and we joined in. It had been a time and a time since I'd danced a set, but Sudley began calling, and we went right on through. I purely forgot about the preacher, I was enjoying myself so much. I even lifted up my skirts and did a little hoedown when it came my turn to go in the middle. I used to be good at it, and it came back to me just as natural. My feet flew almost as fast as Tate's bow!

When it was over we were all out of breath and flung ourselves down and fanned and puffed and panted. "I don't know *when* I've had such a good time," Darkus said, leaning so Clayton could fan her with a newspaper.

I took thought of the preacher, then, expecting he would be clouded up, ready to rain, but he was busy changing his reels. I allowed he had got the whole thing on tape and didn't hold us in contempt for it.

Mr. Singleton was over whispering to Tate and Tate was looking at him. He grinned and nodded his head, then he went outside. When he came back he shook his head. He spoke a word to Sudley, Mr. Singleton listening. Then Sudley laid his guitar down and got up and Clayton went over. When he came back he whispered to me and Darkus, "They have run out of whiskey. Sudley and Tate and Singleton are going down in the cove. Sudley says Tate has got plenty down there."

I just said plain out, since he was marrying into the family, "He's got more than plenty down there. That's where he makes it."

Clayton didn't turn a hair. "I had figured it," he said. He looked around. "Well, Willard and me and the preacher will stay here with you women. Maybe Willard can play for us and sing and the preacher won't notice too much."

They slipped out. The preacher noticed, but he didn't let on. I reckon he just thought they had gone outside, the way men do. Clayton asked Willard to play and sing some of his cowboy songs. "We have had some mighty good music tonight," he said, "but it's not been hardly your kind."

"I thank you for noticing," Willard said. He cleared his throat and looked at the preacher. "Aren't you going to tape it?"

The preacher said he would. "But let me put it on a different reel," he said, "then you can have it. You might want to make use of it."

I looked at Clayton and he grinned. We thought the preacher had got out of that one real cute. He didn't want any part of Willard's singing in his collection.

Willard hit off into "Red River Valley" and Darkus rolled her eyes up. It's the plainest song ever written, but he couldn't even stay on the tune with it. I set myself to endure until our men got back. It went on and on until the preacher began to get fidgety and I commenced to wonder what was keeping them. The preacher kept looking at his watch. "It's growing late," he said, finally, "I ought to be going. Where are Sudley and Tate?"

Clayton said, "Oh, just outside. You want me to step out and call to 'em?"

"I wish you would," the preacher said. "My wife will be worried if I don't come home pretty soon."

Clayton opened the door, but he didn't go out. He just stood there, his hand on the door knob, for just as he opened the door we could all hear the awfulest clanging and banging and shouting and yelling that ever was. Coming straight up the holler.

I have never seen or heard a raid before, but I knew what it was in one flat second. I rose right up and was out that door in a flash and hit the porch running. Clayton caught on quick and was soon on my heels. Darkus strung out behind him screaming what was the matter and wait for her. I never once thought of the preacher — or Willard, for that matter. All I could think of was Sudley and Tate in the middle of a raid and my ears kept flinching from the sound of a shot that might mean the end of one of them.

Not till we got to the bottom of the holler did I know the preacher and Willard had followed on and I only halfway noticed then, for what we saw when we got there was a sight to sicken a body. The place was all lit up with fires burning high, and there in the light, plainer than day, was that Mr. Singleton with a gun in his hand pointed at Tate. Sudley was standing to one side — in a trance it appeared. His mouth was slack and he looked to me like he would faint any minute. There were six other men. Three were standing around with their guns drawn and the other three were using axes and crowbars and mauls, breaking up the still. It hurt to see them smashing it — all that good copper beaten up. They about had it done when we got there. They had lined up a few jugs of likker to take in as samples and they had broken all the rest. It was running like a river all over the place.

I scrambled over to brace up Sudley before he fell. He looked at me, dazed and unbelieving. "He is a revenuer," he said. "Frony, that Singleton feller is a federal man. He has arrested my boy."

"He's a yellow dog," I said. "Try to take it as easy as you can, Sudley. Don't swoon. I'll brace you up and you can stay on your feet. Don't let 'em see it's bothering you."

Then I noticed the preacher, just standing there, goggle-eyed. Lord, Lord, I thought, how come him here — but I had no time for him beyond that. Willard let out a squeak about then. On account of his high heels he had got left pretty far behind and just come puffing into the light. He saw the guns. "Oh, my God!" he yipped and ran to get behind Darkus. "Don't let 'em shoot, Darkus! Don't let 'em shoot!"

"Quit twitching my skirt," Darkus said. "They ain't going to shoot. They are just great big he-men that have got to threaten folks is all. It taken seven of them, all with guns, to take my brother."

Singleton looked at her and grinned. "No," he said, "it took your brother being a damned fool. You've been pretty hard to catch, Fowler, and I thought you were smarter than you've been tonight."

Tate just stood there. He said nothing and his face showed nothing, but I could see his jaw working and knew he was gritting it back with his teeth. They had him, red-handed, but he wasn't begging them for one thing. And he wasn't making excuses. I was proud of him for not acting cowed to them. I thought of what Sudley said about the good blood in us. It was showing in Tate. He wasn't a Muley Fowler for nothing.

All of a sudden Sudley jerked loose from me and straightened up. "That's my boy you're talking about being foolish," he said. "It wasn't him. He is still too smart for you to catch. It was me that was foolish. I was the one swallered your lies and led him into a trap. You — passing yourself off as a Lonely Hearts. Fooling folks. Eating my bread and sitting under my roof. How was you raised, man? We don't do such things in this country. When we eat a man's bread we are obliged to him. You ought to be ashamed of yourself. You would stoop to anything, wouldn't you?"

"I didn't pass myself off as anything," Singleton said. "You passed me off. When I stopped at your house I had got off the road and only wanted to ask the way. You jumped the gun and pointed it straight at your own boy. You broke the case for me."

"Which I will never forgive myself," Sudley said, and he slumped down so I had to hold him again.

Tate said the only words he opened his mouth for, then. He said, "And I don't know as I ever will, either."

Clayton spoke up, then. "What happens next?" he said.

"Why," Singleton said, "you people can go. I have all your names. You'll be subpoenaed as witnesses when the trial comes up. I'm taking Tate into town."

"What do you aim to do with him?" Darkus said.

"What we usually do with people who break the law," he said, "put him in jail until he can make bond."

"I'll make bond for him right now," Sudley said, "if you'll just not take him. He won't like that old jail and I know he won't."

"He has to be arraigned," Singleton said. "If you want to see an attorney tomorrow, that's your privilege."

"I'll do better than see an attorney," Sudley said, "I'll see Job Rigdon. We'll just see who's going to put my boy in jail and keep him there."

The preacher had been standing there all the time, not moving, not saying anything, just looking on. He appeared to be in almost as much of a daze as Sudley had been. All at once he kind of jerked himself up. "I am not sure I understand all this. This equipment . . . this machinery these men have broken up . . . this was a moonshine still? And Tate Fowler was operating it?"

"You've got it exactly right, sir," Singleton said. "One of the biggest operations in the country."

"And you are a federal agent. You have made a raid," the preacher said.

"Right again," Singleton said. "You have witnessed what few people ever do — a federal raid on a moonshine still. Never expected to get involved in something like that, did you, sir?"

The preacher looked dumbfounded. "I am *not* involved. I've had nothing to do with all this. You can't call me as a witness."

"I'm afraid we can, sir," Singleton said. "You've been on this party all evening, when the men were drinking Tate's moonshine, and you have seen us breaking up the still. You can see those jugs of liquor right there on the ground. You are a very important witness, sir."

"But I saw no drinking," the preacher said. "I can't testify to that. And I wasn't present when you captured this man . . . or the still . . . and I was on this party . . ." He shook his head and changed his words, "I am not involved. I was merely taping some folk music."

"You got some fine tapes, too," Singleton said. Then he grinned. "But good music isn't all the people in this country make, sir. You should have sampled the moonshine. Though I have to arrest him, Tate Fowler makes the best white lightning I ever drank."

"Don't worry, Preacher," I said, "we'll swear you never touched a drop."

The preacher began to sway a little, like a tree that has felt the ax. "Me," he said, "a minister of the gospel . . . involved in a raid on a moonshine still . . . what will the bishop. . . ." Then his knees buckled under him and he swooned dead away on the ground.

Willard squeaked again and got out of the way. "I've not done nothing, either," he yelped. "You can't hold me. I've not done a thing. I'm going to get out of this place. This is the craziest place I ever saw." He turned around to run.

Clayton retched out his big hand and yanked him back. "You ain't going nowhere, buddy. Not till we all go."

"All right," Singleton said, "let's get this show on the road." They commenced taking pictures, then — pictures of the smashed-up still and pictures of the evidence and pictures of Tate and pictures of the whole crowd of us. I did wish the preacher had been standing up. It would have looked better.

Then they loaded up with the jugs and marched up the path. Tate went without making trouble. Just walked out in front of them and commenced climbing. Like a lamb led to the slaughter. He passed right by Sudley and didn't say a word. Sudley retched out his hand to touch him, but he sort of jerked away. "Don't you worry, boy," Sudley said, "we'll be right on over. Me and Job Rigdon will take care of this, you'll see. They'll not keep you behind bars."

We watched till they got beyond the light from the fires, then their flashlights went on and we could see their light darting about. I remembered how Singleton had flashed his that way coming down. Signaling to the others that were hid out, no doubt.

Darkus began crying then and Clayton put his arms around her. Over her shoulder he said to Sudley, "Is this his first offense?"

Sudley was shaking and the tears were flowing down his face too hard for him to speak. I said, "Yes, it is."

"It won't go hard for him, then," he said. "He'll get off light."

"There ain't no such thing as light, for a Fowler," I said. "One day behind bars will be an eternity. Fowlers are used to traipsing. Shut one of 'em up, where he can't set foot where he pleases, and it'll kill him."

"We'll get him out as soon as we can," he said. "But he's going to have to do time, Frony. He was caught flat-footed. There's not going to be any getting him off scot-free. You'll have to prepare Sudley."

The preacher stirred and let out a groan. I said, "My goodness, I had clean forgot that one. Here, Darkus, hold onto your father. Let me get some water from the branch and bathe the preacher's face."

Clayton began to laugh. He laughed in the nicest way — sort of all over, shoulders, belly, all his body. "I don't know," he said, "as I ever heard of a preacher being caught in a raid on a still before. It sure is going to be news, isn't it?"

It mortally was. But we didn't know the half of it yet.

16

WE CLUMB out of that old holler considerably sadder than we had gone down. Sudley and me went first, carrying the lantern. Darkus and Clayton braced up the preacher and helped him along, and Willard tottered along behind on his high heels. He kept calling out, "Wait. Wait, I can't see. I'll fall over in this canyon!"

Darkus finally turned on him and said, "I wish you would and get it over with. Now, come on and keep up!"

When we got to Tate's cabin we were just going to pass it by. "We can get the preacher's tape machine and the guitars tomorrow," I said. "We're all too worn out to be burdened with 'em tonight."

I knew Sudley was beginning to feel like himself when he said, "My land, yes. I don't want to pack anything but my bones tonight. I feel like a horse that's been rode hard and put up wet."

It suited the preacher. I a little doubt he even wanted to see a tape machine again. But Willard raised objections. "I want my guitar," he said. "You all wait, now. I know right where I put it. I am not going to leave it down here, for I don't mean to come back to this place."

We gave him the lantern and waited in the dark. The preacher kept saying, "Oh, my! Oh, my!" under his breath, and once he said, "Lord, give me strength!"

That turned Sudley on and he began wailing and quoting the Scriptures. "The Lord has turned away his face," he said, "to bring this on me and mine. He has poured me out like milk, and curdled me like cheese. He has made my flesh and skin old and he has broken my bones. He has compassed me about with gall and wormwood. He has bent his bow and caused his arrow to enter my reins. He has broken my teeth with gravel stones and he has covered me with ashes."

"Don't take on so, Sudley," I said, "it's not the worst that could happen."

"What could be worse?" he said.

"Well," I said, "Tate's alive. If he'd tried to shoot it out with 'em, he could be dead. It's trouble that he's arrested, but not the worst trouble."

Sudley turned on Clayton. "It looks to me," he said, "you could of hauled out your gun and *did* something!"

"Me?" Clayton said, surprised. "I don't carry a gun, Sudley."

"You're the first McCoy I ever heard of that didn't," Sudley said.

"I didn't know you were acquainted with my relations," Clayton said.

"I'm not," Sudley said, "but everybody has heard of them. *And* the Hatfields."

Clayton was quiet for a minute. Then he said, "The Hatfields . . . and the McCoys. I see. Where do you think I'm from, Sudley?"

"Pike County," Sudley said. "You told me."

"Pike County, *Alabama*," Clayton said. "I never set foot in Kentucky before in my life. If I'm related to the Kentucky McCoys, I don't know it."

Darkus began laughing and I began laughing and finally Sudley joined in. "Well," he said, "I am proud to know it. I mistook you for somebody else." He started in to tell about the Hatfield-McCoy war, but about that time Willard came back with the lantern. He had his guitar slung around his neck.

"That can wait, Sudley," I said, "let's get on out of this old holler."

It was a great relief to reach the top and get to the car. I don't know as I ever felt more footsore in my life. We piled in and Clayton got behind the wheel. "My," I said, "I am sure glad to set down."

My relief didn't last. The car wouldn't start. Clayton ground down on the starter and ground down. The engine just growled. Sudley said, "Darkus, I have told you and told you . . ."

"You're treeing the wrong coon, Pap," Darkus said, "Clayton put gas in this afternoon."

"She's right, Sudley," Clayton said. "I filled her up when we got through fishing. She's not out of gas."

The preacher moaned. "Why didn't I bring my own car? My own good little car that never fails to start! I might have known . . ."

Clayton tried a time or two more, then he lit the lantern again and got out to look under the hood. He fiddled around a little, then let the hood down. "Somebody," he said, "has made sure we wouldn't go anywhere. The distributor arm is gone."

"Them low-down skunks," Sudley said, beginning to storm, "them low-down skunks! It's not enough they've took my boy off, they have got to steal part of my car! You wait till I tell Job Rigdon! He'll make it hot for 'em!"

We know now it was Tate that did it. Out of pure meanness to get even with Sudley. But it was Singleton let him. I reckon they both thought it would be a good joke on us.

"Well," Clayton said, laughing, "it's shank's mare the rest of the way, folks. We just as well start putting one foot in front of the other."

"My feet are hurting me," Willard said, "I don't know as I can walk another step. Why don't we just stay the night here? Some can sleep in the car . . . and some on the ground . . ."

"Stay if you want to," Clayton said. "I reckon the rest of us will go on. How about you, Preacher?"

"Oh, I couldn't stay here all night," he said, "I'll walk with the rest of you. My wife would die of worry."

"I ain't going to stay by myself," Willard said, "now, wait for me."

"Willard," I said, "we have come to the road, now. Why don't you slip off them high-heeled boots and walk in your sock feet. It'll be easier than them boots."

"I believe I will," he said. We had to help him get them off, they were so tight, but then he was ready to trudge, guitar around his neck, ten-gallon hat, fancy shirt, and a boot in each hand.

There is a long stretch of the lonesomest road on the ridge between the head of the holler and my house. Not another dwelling. Just two miles of road with the woods coming right up to the edge on both sides. Even in the daytime it's lonesome, but in the pitch of night it's just plain spooky. We

limped along making as good time as we could and we talked
pretty steady just for the company of it. Truth is, we made a
considerable amount of noise. Clayton had a big, hearty laugh
and he was trying to keep us all in good spirits. When he
laughed you could really hear him.

We finally came to the end of the woods, into the open a
little piece, and I had just said, "This is my fencing we've
come to and the house is right over there. We'll just all bed
down at my place for the night."

And the preacher had just said, "I can't . . ." when all of
a sudden there came that high, whining zi-i-i-ng that a rifle
makes and a bullet thudded *whump* into the trunk of a tree
behind us. We all froze in our tracks. "What was *that?*" Darkus said.

Another bullet went singing by, then, and Clayton hit the
dirt, pulling Darkus down with him. "That's a rifle!" he said,
and he yelled, "Down, everybody! Down! Sudley, douse
that lantern!"

Instead of dousing it, Sudley commenced waving it around
like he was flagging a train. "It's that revenuer," he yelled.
"They have got a whole posse after us! They got us surrounded! Hit the dirt, everybody! Head for the timber!
Run for your life!"

He took off back down the road towards the woods, the lantern going like a windmill. Willard sprinted off after him,
right on his heels and catching up with him. The preacher
said, "My God!" Then he took off. I don't know to this good
day why I ran after them. I was just used to being where
Sudley was, is all I can make of it. Whatever the reason, my
legs commenced churning the road, too. Clayton was still

yelling at us to get down and put out the lantern. But another bullet really did put wings on my feet and I couldn't have made myself lie down and be still. I wanted to get behind some trees.

All at once I saw Willard begin to stumble. When you get to stumbling whilst running that fast it's just one long stumbling fall. I knew he was going down. I yelled at the preacher to look out, but he either didn't hear me or couldn't stop. Him and Willard went down together in a rolling tumble and I had to dig in my heels to pull up. I heard a great crash. I thought, there goes Willard's guitar. Then something went whuuuuuung, and snapped me on the cheek, and I thought, there goes the G-string. Then there was a long groan and some arms and legs commenced flailing around. I retched down and got hold of a leg and hauled back. It was the preacher I disentangled, but he was wearing Willard's guitar around his neck and the blood was pouring down his face. Another bullet went singing past and I thought, this is no time to ponder busted guitars and cracked heads.

I yanked the preacher up onto his feet and began pulling him up the road. "Willard," I yelled back, "you'll have to make it on your own. If you can't walk, crawl!"

"My guitar," he was moaning, "my guitar! Where is my guitar? It's gone. I had it just a minute ago and now all I've got is a busted strap. I got to find my guitar."

"Forget your guitar," I said, "the preacher is wearing it for a collar. Come on into the shelter of the woods before that sniper fills you full of lead!"

He scrabbled along behind me and we made it to the first clump of trees. I propped the preacher up behind the trunk of the biggest one. "You stay there," I said, "and you'll be all right."

He was groaning and taking on so much I knew he wasn't killed and I couldn't take the time to see to him right then. I had to get to Sudley and the lantern. But Willard came flinching up and tried to shove the preacher over. "My guitar," he kept moaning, "my poor guitar. I just got done paying for it. It was the best I could buy. Oh, Lord, what will I do without my guitar?" There was another shot just then and he hunkered down and changed his tune. "Lord," he said, commencing to pray, "just let me get out of this crazy place and I'll never leave Texas again."

"I wish you'd never left it in the first place," I said. "Now, you quit shoving the preacher. Leave him be. Come over to this other tree."

"It ain't as big," he said.

"It's big enough for you," I said.

I got him hid behind it and then I started crawling over to Sudley. I guess I came up on him too quiet, for when I called his name it startled him and he dropped the lantern and it rolled down the bank into the middle of the road. I hoped it would go out, but it didn't. It kept burning, and the light drew two or three more shots. The light it made seemed bright enough to show us all up. "Sudley," I said, "we have got to douse that lantern. They're shooting at the light."

We both looked at it. There it lay, on its side, burning as bright as a flare, right in the middle of the road. "Whoever tries to douse that lantern," Sudley said, "is going to get killed. It's too good a light for anybody to miss. I lost my head, Frony. I ought to doused that lantern first thing. I didn't hardly know I had it in my hand, though."

"Anybody would have forgot," I said. "It's too startling, being shot at."

We sat there for a spell. "Maybe they'll shoot it out," Sudley said.

"I a little doubt it," I said. "That's what they've been aiming by. How long will it burn?"

"The rest of the night," he said. "I just filled it up this morning." He made a move. "Well, goodbye, Frony. Tell 'em all goodbye for me. Tell 'em to live by the Good Book and the Lord will spread his wings over 'em. Tell Tate I said I was sorry and not to hold things against me. Help Lissie raise up my little chaps, Frony. Oh, Lord, I don't know who will look after my family, now. All my boys and girls!"

I grabbed him. "Where do you think you're going?"

"To put out that lantern," he said.

"Over my dead body you are," I said. "We can lay it out right here till morning if we have to. Take our chances. You strictly are not going to get yourself shot."

About that time I heard some leaves rattle and was just squaring myself around, scrabbling for a limb or rock or anything to hit with, when Clayton said, "Pst-st-st, Frony. It's me and Darkus."

I retched out and pulled Darkus under the tree. "How did you get here?" I said.

"Crawled," Clayton said. "I learned that much in the Seabees. We crawled in the ditch till we hit the woods."

"Well, I am glad to see you," I said. "Now you talk some sense into Sudley. He's aiming to try to put that lantern out."

"No," he said, "leave it alone. Let it burn right where it is. It'll draw their fire while we get away. Darkus says there's a little draw some place here and it goes around in back of your house, Frony. Reckon you could lead us to it? If we can find that draw, we'll have to cover to your house."

"I can find it," I said, "and will. Now, why didn't I think of that? We'll outfox 'em yet."

"We'll have to take care till we reach the draw," he said. "We'd better crawl, I expect. Where's the preacher? And Willard?"

"Right over there," I said, "behind two trees."

"I'll get 'em," he said.

"Take care," I said, "the preacher is hurt."

"Did they get him?" he said.

"No," I said. "He rammed his head through Willard's guitar. They fell. He's skun up is all."

He came back directly with the preacher. "Willard," he said, "has gone."

"Gone?" I said, "gone where?"

The preacher was dabbling at his forehead. He said, "He crawled over to my tree and got his guitar, then he went crawling off with it. In the woods."

"Well, my land," I said, "what did he want to do that for? He was safe where he was."

"He said he was getting out of here," the preacher said, "and I can't say that I blame him."

"Your chances of getting out of here," I said, "are better if you stay with us, Preacher. We've got a plan."

"I hope it's better than any other I ever knew a Fowler to make," he said.

"It happens," I said, "a Fowler didn't make it. It was Clayton's idea. Have you got a handkerchief, Clayton? I can bind up the preacher's head a little and the blood won't run in his eyes."

He had one and we bound up the preacher and then with me leading and the others following, Clayton helping the preacher, we made our way towards the draw. Every once in a while there was another shot, but the farther from the light we got the farther from the shots we were. My, but it was good to hit that draw finally. It was the upper end of the long holler that goes off back of my place and the nearer the house we came the deeper it got. Soon we could stand and begin walking, for the sides of the draw were higher than our heads.

"Frony," Sudley said, then, "I hope you have got plenty of cartridges for William's rifle for when we get to your house I aim to load up that gun and commence doing some sniping myself."

"If Barney hasn't used 'em all up these last few days . . ." I was starting to say, when it hit me. Rifle. Barney. Scared of the strange men. Scouting around the woods the last several days. Then — Barney home by himself whilst we were all away. Us coming down a dark old road making all sorts of noise. I could almost see Barney waking up and hearing us and thinking . . . and then getting scared and grabbing the rifle and making for the woods.

I hoped I wasn't right. I hoped he'd be in bed asleep when we got there. But I was about as sure as a mortal could be without certain knowledge who our posse had been and who had surrounded us. One scared boy. But dear Lord, one scared boy could kill.

I kept my thoughts to myself, though. No use saying anything till I was sure. We clambered on down the draw. It was rough with a lot of big rocks to climb around and lots of tree roots and briars. We all fell a time or two, in the dark, and got scratched up considerably. The preacher wasn't in too good shape to begin with, and even with Clayton helping him he took more falls than any of us. Every breath he took was a groan and I wondered if Clayton might not have to carry him before we got there.

We finally came to a big flat rock and I knew there was a path that climbed out. It was steep, but it would bring us out in my back pasture. I said, "This is where we climb out, Clayton. I don't know how we'll ever get him up the path, though."

"Have you got a petticoat on, Frony?" he said. "One of them big old-fashioned kinds?"

I knew exactly what he wanted it for. "I sure have," I said, and I unloosened the waist band and let it drop around my feet. "It's a good thing I've not took to them little silk slips, ain't it?"

"A mighty good thing," he said.

We made a twisted rope of it and Sudley took one end and Clayton took the other and they passed it behind the preacher and just levered him up that path with it. All he had to do was move his feet.

When we reached my back gate I said, "I'd appreciate it if you would all let me go inside first."

"No," Clayton said, "I'll go first."

"You will do me a favor," I said, "if you'll stay back."

He retched out and took my hand. "Frony," he said, "this is one time I can't favor you. I'm going with you."

We went together. Out of hearing of the others, he said, "It's Barney, isn't it?"

"When did you guess?" I said.

"Not for a while," he said. "Not till I realized one man was doing the firing. He was moving around, but one gun was doing all the shooting. I didn't see how it could be anybody but him, then. There was no reason for Singleton's men to waylay us. And Tate couldn't have got away from six of them. It almost had to be Barney."

"Try not to hold it against him," I said.

"You think I would?" he said. "Darkus has told me about him. She said he was afraid of us strange men."

"Scared to death," I said, "and I can't figure why. He's shy with strangers but he's not commonly scared of 'em."

We walked up on the porch. "Frony," Clayton said, "I'll go inside first."

"You think he might have come home?" I said.

"There's been no shots for a while," he said, "he might have."

I didn't wait. I flung the door open and called out to him. "Barney?" I said. "You here?"

"In my bed," he called back. "In my bed."

"You stay outside," I told Clayton, "till I get my hands on that gun. He might shoot if he saw you."

I marched in his room, switching on the lights as I went. He was in his bed, but he wasn't even undressed. Clothes and all he had crawled in. The gun was standing in the corner. I went over and took it up, broke it and slid out the clip. Then I stood it back in the corner. Barney smiled at me. "I scared 'em," he said. "I run 'em off."

"What made you do it?" I said.

"They was going to get me," he said. "They come after me."

"What made you think such a thing?" I said. "I told you they had come to see Darkus."

"No," he said, shaking his head. "Sudley said so. Sudley said we would run 'em off. Sudley said me and him would run 'em off. He wasn't there, though. I had to run 'em off myself. They're gone now."

I could have cried. Poor Sudley. Wanting to keep Darkus from going away. And poor Barney, so easy scared. Little did Sudley know how he had stirred him up. I smoothed his hair back and said, "It's all right, now. They are all gone except the one that is going to marry Darkus. You have got to believe me, Barney. His name is Clayton and he is a fine man and he likes you and he is going to marry Darkus."

"He won't take me away?" he said.

"I give you my word and honor, he won't take you away. Now, why don't you take off your clothes so you can sleep better," I said.

He got right up and slipped out of his overalls and I tucked him in and left him. He was half asleep as soon as he got back in the bed.

The others came in, then. I felt like letting Sudley have it with both barrels, but the preacher was there and I didn't want to air family troubles before him. I didn't see any good would come of letting him know who had been taking pot-shots at us.

We couldn't talk the preacher into staying the night, though, and I thought maybe it was best he went on home. His head needed tending. Clayton took him. Walked him over to Sudley's and then drove his little compact car for him. Then he walked all that long way back. The preacher didn't even think to offer him the use of his car. Clayton could have driven it back and taken it home the next morning. But we understood. The preacher was too distracted. Clayton said his woman had hysterics all over the place and he had to get the man to bed for her. He told her then she would have to get hold of herself and do for him, he couldn't stay.

My fire had sort of got damped down by the time we got the preacher off our hands and I didn't make too much of a fuss with Sudley. I did tell him I thought it was a sorry thing for him to do — use Barney for his own ends. He said he had changed his mind after Clayton was so good when Junior drank the coal oil, and he had told Barney so. Told him it was a mistake and for him to forget it. "Put an idea in Barney's mind one time," I said, "and he don't let go of it. Have you forgot how he hung onto that notion of moving to Tate's? We like to never got him out of that notion. Right now I don't know whether it's safe for Clayton to come around. Except I have got the clip for the gun. And you make certain your gun is unloaded and the shells well hid, too."

"Frony," he said, "I won't ever get done repenting of this. I'll see he can't make use of my gun. I'll do whatever I can to make up for it."

All told, it was a night. It mortally was one more night.

17

WE DIDN'T see hide nor hair of Willard again, but we had news of him. The Carnation Milk truck picked him up down on the pike about daylight the next morning. Arlie Newburn that drives the truck said he was the sorriest poor little man he ever saw, carrying that busted guitar and limping along in them high-heeled boots. Arlie said he was a little afraid of him after he let him in the truck, for he acted like he was out of his mind. But he calmed down and rode peaceful into town. We lost track of him then, but as I told Darkus, "Texas, make ready. Your boy is coming home."

Sudley and Clayton walked down to Tish's next morning and borrowed Witchie's car to go in and see Job Rigdon. They bailed Tate out of jail but Sudley came home downcast anyway. For one thing, Job told him Tate's was a federal offense and he would have to be tried at the federal court and he would do what he could for him but he was a little afraid it wouldn't be much. Tate was bound over for the Grand Jury.

What bothered Sudley more than that, though, was that Tate was mad at him and whilst he rode out with them coming home, he wouldn't talk to Clayton or Sudley either. It grieved Sudley for Tate to act so. "If I knowed how to make amends," he told me, "I would, for I didn't mean to get the boy in trouble. Lord knows I would have cut off my right arm before causing him the least little bit of trouble. Looks like he would know that and make it up with me."

"In time he will," I said. "He's just feeling sore and bothered right now. Human beings are all built alike, Sudley. We can't bear our own blame and have got to find somebody else to lay it on. When this trouble is over Tate will be himself again. Not that that's much comfort to you, for he's not overly easy to get along with any time, but it will be better than right now."

When they had taken Tate home and Clayton had put a new distributor piece in Sudley's car, he spoke to Sudley about his intentions with Darkus. "We want to get married," he said. "We have been keeping it secret because Darkus thought you would try to stop us. I don't see any use of it now and I don't admire doing things behind a man's back. I'm glad I can come out in the open and tell you plain."

"I had guessed it," Sudley said, "but I am proud you told me. I reckon you'll be taking her to Florida to live."

"That's my intentions," Clayton said.

"You're a fine man, Clayton," Sudley said, "and I've got no objections to you, but I do hate to see my girl go so far away to live. I don't rightly know how I'll stand it. She's the first to go away, except Andrew and James and John in Vietnam, and that's not the same thing. They'll be home — in time. But I won't stand in her way. I won't ruin her chances. When did you aim to get married?"

"We had planned to do it today," Clayton said. "We got

our blood tests three days ago and the waiting time is up now. If you don't care, we can go ahead with it and go on to Florida. There's a piece of work I promised to do. We'll have to come back for Tate's trial, but I could get in a good season of work before then. It'll likely be several months before the trial."

"It sounds sensible," Sudley said, "but it's awful sudden for me."

Darkus had been hanging her head, embarrassed to be talked about in front of herself, but she spoke up then. "Pap," she said, "would it make you feel any better if we waited over a day? And if we had the wedding here at home instead of going to a justice of the peace?"

"I believe it would," Sudley said, brightening up. "I believe it would seem more real to me that you was married."

"Would it hurt, Clayton?" Darkus said. "It wouldn't make much difference, would it, to wait one more day?"

"It won't make any," he said. "If that's what you and Sudley want, that's the way it will be."

Well, we all went in town and Clayton and Darkus got the license, and then Sudley just poured out the money. He let Darkus get a white dress, the best she could find, new slippers and underclothes, and two more dresses, because on the TV they said brides had going-away clothes. I didn't see how she could go away in two, but if she wanted to try it, I didn't doubt she would. Sudley bought her a new grip to carry her clothes in. Oh, there was naught she wanted Darkus didn't get that day. Clayton bought her a bouquet to carry whilst they were being married. We had to take it with us because there's no delivery on the ridge, but we knew we could keep it in the refrigerator. It was the kind of day to send a girl straight through the pearly gates. We got to singing going home — "All God's Chillen Got Shoes" — and Darkus laughed and said, "And a starry crown, a harp and snowy wings. All mine today!"

Just before we got to Broke Neck Creek and the mission, we all had the same thought. We hadn't made any arrangements for a preacher to perform the ceremony. "I a little wish," Sudley said, "the preacher at the mission could do it."

"I'd just as soon," Darkus said. "Whyn't we stop and see if he is feeling up to it."

That was when we learned they had taken him to Louisville to the hospital. They said he was totally out of his head. They had to carry him in an ambulance because he couldn't even walk to the car. His woman had gone with him but one of the Cahoon women was at the parsonage staying with the young ones. She was the one that told us. It made us all feel bad. "But I *don't* see," I said, "how in the world ramming his head through Willard's guitar could have hurt him that bad."

"Maybe it gave him complications," Darkus said.

"They don't show up this soon," I said. "We ought to do something nice for him."

"Send him some flowers?" Darkus said. "We could do that."

"And we will," I said. "When we take you and Clayton to the bus tomorrow we'll buy him a nice get-well card and stop at the flower shop and order him a pretty bouquet and put the card with it. My March roses are blooming the best, now. I wish I could send him a bunch of them, but I a little doubt the flower shop would appreciate using them instead of their flowers. He always liked my March roses. But he called 'em jonquils."

"Well," Clayton said, "the truth is, Frony, they don't even use their own flowers. They don't send flowers off that way. They just telephone or send a telegram to some flower shop in the other place and have them to fill the order for 'em. If you want to send him a get-well card, you'd better mail it. They couldn't send your card with the flowers, either."

"Who'd have thought," I said, "sending a little bouquet would be so confusing?"

"It's not," he said. "Just place your order and they do the rest."

"Well, anyway," I said, "we can see to it that Veeny Cahoon has plenty in the house to fix for the young ones to eat. We've not hardly made a dint in my canned stuff and I've got one side of meat left."

"I'll break his garden for him," Sudley said, "and drop his potatoes and set out his onions. He won't be behind with his work when he comes home."

We got Preacher Simpson to perform the wedding. He is old, but we all know him well. He is a distant relation, by marriage, and he has held many a meeting in our meeting-house.

Lissie and Darkus and me flew in and cleaned the house till it sparkled. Even Tish came up and helped. Darkus said she wanted her and Clayton to stand in front of the fireplace, so we cleaned out the ashes and filled the firehole full of ferns and laurel and buckbush limbs. It looked so pretty. Then we gathered all my March roses and put two bouquets on the mantelpiece and laid sprays of calycanthus and bronze bush between. I wished the lilacs had been in bloom, for they make the prettiest bouquets, but it was too early.

The bus left at twelve o'clock, so we set the time for the wedding at ten, so as to give them plenty of time. Darkus said we ought to have a wedding breakfast but I said, "Are you out of your mind? Sudley has sent the word around and there'll be two hundred people here. It would take us two days to get ready to feed that many. We'll be pushed to do up the work and get you married and off on the bus the way it is."

"I reckon you're right," she said, "but that's the way they do it — off."

"This ain't off," I said, "and thank goodness. It'll cause talk no more than we're doing. Everybody is going to say Sudley's have got mighty highfaluting."

"I don't any more care," she said. "I want a nice wedding."

She had one, if I do say so myself. She and Clayton stayed in the back room till everybody had got there and Preacher Simpson was standing in place. Then Preacher Simpson raised a hymn and we all sang whilst they came in together. "Lead Me, Jesus, Lead Me, Everywhere I go." Sudley had to quit singing, it made him feel so bad. For she was going a far piece away. I was afraid he would break down, he was taking it so hard. But he didn't. He braced up and stood straight whilst Preacher Simpson said the words.

Darkus looked nice in her new dress, carrying her bouquet. Clayton had got red roses and they looked bright and pretty against her white dress. Clayton looked solemn and a little scared, but they both said their part clear and plain. Didn't either one of them mumble. I thought the Lord had kept

Darkus in his keeping and led her straight to this good man. It did my heart good to think it had all turned out so well for her.

The grandboys and men had tied old shoes and tin cans and bottles to the back of Witchie's car, and when Darkus and Clayton came out to go away all the people lined up and showered them with rice. Witchie drove off with them, and we followed in Sudley's car. Sudley's tears didn't stop till we got to the edge of the town. Then I said, "Now, Sudley, take hold of yourself. You don't want to make Darkus feel bad about going."

"No," he said, "I don't. I want her to be happy, Frony. I'll try to keep hold of myself."

But they both broke down when it came time. Darkus commenced wailing and flung herself into Sudley's arms and said, "Pap, I don't know if I want to go!"

He strengthened up the best. He put her away and handed her to Clayton and he said, "Yes, you do. You've married your man and it says in the Bible whither thou goest I will go. And you have to go with him." His chin was quivering but he said it strong. He gave her a pat on her head, the way he used to do when she was little, and he said, "Why, you'll be back before you know it. It won't be long till you and Clayton will be back for the trial. Hold hard to that if you get to feeling homesick."

"I'm homesick already," she said, but she snubbed up and tried to smile. "Pap, you take care. You be right here, the same as always, when I come back."

"If the Lord's willing," he said, "and nothing don't happen."

"Frony," she said to me, "I'm depending on you helping with Junior till we come back and take him with us."

"He'll not want for ary thing me and Sudley can do for him," I said.

It was then, that very minute, that a bunch of newspaper reporters and photographers came barreling up and then we noticed that right there in the bus station was a TV camera already set up and a TV reporter came over amongst the others with a microphone and the flashlights commenced popping and the questions commenced coming.

"Are you the Lonely Hearts man that won out?"

"Put your arm around her, Mr. McCoy."

"Kiss her, Mr. McCoy."

"Are you one of the Pike County McCoys, sir?"

"Were you present when they raided the still?"

"What connection is there between Tate Fowler and you, sir?"

"Ma'am, did you see the raid? Were you there? Are you the one in the picture?"

"How did you find out about the Lonely Hearts, ma'am?"

"How many men came?"

"Where were they from?"

"How long did they stay?"

"Sir, how did you happen to mistake the federal agent for one of the Lonely Hearts men?"

"Turn this way, please, sir. Ma'am, please. This way. Just a little more. Thank you."

"Is it true there was a minister involved in the raid?"

"Was he drinking?"

"Did he marry you, Mr. McCoy?"

"Ma'am, will you stand over there beside the newlyweds, please. Sir? Please. Thank you."

"What did you think of the report in the paper this morning, sir?"

"Was it your son that was arrested?"

I never felt so bewildered in my life. They shoved us around here and there and mashed Darkus's bouquet and stepped on my foot and took pictures from all sides and fired questions at us so fast we couldn't even think! We just stood there like dummoxes, not able to say a word.

It was Clayton came to himself first. It made him mad when the TV man shoved his microphone up in Darkus's face and she had to duck back. He shoved the fellow away. "If you don't stand back with that thing I'll clobber you with it," he said. "Now, what is this all about? What report was in the morning paper? Where did you get this story?"

One of the men spoke up. "The federal agent called the Louisville paper and said he had a whale of a story. Said he had fine pictures to go with it."

"Singleton!" I said, mad enough to spit. "Thank goodness he didn't know nothing about the shooting!"

That did it! And the minute the words were out of my mouth I knew I had put my foot in. But I wasn't used to reporters. Clayton gave me a look and I shut up like a clam. He made light of it and said all it amounted to was somebody took a few potshots at us as we went home the night of the raid. Nobody was hurt, he said. He let them think what they would of who had done it and I appreciated that. He a little bit led them to think it could have been one of Singleton's men sniping at us.

Then another one of the reporters piped up and said, "Singleton gave us an interview late yesterday. We tried to get out on that ridge last night to follow it up, but we got lost. Where in the name of God *is* Broke Neck Ridge?"

"Up Broke Neck Creek," Darkus snapped at him. "Now, try and find where *that* is."

Clayton nudged her to be quiet. "How did you learn we were leaving on this bus?" he said.

"Oh, the florist tipped us off," the man said. "Said you were being married yesterday or today and planned to leave by bus. We covered the morning bus and when you didn't show up figured you'd be leaving on this one."

"I am sorry," I said, "you bought that bouquet from that flower shop, Clayton. If we had but knowed what a traitor the feller was, Darkus could of carried March roses."

"Or dog fennel," Darkus said, "and I'd of ruther." And she threw her red roses on the floor. The TV got a picture of it.

"I especially hate," I said, "that we sent flowers to the hospital for the preacher from that place."

They pounced on that, then. It was the first they knew he was in the hospital. "Was he shot?" they wanted to know. "How did he get hurt?"

I was so purely outdone I blurted it out. "He rammed his head through the Texas Ranger's guitar, that's how he got hurt."

"Frony!" Clayton said.

"I don't care," I said, "I am tired of all this pestering. Let 'em write what they please."

Some of the men turned to leave. "Let's go," they said. "Let's talk to that preacher."

"It won't do you no good," I said, "for he's out of his mind."

That wasn't thoughty of me! But I was so mad I didn't care one bit. Coming pushing in about things that weren't any of their business — shoving folks around — taking pictures — asking nosey questions. In *my* opinion the newspapers and TV are going to be the ruin of this country. If they didn't always stick their noses in and make a lot of big to-do about things, a lot of troubles would die out a natural death and not much harm to anybody. But let the least little thing happen and they have to blow it up bigger than the Vietnam war!

The bus to Louisville makes up in our town. It's the end of the run. It comes in and waits around an hour then turns about and goes back. The bus driver finally came over, though, and poked Clayton and said, "Time to leave."

"And not a minute too soon," Clayton said. "I wish it had been time thirty minutes ago."

The driver — he was Jeff Harbin's boy, Mark, and I've known him all my life — laughed and said, "Looks like you folks got to be celebrities overnight."

"Which I wish we hadn't," I said. I still felt hotter than a hen in a wool basket and mad and outdone.

"Didn't you see the Louisville paper this morning?" he said.

"No, we didn't," Sudley said, "but I'm aiming to buy one soon as you leave out. I aim to know what they've said about us."

"It's a plenty," Mark said. "All right, Darkus, get aboard. We're leaving a little late."

One thing the ruckus did was take Sudley's mind off Darkus leaving. He just waved at her and said, "Let's go get the paper."

The story took up the whole left hand corner of the Kentucky page. They always put the Kentucky news on the front page of the second section, and there it was, three pictures big and bold and glaring at us. There was the still, all broken up, Singleton's men posing with their axes held over it. There were the jars of likker in another picture, Tate standing by, hands behind him and it was the first I knew they had put handcuffs on him. He had stood so we couldn't see them, but they showed plain in the picture. The worst was the biggest picture — of all of us. We looked scared to death. Eyes bugged out, faces long, my hair half down where the pins had fallen out whilst I was dancing. If we didn't look one more sight. Darkus was caught with her mouth hanging open, which made her look stupid. Willard was scrooched down behind her. And there was the preacher laying on the ground for all the world like a poleaxed ox.

And the things they said in the story! The biggest headline, going all across the top, said:

MINISTER AND LONELY HEARTS
INVOLVED IN RAID ON STILL

In littler headlines underneath it said:

LOVE AND A PREACHER CAUGHT
IN BROKE NECK RIDGE RAID

The story commenced with John Singleton's name and it ended with it. He had really blown himself up. He made it

sound like he was the smartest man in the world and we were
the most foolish. Which may be true, but a body oughtn't to
brag about it. We had been foolish one way, I will admit. To
trust that Singleton fellow. If everything you read in a newspaper is as mixed up and undependable as that story was, I
don't know as I'll ever believe one again.

Part they got right, but the way they told it, it didn't sound
right. They got the Lonely Hearts right, but they made it go
like Darkus was as nigh being an idiot as could be. All she
was was a loving, heartsore, lonely girl. They got Sudley making a mistake about Singleton right, but they made it sound
like he was stupid and ignorant. Anybody could have made
that mistake. And we took that man in under our roof and
offered him our best and were as polite to him as we knew
how to be.

They got it right about our picking and singing party, but
they made it sound hillbilly and foolish. They got it right
about the preacher being with us, but they left out about his
tape machine. It sounded like he was having a night out with
the boys. Oh, they didn't come right out and say so. My, no.
They didn't do anything that honest. They just made fun.
The whole story just made fun of us and our ways and the
preacher and all of us. It was the cruelest story you ever saw.
It made me cringe to think of what would be in the papers
the next day.

We watched the TV that night and on the Louisville news
there we were. Big as life and in color! Sudley was gape-
mouthed and shaky, his eyes were swollen from crying over
Darkus. Instead of looking grieved, which he was, he looked
drunk. His hat had even got shoved over one ear. What I
looked like I wouldn't know, for I wouldn't even look. But I

could hear and I sounded like a dog snapping at them. I wished I had bitten them.

Darkus and Clayton looked pretty good and they were dressed nice and appeared to a good advantage. But the questions went so foolish. To be asked such questions before everybody! To be made to appear so unseemly! I have read about something called the invasion of privacy. They invaded it, all right. They landed the Marines and invaded right up to the hilt.

When it was over I told Sudley, "I know, now, how they make them TV stories for the War on Poverty. How they pick people out at their worst and show 'em up. And have no mercy on their feelings. To degrade people, Sudley, is a sin. I don't doubt it is a mortal sin. News! You know what news is, Sudley? It is mostly somebody's misery, or somebody's shame, or somebody's sorrow. I hope," I said, "Huntley and Brinkley don't get a hold of this."

"I a little doubt they will," he said, "we ain't that important."

"They can make you that important," I said. "Remember how they showed those people that wanted that road? Over at Lovely?"

"Oh, that was bleeding heart stuff," he said.

"Well, my heart's bleeding right now," I said.

"Frony," Sudley said, "I have made up my mind. All this comes of trusting strangers. I don't aim ever again to let nobody from off step foot on my place. Except Clayton and he don't count for he's in the family now. And I hope you will bear me up in it. If somebody from off so much as crosses my boundary, I am going to let him have it with my gun. Both barrels. Loaded with buckshot."

"I hope you will," I said. "Me and William's gun will be standing right beside you."

Witchie went after the papers the next day. He got three, for it had spread to Lexington and Nashville. The preacher had come to his senses by the time they got to him and he had told his side of it. I wouldn't have believed he could be so bitter. He mortally did lay with it. Heathen, he called us — so-called Christians. Because of our religion. Lawless — because of Tate. Corrupt — because of the election. Immoral — because of Junior. Lazy — because we don't tear around over the country. Beggars — because of the giveaways. And his woman even told about Barney and my old piedy cow!

But I reckon the reporters figured he was as funny as us. The headlines said:

PREACHER RAMS HEAD THROUGH
TEXAS RANGER'S GUITAR

Down littler it said:

DRIVEN OUT OF HIS MIND!

You could tell they didn't think he had much to be driven out of!

The only good thing about being in the public eye is that it don't last long. Two days and it was over. It was old news, then, and they had to find somebody else to bother and torment. There was some talk around here, and behind our backs doubtless there was some laughing. There are two ways you can meet such as that. You can either hunker down under it and wait till it passes, or you can laugh first and take the sting out of it. That's what we did. Fowlers have always been that way — never afraid to laugh at their own selves. Except for death, there's little can happen to you that can't be borne that way, and better so than to weep.

The preacher never did come back. They said he had a nervous breakdown and would have to give up pastoring for a while. When his woman came to pack their things she said there wasn't enough money to make him come back. Said the whole six years they had been in the country they had suffered untold mental anguish from Sudley Fowler and his family.

That just went in one ear and out the other amongst the people. The truth is, *he* had caused them considerable anguish. And they were seeking a way to shift him out. Nobody wished that man ill. Everybody was as kind to him as you could be to somebody that kindness just pours off like water off a duck's back. But in the settlement, when it was known he wouldn't be back, it was like a soft rain had come after a long dry spell.

Nobody would have to watch that little compact zipping around the roads and have to jump back out of the way. Nobody would have to listen to that quick talk chattering away ninety miles a minute. Nobody would have to explain why we did things our way any more, and nobody would have to turn their faces for pure shame of his ignorance. It seemed like everybody sort of loosened up and drew a good long breath and felt free and good-humored and easy again. Maybe we ought to be ashamed to feel so relieved, but there is no denying that's what everybody felt — plain, pure relief to have him gone.

18

THEY penitentiaryed Tate.

Not for long, because it was his first offense. He got six months and they fined him three hundred dollars. Sudley did all in the world he knew to do and so did Job Rigdon and all the other boys. He spent money like it was water and Job went over to federal court himself. Job said he didn't know but what he worsened things for Tate by going. He said a federal judge sat on the right hand side of the Lord himself, and the man come nigh to throwing him out when he mentioned that a friend of his was coming to trial soon.

Darkus and Clayton came back for the trial and all of us testified except Willard and the preacher. They couldn't find Willard and they let the preacher off because of his health. Just read out in court what they called his deposition. There wasn't a thing we could do. Sudley got the best lawyer he could find, but it was purely an open-and-shut case. Tate had just walked in a trap and there was no two ways about it. When it was over Sudley paid the fine and they took Tate off to serve his time in that federal penitentiary in Ohio.

It was sad for Sudley, but having Darkus home, already in

the family way and showing, heartened him up. What really pleased him the most was that Clayton said they were going to stay. Said he had taken a liking to the country and wanted to live here. And Darkus had been so homesick he didn't think she could live if he took her back to Florida. "Be satisfied," she told me, "to look at such places on the TV, Frony, so you can turn 'em off when you want to. They are not what they are cracked up to be. Florida is mostly sand and flies and fleas and a lot of other things that sting and bite, and trees that look like feather dusters, and flat and no hills, and black water rivers, and worst of all, the most people you ever saw, pushing and shoving around. It was the longest seven months I ever spent — down there. I felt like the foreign lander in the song, serving out seven long years."

They had already sold their place down there when they came. It tickled Sudley the best. He said, "I am glad to hear it. You couldn't have come at a better time, Clayton. What with this War on Poverty and the Happy Pappy program and all the giveaways, these old Kentucky hills are purely the land of opportunity. I tell you, it don't *pay* to live off and do public works no more. I can get you on the Happy Pappies in no time. Job Rigdon will take care of it for me."

"What," Clayton said, "are the Happy Pappies?"

"They go a lot like the old WPA," Sudley said. "You recollect back in the old days, during the depression, when the WPA come in? We called it the We Piddle Around program. Well, the Happy Pappies is the WET. I don't know exactly what that stands for — something like Work, Experience and Training. But the boys call it Without Even Trying. They do about what the WPA done — make roads and clean up the

brush and stand around and lean on their shovels. A few —
and Job will see to it you're one of 'em, never fear — get to
go to school and get paid for it. Learn some kind of work. Of
course you don't need to learn no kind of work. You already
know plenty. But the main thing is to draw the benefits as
long as you can. If you're a family man, and you are on account of Junior, and soon will be on your own, you qualify.
All you have to be is ninety days out of work and a family
man. You get work and you get free doctoring and medicine
and hospital, free dentist. If you want to, they will send you
away to school and pay you for going, even pay your board
and room. And it's all, every last penny of it, tax-free. You
don't pay that first thin dime of taxes on it. I tell you, Clayton, it is one of the *best* giveaways the government has come
up with."

Clayton laughed. "Sudley," he said, "if I was looking for a
giveaway I wouldn't go for the Happy Pappies. I would go
for *running* the Happy Pappies. If you're going to feed out of
the tax trough, Sudley, you just as well feed hearty."

Sudley blinked a few times, then he said, "You are a sensible man, Clayton. We can do it. Job Rigdon is old — he's
older than me. By the time the folks know you well enough
for you to run, he'll be through."

"And so will the Happy Pappies," Clayton said.

"Oh, likely they will," Sudley said, "but they'll come up
with something else. I tell you, boy, this government has got
a tiger by the tail and it can't never turn loose. Why, I don't
look for my boys, Nathaniel and Whitley to *ever* have to
work. Time they get big enough, the government will be
paying folks *not* to work!"

"I don't doubt it at all," Clayton said.

"If they was really wanting that anti-poverty program to work," Sudley said, "they would quit all this patching and piecing around and pass that guaranteed annual income law. Guarantee everybody a little they could count on and throw all the rest out. It would be a saving in the long haul. And then they could quit trying to change everybody and make us all alike. Go away and let us alone."

"They ain't going to do that," Clayton said. "It would throw too many welfare people and government workers out of jobs and besides it wouldn't be good politics. Why, what would a politician have to campaign on without promising to get more federal money to fight poverty and build roads and bring in industry? It would upset politics worse than anything."

"I reckon it would," Sudley said. "But it would work if they would just ever get over the notion we all got to be alike, and worst of all, like them. They got National Parks and National Wildlife areas, I don't see why we couldn't have some National People areas, so folks could live according to *their* lights. Looks to me like people, like them Indians out west, and us, would be as important to the country as the animals and rivers and trees and sandy dunes. But maybe I've not got the straight of it and a man don't count like he used to."

"Not by himself, he don't," Clayton said. "Only way he can count any more is to get in step with all the others. Look like 'em, act like 'em, live like 'em."

"Like convicts," Sudley said. "It gives a body the cold chills."

Clayton and Darkus stayed with Sudley until they found a

place. It's down on the pike. The government is building a dam on the river and going to make a lake. Clayton says where he bought will be on the water when they fill up the lake. He had to pay a terrible price for it, to my notion. There never was a piece of land worth that much. But he says he will make it back the first year. He aims to run a bait shop and boat dock.

At first it didn't set very well with our people to build the dam and make the lake and change the river and take a lot of people's farms and homes. It would have set better if they hadn't known it was mainly because the Democrat courthouse in the next county had figured a way to get a recreation park and what they call water sports and a new water system for their town. All out of tax money. To attract industry. They weren't pikers, them men. They really fed hearty out of the tax trough. Fifty million dollars' worth of pure pork. It ought to fatten them considerably.

But as Clayton says, if you can't lick 'em, jine 'em. So Sudley has bought some land on the waterfront, too. He and Clayton are going to build cabins on it. To rent to tourists. Clayton says people have got more time and money than they've got sense nowadays and they run around like chickens with their heads off trying to find a way to spend both. Likely he is right.

Now, I have told you the straight of it . . . the pure truth and straight of all that happened during the time of our trouble. I just hope you get it down straight. When you get your book finished, if you peddle it through here, stop by. We'll likely buy one from you. I had to plead with Sudley to get to tell you the story. He will want to know if you've told it right.